Praise for M

'An emotional landslide or a nov...
gripped from first page to last.'
Clare Lydon, bestselling author of *Before You Say I Do*

'A compelling story of second chances and being
true to yourself.'
Harper Bliss, bestselling author of *Seasons of Love*

Readers Love *The Secret of You and Me*

'[O]ne of the best second chance romance stories I've ever
had the pleasure of reading!'

'With all the twists and turns I couldn't put it down until
I got to the HEA. A really good read that had me in
tears quite a few times.'

'Fantastic book, beautiful plot and very relatable characters.'

'This was a wonderful read. A love story with a difference.'

'Wow, what a fantastic book this was to read. A fantastic
story that gripped you from the start as the story slowly
unravelled itself.'

Melissa Lenhardt splits time between Europe and Texas, her lifelong home. *Run Baby Run* is her ninth novel.

Also by Melissa Lenhardt

The Secret of You and Me

Run Baby Run

Melissa Lenhardt

MILLS & BOON

This novel is entirely a work of fiction. The names, characters and incidents portrayed in it are the work of the author's imagination. Any resemblance to actual persons, living or dead, events or localities is entirely coincidental.

Mills & Boon
An imprint of HarperCollins*Publishers* Ltd
1 London Bridge Street
London SE1 9GF

www.harpercollins.co.uk

HarperCollins*Publishers*
Macken House, 39/40 Mayor Street Upper,
Dublin 1, D01 C9W8, Ireland
This edition 2023
1

First published in Great Britain by
Mills & Boon, an imprint of HarperCollins*Publishers* Ltd 2023

Copyright © Melissa Lenhardt 2023

Melissa Lenhardt asserts the moral right to be
identified as the author of this work.
A catalogue record for this book is
available from the British Library.

ISBN: 978-1-84845-818-5

This book is produced from independently certified FSC™ paper
to ensure responsible forest management.

For more information visit: www.harpercollins.co.uk/green

Printed and Bound in the UK using 100% Renewable Electricity at
CPI Group (UK) Ltd, Croydon, CR0 4YY

All rights reserved. No part of this publication may be reproduced, stored in a retrieval system, or transmitted, in any form or by any means, electronic, mechanical, photocopying, recording or otherwise, without the prior permission of the publishers.

This book is sold subject to the condition that it shall not, by way of trade or otherwise, be lent, re-sold, hired out or otherwise circulated without the publisher's prior consent in any form of binding or cover other than that in which it is published and without a similar condition including this condition being imposed on the subsequent purchaser.

Roses are red,
Violets are blue,
Hey Sugar Britches,
This one's for you.

Run Baby Run

PROLOGUE

My name is Darcy Evans, I'm thirty-three-years-old, and I've seen some shit.

I've visited seven continents, walked the Great Wall of China, taken selfies with turtles on the Galapagos Islands. I've ridden in the back of a truck through the Amazon with a goat named Jesus, a coop stuffed with six chickens, and a twelve-year-old boy with a submachine gun. I was almost arrested in Russia when I got caught up in a Pussy Riot demonstration. I've eaten monkey brains in India, got into a shouting match with a racist at Monticello when they said Sally Hemings was in love with Thomas Jefferson, and accidentally boarded a ferry in Tasmania that was celebrating a lion god with an animal masquerade orgy.

After traveling almost nonstop for a decade, nothing much fazes me. But none of my experiences prepared me for six days in October that started with a road trip in a 1969 Mustang with my mother, an incontinent, evangelical dog, and a woman from my mother's past who may or may not be who she seemed to be, and ended with…well. You'll have to read on to find out.

Most of this story is true.

PART ONE

ONE

As soon as I walked out of the airport, I remembered why I didn't miss Texas.

The freaking heat.

I'd barely taken five steps out of the terminal when my eyes were blinded by the bright Texas sun and my pale skin singed in the dry heat. I found an out-of-the-way spot to stand in a sliver of shade, rolled down my shirtsleeves, and searched through my backpack for my sunglasses. My eyes have always been sun-sensitive, just like my skin. *That's* why I needed my sunglasses, of course it is. Not because my head was pounding, and my mouth felt and tasted like the bottom of Don Draper's ashtray. I dug in my backpack but found no joy. Of course, I'd forgotten them. Just as I'd forgotten my driver's license and passport.

For the record, you can get through TSA without an ID, but they get personal. Very personal.

I know, I know. You're probably wondering what kind of professional traveler I am.

That Saturday in October I was the kind of ten-year pro

who woke up ninety minutes before my flight, hungover and vaguely ashamed of my behavior the night before, and delayed the plane at the gate because I was puking up red wine and chocolate cake in the washroom before takeoff (and was thankful to make it, truth be told). We all have those days, admit it, and I'd had much worse traveling days than that, I can assure you. In fact, as much as I hate to admit it, getting myself out of travel jams is kind of my brand. Sometimes it doesn't matter how much you plan, sht happens. I wrote a book about it, in fact. *Sht Happens or Why It's More Important to Be Flexible than Prepared*. My first NYT bestseller. Don't get me wrong; I'm a planner and a little obsessive about it. I'm also willing and eager to throw out a plan if needs must, and too often needs must. I am absolutely, 100 percent the woman you want to be with when you sprain your ankle in Venice, have a flat tire and no spare in western Iceland, or get lost on the Walk of the Gods trail in Italy. Nothing phases me and, so far, there hasn't been a situation I haven't been able to problem solve my way out of. Sometimes, I can even charm my way out of tight spots, though I usually leave that to Chloe.

Which brings me to my go bag, the bag I always have packed in case of a last-minute trip or weekends away. All the Wander Women have one—me, Chloe, Jess, and Ella. We used to prank each other by switching clothes around so Jess would be stuck with Chloe's wedges and sundresses when she showed up to an outdoor gear convention, or I would have flannels and hiking shorts when going to LA to review the latest luxury spa resort. We'd all gotten wise and started checking bags before we left, so it took a special set of circumstances for anyone to be able to pull it off.

Like being hungover and late for a flight on a Saturday

morning to see my mother, to *speak* to my mother, for the first time in three years.

So, instead of a weekend bag for a tall woman with skin so fair I almost qualify as handicapped, I had all the clothes and makeup for a petite, Desi American chef. I mean the snacks are great, but Ella's style tends to animals prints and chef whites. My capsule wardrobe is full of neutral basics and colorful scarves. And underwear Ella, I had no idea.

On the bright side, I'd already written, "Up Close and Personal: How to Get Through Airport Security Without Your ID" on the plane. Who knows how many articles I'd get out of my first road trip with Marja in years? Writing about our poor man's vacations had started my career, and I'm not going to lie; one of the only reasons I agreed to this road trip was to get an article or two out of it. #AdventureswithMarja had always been good for a laugh or two and lots of engagement.

I scrolled through the alerts and messages that came through while I was in the air. Instagram likes and messages. TikTok and Twitter notifications. Jess and Ella checking on me in our WhatsApp group. A text from Michael asking me to let him know when I land. Nothing from Chloe. Headline news that everything is shit and the world is ending.

That headline hit a little too close to home.

The night before, the well-ordered, successful life I'd worked so hard to achieve, and the future I'd planned out, had been hit with a truth bomb that I never expected and have no idea how to manage. I shouldn't have gotten on the plane that morning. I should have stayed in Chicago and managed this crisis, because it absolutely was a crisis. Chloe was the only person who I want to talk to, the only person who could help me, and was the one person who'd gone radio silent.

The only person I *didn't* want to talk to was Michael, my

fiancé. All the confusion and uncertainty I'd been ignoring since I'd reluctantly agreed to a big wedding were front and center in my mind, and in my heart.

Oh, by the way, Chloe is my best friend and has been since we met the first day of freshman year at the University of Texas.

Did I mention that Michael is Chloe's brother? I didn't, did I?

And, since I'm oversharing, I should probably just come out and tell you that Chloe dropped the truth bomb, telling me she loved me, was in love with me, and had been for years.

So, yeah. My mind was spiraling out of control with what it all meant, what I felt, what I should do. I needed to sit in a quiet room and think. Write a pros and cons list. Freewrite in my journal so I could figure out what I needed to do. What I wanted to do.

The last thing I wanted was to be in the same car with my mother, Marja Evans, for twelve hours with no privacy and no means of escape.

I looked at my watch. My flight had been on time but was Marja? No, of course not. I gritted my teeth. One of the reasons I loved traveling alone was that I was never at someone else's whim or on their timetable.

A text popped up from Michael. Thank God he didn't call. Knowing me, I would have blurted everything in one breath. Managing the fallout from that when I was a thousand miles away would've been too much for even me to manage.

How was your surprise shower? Get anything interesting? *wiggles eyebrows*

You knew it was a sex toy shower, didn't you?

Lol. Of course, I did. I put in a lot of requests I'll have you know.

And here I thought the strap on with the enormous rainbow dildo was a gag gift from Jess.

...

...

You can pass that off to Chloe. I'm sure she'll get some use out of it.

I ignored the message, and my plummeting stomach.

How's Marja?

Late, as usual.

Uh-oh, the forgiveness tour is off to a bad start, I see.

Told you. How's the bachelor weekend so far?

I'm too old for Vegas with a bunch of guys. The golf is great, but I don't like to gamble, and I've had about all the bottle service I want for the rest of my life.

It's only been one night!

Like I said. I'm old. I'm doing this for Tate, not me.

I rolled my eyes. Michael's childhood friend, Tate, was an a-hole. A recently divorced (shocker) a-hole who was using Michael's bachelor party as an excuse to go to Vegas and probably pay for a hooker or two.

17

You're right. Tate's an a-hole. Lol

I smile. Michael knows me so well.

I'm not saying a word, though what do you expect with a name like Tate Rivers? How none of you called him Tater is a mystery to me. I mean it was right there.

My phone rang. I expected it to be Michael, but it wasn't. Chloe.

"Sht, sht, sht, sht."

I didn't want to answer, not really. I'm not nearly as brave as I let on, especially when it comes to being vulnerable with people. But I needed to answer. My wedding was in a week, and I couldn't say I do until Chloe and I finished the conversation we started the night before. I swiped my phone with a shaking hand.

"Hang on, Chlo."

I switch apps and send a quick text to Michael.

Gotta go. I'll text you from the road. ♥ you.

I sent it before I could second-guess myself.

I took a deep breath and put a smile on my face. Brazen it out. Ignore the albatross over our heads for as long as possible. "Hey."

"You arrived safely." I could hear humor in Chloe's voice, which was a relief considering. At least she wasn't angry.

"The go bag prank? Really?"

"That's all Jess and Ella. I wasn't there, remember?"

"Yeah."

There was a long pause. Was this her testing the waters? Did she want to talk about it? Or pretend it didn't happen and move on with our lives and friendship the same way they'd been a little over fourteen hours ago? Had it only been fourteen hours? It felt like much longer, and it felt like it had just happened. I touched my lips.

"How do you feel this morning?" Chloe asked.

One question, two different meanings, and God only knows how many answers. I took the coward's way out.

"Do you feel as hungover as I do?" I asked.

"No, but I drink more than you do on a regular basis," Chloe said.

"I puked in the airplane washroom."

"I saw that on the group message. Even *I* haven't done that."

"I vomited so much I delayed the plane."

Chloe laughed. "I'm sorry, Fitz."

"No, no. It's fine. I'm sure I'll laugh about it eventually, but right now I'm sweaty and angry and nauseous."

"Marja hasn't shown yet, huh?"

"Nope."

"Take a deep breath and remember what we talked about. Don't get angry because then she'll clam up. You probably won't get all the answers at once so..."

"Pepper the questions I want answers to in with easy ones."

"Right. People like to talk about themselves."

That was true in theory, but Marja wasn't like most people. She'd learned a long time ago that there wasn't any use trying to set people straight about the kind of woman or mother she was, so she stopped trying. She knew who she was, and I knew who she was, and that was good enough. I would have agreed with her until three years ago when she stopped calling or texting or returning mine. The mother I knew wouldn't do that.

"This is going to suck."

"Darcy Elizabeth Evans, you are the strongest person I know. You've got this."

Affection for my best friend swelled in my chest. "Thanks, Chlo."

"Now for the good news," Chloe said.

"Oh my God, yes, please."

"Kate Murphy called. Athena Capital is in."

"What? Already?"

"Already." I heard the smile in Chloe's voice. "She's sending the contracts to our lawyers today, and she wants us to get together for a drink Monday night to get to know each other better."

I put my hand on my head to keep it from spinning off my body. "Holy sht."

Chloe laughed. "I think this news warrants the full shit, Fitz. We just secured funding from the hottest venture capital fund in the country. I told you we crushed that presentation."

We *had* crushed the presentation. It was a nice change of pace, giving a presentation to a woman and her all female team who understood our mission. We didn't have to spend the majority of our time justifying WanderWomen.com's right to exist and answering inane questions like, "Aren't you leaving 50 percent of the travel market out by focusing your website only on women?" and "I don't know one woman who travels by herself" and the inevitable gem, "What about family travel? That's a huge market you aren't tapping into."

I sat down heavily on the bench nearest me trying to come to grips with all Chloe, Ella, Jess, and I had been through and done to get to this point. It all started with a podcast idea born one boring Tuesday night when we all happened to be in town and decided to kill a bottle of wine. It turned into five bottles by the time we'd finished giggling our way through telling each other our most ridiculous travel stories. I won with the boat orgy, of course. I *always* win with the boat orgy.

"We should start a podcast," Chloe had said. No surprise. All of our crazy ideas started with Chloe.

"What will we call it?" Jess said. "Four Drunk Millennials?"

"Not a bad title," Chloe said.

"My mother's head would explode," Ella said.

"Wander Women," I mumbled, eyes closed.

And Wander Women had stuck. We started it as a biweekly podcast, calling in from wherever we were in the world to tell stories of our trips. Over time, we honed the format, with me as the primary host because I prepared for the podcast whereas Chloe and Jess, especially, were more fly by the seat of their pants podcasters. Ella had been in the midst of opening her first restaurant and had to bow out, but had returned occasionally to check in, especially when I had a food traveler guest on. Our audience grew slowly at first, then exponentially, and the website we created for the podcast archives morphed into a blog and then into a full-fledged women's travel site. Between our jobs that paid the bills, freelancing jobs that paid for avocado toasts and $10 lattes (/sarcasm), Wander Women had grown as much as it could. Now, Chloe, Jess, and I were making the jump into Wander Women full time, but we needed venture capital money to do it. Which is where Athena Capital came in.

"Yes, it's really happening. I told you so," Chloe said.

"You were right," I said.

"Say that again?" It was nice to hear teasing in Chloe's voice.

"Absolutely not. Your ego is big enough already."

I stood up from the bench and swiped my hand across the back of my linen pants, worried that the sweat from sitting for a few minutes had soaked through. Freaking Texas. "I bet I can catch the next flight back."

Chloe pulled the phone away from her ear and shouted, "Ella, you owe me ten bucks!"

I heard Ella's voice in the distance. "Dammit!"

"It was a sucker bet," Jess's distant voice said.

"Ha ha," I replied.

"You don't need to come back," Chloe said.

"There's so much to do. And to talk about."

Chloe took her time answering. "No, there's not."

My stomach dropped. I wasn't expecting that answer. "There's not?"

"There will be after we meet with Kate on Monday. Until then, forget about everything else and enjoy your time with your mother."

I was too stunned to reply. I mean, it was what I wanted, right? Pretend nothing happened. But I didn't want Chloe to want the same thing. I wanted her to...tell me she loves me again? Beg me to not marry Michael? She'd apologized last night and said she'd made a mistake. That she shouldn't have said anything, taken her secret to the grave. I suppose she meant it. Obviously, she meant it.

I'm not sure how I feel about that.

"Speaking of, tell Marja I said hi."

It took me a moment for the change in subject to register. "Right. Yeah. She still isn't here. I could kill your mother right now," I said, needing to focus my anger on someone.

"She'll be disappointed she's not your favorite anymore," Chloe said.

I'd idolized Eloise Parsons from the moment I met her as Chloe's new friend at the University of Texas. Eloise was beautiful and successful and oozed confidence and charm, and Chloe was just like her. I'm still not sure what Chloe saw in me, a small-town bastard whose wardrobe was a combination of Goodwill and Walmart, but we've been best friends from almost the moment we met. I guess it wasn't much of a surprise that I idolized Eloise; she was everything Marja wasn't. And, as long as I was being completely basic, it's not much of a surprise that I fell in love with Chloe's older brother, Michael, the first time I saw him. On his wedding day. It would take ten years for his marriage to end and him to finally see me as anything other than his little sister's friend. Within six months we were engaged. Within a week we will be married.

That was the plan anyway.

What was never part of the plan was Marja attending my wedding. I had specifically told Eloise that I didn't want her there. I didn't want the wedding either, but that's a story for another time. She agreed with but she decided later and without consulting me that Marja was my mother and should be invited. After Marja accepted, and cooked up this ridiculous road trip to trap me in the car with her for twelve hours, Eloise told me that she never expected Marja to accept. "Inviting her was the right thing to do, Darcy. She's the only family you have in the world." Until that moment, I thought the Parsons were my family. Eloise and her husband, Robert, had said it often enough. I told myself that she didn't mean anything by the comment, but it still stung. I've moved on from it all, but a part of me still harbors some resentment from my wishes being ignored.

"Chloe, if Marja's not here in five minutes, I'm coming back to Chicago."

"I kinda hope she doesn't show up," Chloe says.

"You do? You just told me not to come back."

"Sorry, Fitz. I'm a little scattered this morning. I shouldn't have left last night."

"No, you shouldn't have."

"I was confused."

"So was I."

It was a relief to know that Chloe and I shared the same uncertainty. *Of course* Chloe and I will be able to sit down and talk everything through when I get back. Last night was the closest to a fight we've ever come. I know that sounds unbelievable, but we've always been able to talk to each other about everything.

"Having a few days to think will be good for us, though," I said.

"It will?"

A red convertible 1969 Mustang with the top down rolled slowly down the drive, as if letting everyone get a good look at its spotless cherry red paint job. The car stopped in front of me.

The driver had short, windblown blond hair and wore aviator sunglasses. She pulled the emergency brake and grinned at me. For a split second I wondered what the heck Charlize Theron was doing in Austin and who she was staring at. I looked behind me, and the only person there was a custodian sweeping up cigarette butts.

I turned back to the woman, who was now sitting on the top of the driver's seatback with her arms open wide. "There's my baby girl!"

My phone slipped from my hand and clattered on the sidewalk.

Marja.

TWO

"Ho-ly sht."

Marja crawled over the passenger seat and jumped out of the car like Luke Duke.

"You dropped your phone, baby girl." The woman, my *mother* for God's sake, handed me my phone. I lifted it to my ear.

"Darcy, are you there?"

"Yeah."

"What happened?" Chloe said.

"Marja showed up."

Marja spread her arms wide and said, "Get off that phone and come an' give your momma a hug."

Dazed, I said, "I gotta go." My arm fell to my side.

I wasn't quite sure what to expect when I saw my mother for the first time in over three years, but Marja Evans cosplaying Charlize Theron in *The Old Guard* (and pulling it off!) wouldn't have been one of a hundred guesses. A thousand.

Look, Marja was a small-town single mother and maid whose hands were chapped from thirty-five years of scouring bathtubs and showers and kitchen sinks, who smelled like lemon not because of L'Occitane but Pine-Sol, and had clients nicknamed the Shittin' Spiveys. People in Frio, Texas, might have called Marja a lot of things, but no one ever called her sexy. This woman walking toward me with short, bleached blond hair, black pants haphazardly stuffed into well-worn, square-toed Dingo boots and a formfitting black T-shirt was sexy as hell.

"Momma? What happened to your hair?"

She ran her hand over the pixie cut. "Oh, you know. Midlife crisis."

"But you *loved* your hair. *I* loved your hair."

Marja shrugged and pulled me into a hug. That, at least, was familiar. Her hair smelled like Prell, and Marja's head settled perfectly on my shoulder, as it had since I outgrew her when I was fourteen years old.

I didn't return Marja's hug. For one thing, my arms were pinned to my sides. But I wouldn't have returned it if I could. Marja couldn't just call me baby girl, throw her arms around me and expect me to forgive her for three years of silence. I was still angry. Pissed. Livid. With myself almost as much as Marja and, truth be told, angry with Eloise Parsons for inviting her to my wedding behind my back and angry at Chloe, Ella, and Jess for talking me into driving back to Chicago with her.

"She's your mother," Ella had said, family loyalty and forgiveness trumping everything else.

"You always have a good time on your road trips," Jess said.

"She ghosted me, guys," I said. "My own mother! There's no way I'm going on a road trip with her."

We'd all looked at Chloe, who'd been uncharacteristically quiet. She raised her eyebrows. "What?"

"You always have an opinion," Ella said.

"And you're usually very loud about it," Jess said.

Chloe lifted her hands in surrender. "I'm Switzerland on this one, guys."

"What?" Said in unison, like so many of our conversations.

Chloe looked between the three of us, and her gaze finally settled on me. She sighed and rose to stand in front of me. She put her arms on my shoulders. "Fitz, I've known you and Marja for fifteen years. I probably understand your relationship with Marja better than I understand my own with Eloise. Lord knows I've spent more time thinking about it. Marja ain't perfect, she'll be the first one to tell you that, but that woman loves you more than anything in the world. What she did was shitty, you'll never convince me it wasn't, but I think she has a good reason for it." Chloe dropped her arms and shrugged one shoulder. "And I know if you go, you'll find a way to get it out of her."

"Marja's pretty stubborn," I said.

There was a short pause before all three of my friends died laughing. I flipped them all off and texted my mother I would go, but I didn't like it. I hated myself for being so easily persuaded.

So, yeah. I was bitter about being in Texas for so many reasons. *So many reasons.* Being hungover just made it worse.

Marja pulled away and held me at arm's length. An expression of concern crossed her face as if she'd read everything that had just passed through my mind, and I knew in my bones Marja wanted to say something. Instead, she smiled. "How's my baby girl?"

So, we were going to act like everything was cool.

"I'm thirty-three years old, Marja. Don't call me that. I'm hungover."

"Go out barhopping last night?"

"No. A surprise wedding shower."

"Oh, I bet you hated that."

I did hate it, as a matter of fact, but I wouldn't admit it to Marja. "Can we have this conversation in the car?"

"Sure thing." Marja grabbed my duffel.

"So, you finally got a Mustang," I said.

"Yep. I figgered if we're gonna go on an epic road trip, might as well do it in style," Marja said. "Whattya think?"

I stared at the car and wanted to glower, but I couldn't. It was beautiful. The chrome shined, the leather seats were soft and supple, the carpets on the floorboards spotless. The knob on the standard gearshift polished. It was the car my mother had dreamed about having all those years ago, but back then we'd barely had the money for a 1980 two-door tan Bonneville. The Mustang was a great car to dream about, but completely useless in real life, especially for a red-haired, pale-skinned, freckled woman like me.

"I'm going to fry before we get out of the airport."

A security guard walked by. "No parking. You need to move along."

Marja opened her mouth to argue (Marja's favorite pastime), but she clamped it shut and smiled. "Sure, Officer."

That was weird. I threw my backpack in the back seat. A dog yelped. "Fucking hell, Darcy," Marja said.

A light-haired dog that looked like a golden retriever but could fit in an oversize Kate Spade tote barked at Marja.

"Bark at Darcy, not me," Marja said. "She's the one who hit you."

The dog turned her attention to me, and I swear she narrowed her brown eyes. "Sorry," I said. I wasn't in the mood to be judged by a yappy dog.

"That's Helen," Marja said. "Helen, this is Darcy." Marja pulled a bag out of the back seat. "For you."

I looked inside. A wide-brimmed straw hat, 100 SPF sunscreen, a lightweight oversize scarf. My instinct was to quote *Dumb and Dumber*, but that would signal camaraderie to Marja, so I kept my mouth shut.

Marja put the car in gear. "Don't worry, we won't be top down the whole time. But when we are...you're set."

"Thanks."

"You're welcome. Let's get this show on the road."

Marja smoothly pulled away from the curb. The engine hummed and quieted with each shift. I put on the hat, draped the scarf over my shoulders and rubbed the sunscreen on my neck and face.

"When did you learn to drive a stick?"

"Couple of years ago when I bought it," Marja said. "I'll teach you along the way."

I laughed. "I'm not learning to drive a stick on the interstate."

"Oh, we aren't taking the interstates," Marja said.

"What?"

"You have a week, right? I thought we'd take our time. See some sights. Go down Route 66."

"But we're going to Chicago."

"It goes East, you know. It *starts* in Chicago."

"I know that. It's just...there's a reason no one goes east."

"Why?"

"Because it's a pain in the ass. The road has been taken over by interstates, you have to get off and back on and there's really not much to see."

"Oh, ho, ho! That's where you're wrong. We are going to stop and eat a corny dog where they were invented."

"Really? That's your idea of an interesting pit stop?"

Marja shifted aggressively but she had a smile on her face. "It'll probably be the height of the fucking trip."

Helen barked, scaring me half to death.

"Sorry, Helen," Marja said.

"What are you apologizing for?"

"Cursing. Helen doesn't like it."

"Neither did I, but that never stopped you."

"I am what I am."

I looked back at Helen, who lay in the middle of the back seat, her front paws hanging off the edge. Helen met my gaze and didn't blink. "I guess she barks all the time, then."

"Pretty often. She loves me."

Helen had turned her evil eyes on Marja. "Are you sure about that?" I asked.

"Oh, yeah. It makes her feel like she's in charge when she scolds me. So, I cuss all the time to humor her. Gives her something to do."

"Will I be in charge if I scold you?"

"Hell, no."

Helen barked again.

"Okay, okay. Settle down. I'm sorry," Marja said.

As annoying as she was, I knew Helen would be a hit in the article I was bound to get out of this ill-fated road trip. East on Route 66. Marja read and planned as much or more than I did. She knew very well the trip east on 66 would be a waste of time and take too much time.

"I have to be back in Chicago tomorrow night," I said. "I have an important meeting Monday morning."

"You said you had a week."

"I have one week before my wedding. We just got VC funding for the website, so this week will not only be dealing with that but also getting as caught up as possible at work. All the while we have a party or happy hour or something every night this week leading up to the wedding. I don't have time for meandering through the Midwest."

"Jesus." (Bark) "I guess rich people have to spend their money on something," Marja said.

"Yeah, I guess."

"Why in the hell (bark) did you to agree to all of that?" Marja's expression was part admiration, part horror.

"Honestly, I don't even remember. It was just easier to agree."

Marja narrowed her eyes. "I'm sure Eloise didn't have to work too hard to convince you."

I turned halfway in my seat to look at her. I wanted to glare, but ended up squinting against the sun. I held the brim of the hat down over my eyes to shield them from the sun, losing any bit of the dirty look I tried to give Marja. "We haven't talked in three years. I've been lucky I had anyone to step in and be a mother figure to me."

"And, now she's going to be your actual mother. How convenient."

"Oh, are we going to have this argument now?"

"I'm not arguing. Just making an observation."

"You never did like Eloise," I said. "You've met her once. You don't even know her."

"I know the type. Here." Marja handed over her sunglasses.

"Thanks. I forgot mine."

"We'll stop somewhere."

I stared at her from behind the glasses, waiting for her to elaborate about why she doesn't like Eloise. Nothing. She kept her hands on ten and two and her eyes on traffic.

I sighed and turned away. I'd forgotten; Marja doesn't have to answer to anyone.

The air whistled around the windshield, the tone rising and falling depending on the speed, and swirled around me like a convection oven. The warm air hit the perspiration on my face, cooling my heated skin a bit. Natural air-conditioning, I supposed. I was still miserable. How could it be so hot at the end of October?

It hadn't been this hot when I was in college a little over a decade ago. I remembered nice fall days, sweatshirts with shorts and flip-flops. Taking blankets to the late season Longhorn games. Me and Chloe sneaking a flask of Fireball into the game in our boots, spiking hot chocolate and feeling the warmth of the alcohol spread through our veins and to our fingers and toes and brains until we were as excited about the game as two women who really didn't like sports all that much could be. But the guys were there, and they were cute and Chloe and I couldn't help but attract a few; Chloe with her heart-shaped face, upturned nose, and chocolate brown hair; me, well. Let's be honest. Chloe pulled in most of the guys. I just tried to stand next to the tallest one so I didn't tower over everyone.

Most people think I'm shy, some think I'm stuck-up. The truth is, I hate being the center of attention, and looking like I do I could hardly help it, even now. Unique. Striking. "Wow, you're tall." That's how people describe me. I do my best not to stand out, and I never take selfies.

"How was your flight?" Marja asked.

"Fine. Sorry you had to get up so early to pick me up." I could kick myself. Why am I apologizing?

"No worries. I stayed in Austin last night."

"Oh. Nice. Where'd you eat?"

"Hut's."

"Oh my God, a Hut's burger sounds so good right now."

"I'd take you but I can't. Last night was their last. They're closing down."

"Get the heck out of here."

"Not kidding. Austin is gentrifying, though the Keep Austin Weird people keep up the good fight. But, everything changes."

"And some things stay exactly the same," I said.

Marja glanced at me with a wry smile. "Why do I think that jab was targeted to me."

"If the shoe fits," I murmured.

Marja chuckled but didn't rise to the bait. "How are Chloe and the girls?" Marja asked.

"We're women, Marja, and we're all good."

God, was our conversation going to be this inane all the way to Chicago? I held my hat on my head and watched the scenery go by, composing an article in my mind.

This morning, I left the crisp air of Lake Michigan and the changing leaves of Grant Park for the gnarled limbs of live oak trees, and the dry, dusty, dark green leaves of scrubby mesquite trees in South Texas. Fields with large plywood signs painted with the name and phone number of real estate agents hoping to make millions of dollars selling these former cattle farms and cotton fields to a developer that would build another shopping center or apartment complex on a stretch of road that, five years ago, had been a two-lane highway with a dangerous shoulder drop-off. Here's the Texas Miracle writ small; squirrels, bunnies, rattlesnakes, lizards, armadillos, and deer and being displaced by a Target. DSW. Home Depot. Chain restaurants. Tract housing. A bank on literally every corner at a stoplight. Fast food...

I sat up. There, between the Wells Fargo and Arby's. How could I have completely forgotten about it? A wave of nausea hit me again. "What time is it?" I looked at my watch and answered my own question. "Pull over. Quick."

Marja obliged, knowing without being specifically told, exactly what I wanted.

Whataburger.

Specifically, Whataburger taquitos.

More specifically, a potato, egg and cheese and a bacon egg and cheese and a cup of coffee. Check that: a sweet tea as only you can get in the South. My mouth watered just thinking about it.

It was impossible to know how many times Chloe and I had

made a Whataburger run after a night of drinking on Sixth Street, but it had been dozens. Maybe over a hundred.

We'd gone out a lot.

Marja called to Helen, who jumped nimbly out of the car, and followed Marja to the trunk. I was a little slower. Lord I was tired, and the heat wasn't helping. When I finally closed the car door, Marja had Helen on a leash and the dog was wearing a little red vest that said Service Dog.

"But…what…? She's a service dog?"

"Close enough. We'll meet you inside," Marja said, taking Helen to the tiny bit of grass available among the sea of concrete.

"That's illegal, you know!"

Marja ignored me. Of course.

A couple of teens who weren't even trying to hide the fact that they were stealing the table numbers held the door open for me. I chuckled; Chloe and I had had our own little collection of the orange table tents. The more things change…

When the door closed behind me, the smile slid from my face.

I'd expected to be met with the smell of nirvana, but my stomach revolted, and I ran to the bathroom. I made it to the toilet, but just barely. I was dry heaving at this point, having thrown up all of my dinner on the plane. I despised throwing up. Was known for having a stomach of steel. But I'd never been hungover like this. I almost wanted to eat something so I could throw it up and feel better.

I rinsed out my mouth, washed my hands, looked in the mirror, and blanched at what I saw. Dark circles under my eyes looked like bruises and made my skin look almost translucent, and more pallid than usual. Why hadn't Marja mentioned it? Lord knows she'd never been one to hold back before. Not that she was ever cruel, but Marja Evans was unfailingly honest. It was what I loved, and hated, about her.

Had I even put on makeup that morning? I didn't think so. Christ. When I woke up, the clock had said 5:30 a.m. My flight was at 7:00. O'Hare was forty-five minutes away, if I was lucky. I hadn't undressed from the night before. Now here I was, in a Whataburger in Austin, Texas, in clothes I'd been wearing for twenty-four hours, makeup left over from the day before if I had any on at all. I was usually better about my postdrinking, pre-bed routine. Lord knows I've used it enough times over the years; face washed, two Advil, full glass of water, plop, plop, fizz, fizz, oh what a relief it will be in the morning when I wake up fresh. I hadn't last night, obviously.

I splashed some water on my face and hoped that taquitos were still a great hangover cure.

Marja looked up from her phone when I came out. She shoved it in her back pocket and smiled. "You okay?"

Not really, I thought. "I'll live. Have you ordered?"

"Waiting on you."

I went to the counter to order and pay but Marja kept me back. "I got it," she said, and rattled off my order from memory. "Do you want to eat here or in the car?"

The idea of getting in the hot car didn't sound appealing. I'd take the AC for a bit. "Here's good."

I found a booth, put my head down on the cool ormica and took a few deep breaths. The smell of the restaurant wasn't pleasant, exactly, but I didn't feel like puking so that was progress. I heard Marja slide into the seat across from me. I looked up and shook my head.

"What?" Marja said.

"I can't get used to your hair."

"Me either, to be honest."

"When did you get it done."

"Last night."

"What?"

"Last night. At some barber shop down on South Congress. The guys had short hair and lots of tattoos so I figured they'd know what they were doing."

"Did you get a tattoo, too?"

"I thought about it, but no. No identifying marks, you know."

I opened my mouth to say what a weird comment that was, when our breakfast showed up. We spent a few minutes dividing the order up, doctoring the taquitos and taking the first bite, which was, quite honestly and surprisingly, heaven. I might have groaned.

"What's going on in Frio?" I asked.

Marja shifted in her seat and said, "Same old, same old," before shoving a honey butter biscuit into her mouth. "Maddie is in jail for writing hot checks."

"Dear old Dad hasn't donated enough to the GOP to get her out?" I said.

"He isn't your dad. He was an accidental sperm donor," Marja said. "Rumor has it he's teaching Maddie a lesson."

I laughed. "You mean, Chelly is teaching her a lesson, surely." Everyone in Frio, Texas, knew who wore the pants in the family and it wasn't my dear old sperm donor, Russell Clarke. "Now they decide to discipline her."

"Apparently. Twenty-five years too late, if you ask me."

"What an asshole," I said.

"You have no idea," Marja murmured. She took another bite of her biscuit, chewed and swallowed. "You know, Chelly wasn't always so awful. We were friends, once. Well, I guess as much as a high schooler can be friends with an adult. She wasn't from Frio, you know. Houston. I was always fascinated by people who weren't from around there. She and Russell were the It couple, so it was a big deal when they asked me to babysit their little boy. God, he was a terror. Turned out all right, though. Jake's a Green Beret, did you know that?"

"Yeah. He was always really nice to me."

"Same. Only decent one in that family. Chelly's only eight years older than me which, when you're sixteen, is a lot. Not so much when you're fifty."

That's more than she's said to me about Chelly Clarke or the family in my entire thirty-three years on earth. We tended to avoid all conversations regarding that family ever since I figured out that Russell Clarke was my father. There just aren't that many redheads in Frio, Texas. When I asked Marja she didn't confirm or deny it, which was as good as an admission. I was old enough to do the math, too. Russell was older than Chelly and Marja is eight years younger, is what I'm saying. As a child I assumed my mom had been at fault for the accidental pregnancy; as an adult I know better.

"What's with the navel-gazing about Chelly Clarke?"

"Hmm?" Marja looks at me, and after a moment her faraway expression clears. "Oh, nothing. Just that sometimes you misjudge people and sometimes people change. It's hard to know which is which."

"Did Chelly always wear the pants?"

"Well, she was always smarter than Russell, that's for sure." She pulled a piece of chicken from the sandwich and gave it to Helen, who was sitting on the floor so quietly I'd forgotten about her. Helen sniffed the chicken and took it daintily in her mouth. "I don't want to talk about the Clarkes."

"You brought them up."

Marja went silent, fed Helen some biscuit. That was apparently all Marja had to say about my hometown. Fine by me. I'd only been back there a handful of times since I graduated high school. I will give Marja credit for realizing how much I hated the place and being willing to meet me somewhere else when she wanted to see me. Hence the road trips.

Marja piled wadded up wrappers and empty salsa packets onto the tray and sat back, waiting for me, staring into the distance. Not angry or irritated, but thoughtful. I abandoned my food and stood. "Let's get going."

"Finish your breakfast. We have time."

"No, we really don't. I need to stop by Target to get a few things."

Outside Marja said, "Why? Didn't you write a book about how to pack for every situation?" Without discussion, we both started putting the roof on the car.

"Yes, and it still sells very well, thank you. They switched my go bag with Ella's last night."

Marja laughed. "How is Chloe anyway?"

I didn't correct her. "She's great. Same old Chloe."

Marja folded her arms across the roof of the car. "I'm looking forward to seeing Chloe. All your friends. It makes me happy that you've found your people."

"They're looking forward to seeing you, too."

Marja looked off into the distance, a shadow crossing over her face.

"Momma, what's wrong?"

Her gaze met mine, and after the briefest of moments, she grinned. "There's a Walmart right there," she said, pointing, and got into the car.

My shoulders slumped, I groaned, and got into the car.

I don't like shopping at Walmart. I'll go to one if I'm on the road and have forgotten something (like now), but there isn't one near where I live and it's more convenient to shop at the corner drugstore (its own kind of problematic corporate behemoth; is there any other kind?) on the way home from the office.

That's *a* reason I don't shop there, but it's not *the* reason.

The reason is something I never told anyone, not even Chloe.

There was a time, and it wasn't so distant that I don't remember the joy of it, that shopping at Walmart was an aspiration for me.

It's a special kind of poor to not be able to afford Walmart clothes, but that's what life was like for me and Marja. I wore hand-me-downs given to Marja by the women whose houses she cleaned. Until the day the kids who originally wore the clothes recognized their castoffs and that was it. I became the outcast. I was small and skinny and ugly, an easy target on my best days. Though I tried my damnedest to be invisible all day every day, the day I punched Maddie Clarke in the face I was feeling it because my outfit was awesome. Dark Lee jeans ironed to a crisp, a coral Hawaii t-shirt, and Chuck Taylors. Maddie had a special sort of hatred for me, learned from her mother, that neither one of us understood until years later.

Sitting in the principal's office, waiting for Momma, wearing my now hated outfit, trying not to cry, trying to be invisible, so the principal wouldn't look at me from over the top of her glasses and tell me, yet again, that fighting wasn't the way for nice little girls to behave, dreading like the dickens the moment when Momma walked through the door and gave me The Look and knowing, with all of my little seven-year-old heart, that I was going to hear it at home because Thursdays were Momma's busiest days and tough for her to complete in time to pick me up from school when everything went well, which considering she had the Shittin' Spiveys on Thursdays, never happened.

Momma didn't disappoint. She came into the principal's office like the Tasmanian Devil, her hair coming undone from her ponytail, a strand of it stuck to her sweaty face like an upside-down question mark, damp patches on her jeans near the knees, her hands and fingers shriveled from damp despite the fact she wore gloves, and a thundercloud of an expression on her face. I should have been scared, would have been but for two things. Momma's lemony scent calmed me, and that thundercloud of an expression was zeroed in on Principal White.

"Mary Verne." She spit the words out as if they were sour on her tongue.

Principal White's eyes narrowed over her half-moon reading glasses and her thin nostrils flared. I didn't move a muscle. Momma called Principal White *Mary Verne*! I just knew Momma was in for it now. Maybe that was Momma's plan, to take Mary Verne's dirty looks from me onto herself. Right then and there, my momma became my hero.

"Marja, your daughter punched Maddie Clarke without provocation at recess."

"Without provocation? Really, Mary Verne?"

"The apple doesn't fall far from the tree, does it?"

"And you're still letting the rich kids bully with impunity."

Mary Verne's eyebrows lifted. "Someone's been studying their vocabulary cards. Did you save them when you dropped out of high school?"

Momma turned away from Mary Verne and knelt in front of me. Her expression was soft, but her voice didn't sound right. "What happened, baby girl?"

I looked at Principal White, who was watching me through narrowed eyes, and back to Momma. "Can we talk about it later?"

Momma rubbed my legs. "It's okay, you aren't in trouble."

"Yes, she is," Mary Verne said.

Momma closed her eyes and inhaled. I knew she was counting to ten. When Momma opened her eyes, she smiled. "Be brave. Tell me."

"Maddie made fun of my clothes because they used to be Sandy's."

That was the God's honest truth. It just wasn't all of the truth, and Momma knew it. She patted my knees said good girl and stood up.

"I know it's pointless to try to argue that Darcy was being bullied and stood up for herself."

"Making fun of someone's clothes isn't bullying."

"It is when…" This pause was five seconds, but I knew it was Momma gathering her wandering patience back to her breast. "You know what? Forget it. I'll talk to her. Can she go back to class now?"

"No. She's being suspended for two days. She can come back on Monday."

"Suspended!"

"You haven't even asked how Maddie is."

"I don't give a—" Marja twisted her neck around on her shoulders. "Was she hurt?"

"She has a bloody nose. It might be broken."

"Of course, it's not broken. Darcy's seven."

"Chelly and Russell think, and I agree, that suspension is warranted."

"Chelly and Russell think, huh? Well, by all fucking means, whatever Chelly and Russell want they get, don't they?" Marja put her fists on Mary Verne's desk and leaned over it. She dropped her voice, but I had amazing hearing (a fact I kept to myself). "I know what you, the town, all think about me and what happened. But, you're all wrong. Now, you're making an innocent little girl pay for something her father did."

"Oh, you know who the father is?"

"Fuck you, Mary Verne. Come on Darcy. Let's go get some

41

ice cream. Celebrate your first TKO." She pushed off the desk and stalked out of the office. The main office door hit the wall when Marja barged through, and we ran almost smack-dab into Maddie and her parents. Everyone looked surprised for a millisecond, before expressions became hostile, though I noticed that Maddie looked scared of me and stepped a little behind her mother, which gave me a thrill, so I narrowed my eyes at her. Momma took my hand and pulled me along, raising her other hand and giving the Clarkes the middle finger as we walked off down the hall.

I wasn't about to ask if Momma'd meant it about the ice cream. Momma didn't seem mad at me, but now that she wasn't channeling it toward Mary Verne (I would never think of her as Principal White again) I was afraid her anger would descend on me. True to her word, we pulled into the Dairy Queen. She told me to order whatever I wanted, so I ordered a hot fudge brownie sundae. Momma got a water. She knew as well as I did I wouldn't be able to finish it. Looking back now, I realize that most of Momma's meals were my leftovers, or coffee and cigarettes.

When I'd had my fill, which wasn't much, I was seven after all, Momma dipped the red plastic spoon into the soupy mess and dug out a chunk of brownie. "Tell me what happened, Darcy."

"I'm sorry, Momma."

"Let's see what you have to apologize for first."

I didn't want to tell her, but I knew I would. I'm a terrible liar.

"Maddie made fun of me because she said I was wearing Sandy Walker's old clothes. Am I?"

Momma ate a bit more of the sundae before answering. "Yeah, you are."

I'd never thought about where my clothes came from before.

Momma just showed up with a bag of clothes and we spent the night in my room, trying on every single bit, mixing and matching like Garanimals, Momma said, but I didn't know what she meant. The things that didn't fit or we didn't like we put back in the bag and I never saw them again.

"My clothes don't come from the store?"

I'll never forget the pained expression on my momma's face, or the way she stabbed that red plastic spoon so hard into the last bit of brownie that it snapped in two. She pushed the sundae aside, rubbed her face, murmured something unintelligible.

I hopped down from the booth and held out my hand to her. "Come on, Momma. Let's get you a cigarette."

Marja looked at me with the funniest expression on her face and then she burst out crying, right there in the middle of the Dairy Queen.

If this were a novel, this is where Marja'd pull herself and me up by our bootstraps and we'd be able to shop at Walmart. Yeah, no. Trust me, there was nowhere to scrimp and save. I wore hand-me-downs for years, but luckily I outgrew everyone my age and the older girls either didn't know or care that I was wearing their castoffs. That didn't stop Maddie and her minions. Though I have to note that when Maddie picked on me from then on, she was always a step behind her girl gang for protection.

Marja would tell the TKO story in later years and laugh about my lethal right hook and me being an old soul from the word go. She never mentioned the part where I crawled up in her lap and let her cry and hold me so tight I thought I would suffocate. But I didn't move and I didn't complain. My momma needed me right then, and I have never felt so loved or wanted or…no, none of that's right. I've felt loved and wanted since, but I've never felt so utterly essential to another person's life as I did in that moment.

I've been searching for that same feeling every day since.

My momma cried out all her tears that day, I think, because I never saw her cry again.

THREE

Marja took me to Target. I was in and out in twenty minutes. Sunglasses, joggers, underwear, socks, a Wonder Woman T-shirt. Jess owed me fifty bucks.

"You look exhausted," Marja said. "Why don't you take a nap?"

I *was* exhausted so I took her up on the offer. Three reasons: one, I knew myself well enough to know that before long I would work myself back into a state over Marja's three-year silence and start an argument and two, I was just too freaking tired and hungover to have that argument now. Three, when I woke up, I would be closer to home and being done with this road trip. Of course, all of my problems would meet me there. That was at least twelve hours away, though. I'll worry about it later. I fell asleep fast and slept hard, the benefit of learning to sleep whenever and wherever on the road.

Marja, as usual, had her own ideas.

I startled awake when the car engine died. I wiped drool from my cheek and twisted my stiff neck from side to side.

"We're here," Marja said.

We were in a parking lot in surrounded by scrubby trees.

I hadn't driven north of Austin in years, but I remembered enough to know this was not Waco, Texas. (Oh, good God. Marja better not want to stop at Magnolia Market on the way through Waco. There is no way my head or stomach could take that sensory overload right now.)

It all looked terribly familiar, but I couldn't quite place it. I turned and looked out the back window—Helen gazed at me placidly—and spotted a wooden sign and shelter with a large outcropping rising in the distance behind it.

"Enchanted Rock? Marja, why are we at Enchanted Rock?"

"It's our first stop," Marja said. She opened the door and got out of the car. Helen followed.

"Our first stop?" Was I still asleep? I had to still be asleep. This is the traveler's version of running in quicksand. Instead of moving forward on a trip, getting closer and closer to your destination, you move backward. That's the only thing that made sense. Honestly, I'm shocked it took me fifteen years to have this particular dream.

I got out of the car. Marja was pulling a small backpack out of the trunk. "Water and snacks."

"Water and snacks? Where did you get those?"

"I brought them with me." Marja looked at my feet. "Do you want to change shoes?"

"Oh, so your offer of me taking a nap was about kidnapping me instead of any sort of concern for my well-being."

Marja rolled her eyes. "My God, I forgot how dramatic you can be sometimes."

"Mother, I have to be in Chicago tomorrow. It's now past noon and we are farther away from Chicago than we were two hours ago." I lifted my phone. "Hey Siri, take me to Chicago." I stared at the phone and waited. No service. Shocking.

"We are two hours west of Austin, when we should be two hours north." I windmilled my arms pointing dramatically west and north. "Instead of fourteen hours from Chicago we are eighteen hours." The thought of that much time in a car made me want to heave again.

"Don't worry. We'll make up the time." Marja shouldered the backpack and clipped Helen's leash to her belt loop. "Since we're here we might as well take a look. We might never get the chance again." Marja walked off.

"That's a weird thing to say," I said to her retreating back.

"When was the last time you were in Texas, Darcy?" Marja said over her shoulder.

Okay, she had a point. I'd seen everything in this state that I wanted to. I sighed. I guessed I'd see Enchanted Rock one more time.

I pulled out my phone. I'd written about Enchanted Rock before, it was the first story I'd ever sold professionally, and it was probably time for a follow-up. A bookend, if you will. Not much had changed, by the looks of it. Not surprising since the Rock is one outcropping of a six hundred million-year-old pink granite batholith. Change never comes quickly in nature.

I took photos of the Rock from a distance, of the dry creek bed, trees, a lizard sunning itself on a rock along the short trail through scrub trees and tank-sized pink granite boulders that would lead to where the hike really began. Groups of hikers dotted the face, which seemed to slope easily but once you got on the Rock you realized that yep, it did feel like climbing thirty to forty flights of stairs. One group had stopped for a break about halfway up. A family with two small children was making its way down the lower trail, one child on the father's back, the other being carried by a red-faced, slightly plump mother. Marja stopped and started talking to them. Marja handed the mother a bottle of cold water. The kids had been lowered to the ground and were showering Helen with love, which she received as if it was her just due.

"Oh my gosh, thank you so much," the mom said. She handed the open bottle to her youngest, who stopped petting Helen long enough to take a few gulps. "We just had no idea how hot it would be."

"That happened to us the first time we came here, didn't it, Darcy?"

"It did. I was about your age," I said to the girl the mom had been carrying.

"You're nicer than I was," Marja said. "I wouldn't carry Darcy."

"I had blisters for a week," I said, remembering how fascinated I was as the pus oozed out of the blister when Marja popped it with a needle. I've never been squeamish.

"It toughened her up," Marja said. "Now she's a travel writer and goes on hikes all over the world."

"Wow, really?" the mom said.

"I'm more of city walker than a hiker. I have a friend who writes the outdoorsy articles for our website."

"You have a website?" the father asked. He was tall and lanky and wore a floppy safari hat.

"I do. Wander Women. We specialize in women who like to travel solo."

"Why?" the man asked.

"What do you mean, why?"

"Why are you discriminating against men?"

Oh great. Here we go.

"Chad," the wife chastised.

He looked like a fucking Chad. "Well, we aren't discriminating. Men are welcome to read the articles we write about how women can protect themselves from predatory men as they travel. Maybe you'll recognize some of your own actions that make women feel unsafe in the world."

"Okay. Enjoy the water," Marja said, pulling me along.

"What a bitch," Chad said.

"Well, I think you deserved it," his wife said.

"Proving my point, Chad," I called.

When they were out of earshot, Marja asked, "When did you get so feisty?"

I could tell that Marja was impressed, and maybe a little proud. I grinned. "I've met my fair share of Chads over the last decade."

"Especially the last few years?" Marja raised an eyebrow.

"Yeah. Chads have been coming out of the woodwork since 2016."

"The fuckers are saying the quiet part out loud now," Marja said.

Bark.

Marja continued up the rock. I stopped and took a photo of a group of three hikers at the top, shadowed against the blue sky. I would change it to a black and white, my preferred filter, later. We skirted a vernal pool, indentations in the rock where water accumulated, avoided a cactus or two that grew out of the cracks in the rocks. I took a microphotograph of a small purple flower growing out of a little island of soil in another indentation. I hadn't been here in more than ten years—had it been fifteen?—but it was like I'd been here yesterday. Everything was achingly familiar.

I stopped at the top, letting the wind from the Hill Country swirl around me, drying the sweat on my face, cooling me off. I removed my straw hat, ran my hands through my short hair.

Like I said, I don't like selfies, but I can usually ask a tourist to take a photo of me from behind with a great view in front of me.

"Marja? Would you come take a photo of me?"

"Already been doing it, baby girl."

"From behind," I said.

"That, too."

I sat down next to Helen, who was happily drinking water that Marja had brought her. Marja handed me a bottle of water and her phone. I scrolled through the photos of me. The first few were photos of me standing with my back to her, looking out over the Hill Country. It was perfectly framed and really rather spectacular.

"This is really good," I said.

Marja shrugged. "I read a book about it."

I chuckled and kept scrolling, stopping on a photo of me asleep in the car. I looked small and vulnerable and completely at peace.

"I love that one," Marja said. "Will look good in black and white."

"Yeah," I said. "At least my mouth isn't open. I don't have to tell you to not share it with anyone, right?"

"Of course. Who would I share it with?"

"I'm sure you'd find someone." I scrolled back to one of the ones with my back to the camera. I airdropped it to my phone. "Thanks."

I converted it to black and white, adjusted some settings to heighten the shadows, and posted it with the caption, *To all who have been wanting me to post photos of myself, here you go. My best angle.* I added a couple of hashtags and sent it.

"Nice view," Marja said.

I didn't answer. As far as views went, it wasn't particularly spectacular. Low rolling hills of semiarid land, trees that were more scrubby than majestic, cacti, rocks, plenty of creek and riverbeds (mostly dry), occasional grass fields reclaimed from the brush, but overall unimpressive if you've seen the wider world. But, the view from the top of the Rock had been the first panoramic, bird's-eye view I'd ever seen, and to me, it was magical. As irritated as I was with Marja for the four-hour detour, along with everything else going on, I had to admit I was glad to see the view again.

I'd never admit that to Marja, though.

"I've seen better," I said.

That was a lie. I had this uncanny ability to hike up to views when they were socked in with clouds. Capri, Pike's Peak, One World Trade Center, even Sears Tower, which I could go up any day of the week but still managed to only do it on cloudy days. I kept at it, across the world, trying and failing to capture the sense wonder that I'd found on top of this granite outcropping when I was eight years old.

I felt Marja's gaze on me. "They've never lived up to the first time you saw this, though, have they?"

I glared at Marja.

"I've read everything you've ever written, Darce."

I looked away. "That's nice."

"You're very talented."

"I know."

Marja chuckled and started rummaging in her backpack. She pulled a sandwich (peanut butter and strawberry jam, no doubt), Bugles, an apple, and a Snickers bar. Two of each, except a Butterfinger for her. "I skipped the Capri Suns," she said.

I stared at the lunch in front of me. It was the same lunch we'd eaten on our first trip to Enchanted Rock. Our first vacation. Our first road trip. I'd been eight and easily impressed by the view, and excited about the lunch, especially since Marja let me eat the Snickers bar first. It had been a great day. A perfect day. Short-lived, but still. There are times when I'm able to carve out that day and pretend that it had happened in a vacuum. That before and after didn't exist, that Marja and I could sit on that big ass rock forever, not be touched by the cruelty and judgment of the outside world. Nothing happens in a vacuum, especially nothing in my life.

Was this Marja's olive branch? Bringing me to one of the places we have good memories before telling me what the last three years have been about? Softening me up by tapping into sensory memories I would struggle to resist; fingers sticky with peanut butter and jelly, the cloying sweet taste of nougat and salty peanuts, the crunch of airy corn chips, the smell of summer in Texas—dust and bug spray and sweat—the heat of the sun on your skin, regardless of long sleeves or hat, the way it was ten degrees cooler in the shade, the struggle to find shade, wading in the cool water of the Pedernales River, the tops of Lady Bird's beloved wildflowers tickling the palms of my hands, eating smoky barbecue at picnic tables with an open loaf of Mrs. Baird's white bread for all to share, the sharp tang of pickles and onions and pickled peppers, flies buzzing around, landing on the brown edges of bread, on arms sticky with sweat, lifting your hair up off your neck in hopes of a cool breeze but rarely finding one, snuggling next to my mother in the frigid cold of a cheap hotel room.

Too bad there were as many bad memories entwined so tightly with the good it was impossible to separate the two.

Marja stared out at the view. I waited for her to speak, but she seemed content to be silent.

"I'm waiting," I said.

Her gaze meets mine. "For what?"

"Didn't you bring me here to explain the last three years?"

"No."

"No?"

"Nope."

"No. NO? I could have understood this four-hour detour if you had. It would have been great, in fact. I told Chloe you'd never explain or apologize, and I was right. You are such a bitch."

I stood and started down the Rock to the car, the cotton ball clouds darkening and moving together in the sky around me.

FOUR

I reached the bottom, sat down on a bench in the shade, and did the most mindless thing I could think of: scrolling through and liking the messages popping up on Instagram. There was a comment from Eloise.

We need to see your beautiful face! Hope you're having a wonderful time with Marja. Can't wait to see her when you get home!

I liked the comment and replied: She can't wait to see you, either even though it was a lie. Marja had disliked Eloise Parsons from the moment they met.

Their meeting was accidental. I'd done my best to keep them apart, even though Eloise was sure to say before each of her visits, "I hope I get a chance to meet your mom this trip, Darcy." There was just no scenario I could imagine my white trash momma meeting Chloe's philanthropist mother and it not being a disaster. The gap between the Parsons's Gold Coast mansion and our two-bedroom trailer house was a fucking chasm. Just the thought of them in the same room made my palms sweat. I might have made Marja out to seem like a rags to riches story, a millionaire next door type who didn't see the need to waste her money on a house when she had a perfectly good roof over our head. Her money was better used being donated to charities that helped young single mothers pull themselves out of poverty, like Marja did.

Yeah. I laid it on pretty thick. I was young and stupid and ashamed of my mother, my background, my illegitimacy. If it hadn't been for a particularly bad flu season our sophomore year, I probably would have been able to pull it off. Chloe and I were still in the dorm (I couldn't afford an apartment and Chloe said there was no one else she could bear to live with), and if you managed to get through a semester without getting sick it was a minor miracle. That February, I got the flu first and it laid me low for days. Chloe nursed me between classes, and she was a wonderful nurse, but when you're as sick as I was you just want your mother. Marja rented a hotel room and moved me in, away from the germs, and nursed me back to health with chicken noodle soup, crackers, Sprite, Gatorade and Momma snuggles. When I told her she would get the flu, too, she claimed she had Mommy Immunity and would be fine. Come to think about it, she'd never gotten sick after nursing me. She never got sick, period.

The next morning we were watching the *Today* show in bed. Momma drinking a cup of coffee, me drinking a Gatorade, when there was a knock on the door. Chloe, pale, shivering, and sweaty, stood outside. Momma got Chloe settled in the other bed, asked her what comfort food and drink she had when she was sick, and went to the store. The next day I was well enough to go back to class and Marja stayed to take care of Chloe. When I got back to the hotel that afternoon, Eloise answered the door. My excitement at seeing Eloise vanished when I looked over her shoulder and saw Marja standing there with an expression so benign as to be blank.

Eloise hugged me, said how glad she was I was feeling better. It, uh, went downhill from there.

"When did you get in town?" I asked.

"A couple of hours ago. I was on a business trip when Chloe called so I changed my return flight to Austin instead of Chicago."

"That's...great."

Eloise Parsons was an elegant woman. Patrician. Tall, thin, dark hair in a rich woman bob with bangs swept to the side. You know the expression "no hair out of place"? Well, I'm pretty sure it was created for Eloise Parsons. Her style was understated to the extreme—pantsuits and trousers and button-down silk shirts—but so expensive and well-made you thought she was on the cutting edge.

When you saw her and Chloe together, you knew that this was exactly how Chloe would look in thirty years. I was a little in awe of her. I was probably a little infatuated with Eloise, truth be told. In her I saw intelligence, strength, and determination all rolled up into this amazingly regal package. I wanted to be her, but above all I wanted her to like me.

"And, I've finally gotten to meet your mother," Eloise said.

"That's...great."

"She's just as fantastic as you said," Eloise continued. "In fact, I think you might have sold her a little short."

My gaze, which had been fixed on the ground, shot up to Eloise. Her eyebrows were raised very slightly, and I knew the game was up.

Marja went to Chloe and rubbed her arm. "I'm going to head home now that your mom's here."

"Okay." Chloe grasped Marja's hand. "Thanks for taking care of me."

"You're very welcome." Marja leaned down and planted a

gentle kiss on Chloe's head. "You'll be up and at 'em in no time."

"I'm sorry we had to meet under these circumstances," Eloise said, "and that we haven't had more time to visit."

"Same," Marja said. "It was nice to finally meet you."

"Likewise. Here." Eloise reached for her purse. "Won't you let me pay you for the hotel room? How smart, to get them out of the dorm."

Momma stiffened. "Not at all. I've taken care of it. Stay as long as you need. I insist."

Eloise reached out and took Marja's hand. "Thank you for taking care of my daughter."

"You're welcome. You would do the same for Darcy."

"Yes, I absolutely would."

Marja released Eloise's hand, glanced at me, and left the room without another word.

"Momma wait," I said, jogging after her.

Marja didn't stop until she reached her car. She unlocked the trunk and threw her duffel bag in the back.

"I'm sorry," I said.

She slammed the trunk and looked at me. "What for?"

"For, um…"

Marja waited, arms crossed over her chest, eyebrows raised. I couldn't answer.

"Well, I have to go, Darcy. I have an important meeting with my teen mothers charity."

"I'm sorry, okay?"

"Don't be. I should thank you for making me sound so good. Eloise was very impressed. I'm sending her information about my charity. She wants to donate."

"Momma—"

"Shut up, Darcy. Just shut up."

She pushed me out of the way, got in the car, and left.

★ ★ ★

I spent the first year of my friendship with Chloe secretly terrified she would see right through me to the horrible person I was, someone unlikable, unlovable, not worthy of being anyone's friend. The summer between freshman and sophomore year was its own kind of torture. I went back to Frio, worked for my mom to earn money, and Chloe went back to Chicago, to her rich friends, worked as a counselor at a fancy sleepaway camp she had attended every summer since she was seven years old. Surrounded by people like herself, she would realize she could do much better than a white trash bastard as her best friend.

As you have probably figured out, I didn't give Chloe nearly enough credit. Or Eloise. Neither was as shallow as I feared. And I wasn't giving myself enough credit, either. But it's difficult to get past eighteen years of rejection, of bullying. It took an amazing amount of willpower—oh, who am I kidding? It was pure terror at being alone and friendless in the big wide world—to not cling to Chloe like she was a life raft, to not be jealous of any other friend she might have, or even of her boyfriends (and girlfriends, too, eventually).

I've always considered my first trip to visit Chloe's family in Chicago over spring break my junior year as my first trip out of Texas. Well, my first real trip anyway. Marja and I had gone as far west on our road trips as Carlsbad Caverns and as far to the east as New Orleans.

Chicago was the biggest city I'd ever been to, and Chloe was an amazing tour guide. She showed me every nook and cranny of Chicago, taking me to the tourist spots, as well as the gems that only locals knew. Every night I went home and wrote notes in my journal (which at that point in my life was a cheap spiral notebook), gathering thoughts on how best to put my experiences together into an article with a hook that would catch an editor's eye. In the end, I wrote three articles about the trip. None of them sold, so I started a blog and posted them there. It was the beginning of my career as a travel journalist, though it took me three more years to sell my first story to a major magazine. About my first visit to Enchanted Rock.

I don't think there could have been a culture more removed from my small-town life than Chicago's Gold Coast. As much as the Parsons welcomed me and treated me like family, I was still uncomfortable around their money, even if it was old money and they were more subtle about it. I'd never gotten over the idea that I was a poser, an interloper, and sooner or later they would realize it. I lived in fear of being found out, even now.

I watched Marja and Helen saunter down the trail from the top of the rock as if they had all the time in the world. Marja put her backpack in the trunk and closed it. I stood in front of her, hand outstretched.

"What?" Marja asked.

"Give me the keys."

"Why?"

"Because I've mapped out our route, and I'm driving so you don't do another hour-long detour to Cooper's or something."

"You always did like their smoked chicken."

"I've told you, I have to be in Chicago Sunday."

Marja nodded her head. "I guess I shouldn't have assumed you would take time off to spend with me."

"Marja. I agreed to drive back with you, not to babysit you all week. I'm running a business, getting married in a week, and trying very, very hard to keep my anxiety in check. You aren't helping. At all. So, drop the guilt trip. Now, it takes seventeen hours to drive from Austin to Chicago. So, nineteen hours from here. That's two days if we stop. Trust me, that's more than enough time in a drafty old car with an evangelical dog."

"We're going to have to stop every couple of hours for Helen. She has a tiny bladder."

I closed my eyes and sighed. "Jesus, take the wheel." I looked down at the mutt. "What? You aren't going to bark at that?"

"She knew you were using it as a proper noun."

I held out my hand again. "Momma, give me the keys."

With a smile, Marja handed me the keys. I got into the car and sighed in relief. Finally, we would get somewhere. It was two o'clock. If we were lucky, we'd miss rush hour in Dallas. I guessed we could drive a few more hours north and find someplace to stay the night in Oklahoma.

I put the key in the ignition and turned it. Nothing. I did it again. Nothing. I looked around and saw the gearshift. My head fell forward onto the steering wheel with a thunk, and I let out a growl of frustration that turned into a yell. When I finished, there was a knock on the window.

Marja. Her voice was muffled through the window. "Don't know how to drive a stick, do you?"

"Motherfucker," I mumbled, and got out of the car. Helen barked. "I was using it as a proper noun!" I yelled.

After I settled into the passenger seat, Marja handed me the PB&J and bag of Bugles. I wanted to reject it on principle, but my stomach betrayed me with a loud growl. At least I wasn't nauseous anymore.

"We could be eating BBQ in thirty minutes," Marja said.

"No. Drive."

"My car isn't drafty."

"My God, you have to get the last word in every time, don't you?"

"Yep."

I opened my mouth to reply, saw Marja's shit-eating grin, and clamped it shut.

Will this day ever end?

FIVE

I wouldn't admit it to her but I loved Marja's car.

Marja had been faithful in her restoration, right down to the AM radio in the dash. But, proving yet again that she'd thought of almost all eventualities, she had her phone plugged into the cigarette lighter, and a wireless speaker Velcroed to the floor behind the gearshift gifted us with a steady stream of seventies and eighties rock. It wasn't my first choice for music, but it was the music that I grew up on and it faded into white noise while I worked on my laptop.

"Hey." Marja waved her hand in front of my face.

"What?"

"What are you doing?"

"Working."

"You're on vacation."

I scoffed. "No, I'm riding to Chicago with you. That's not a vacation."

"It could be if you'd stop working."

"Why should I? You aren't interested in having any sort of meaningful conversation."

"Sounds like the next week is going to be nonstop. Take a day off now. Watch the world go by."

We were north of Waco, which is not scenery worth looking at. Though the house built like a caterpillar is interesting enough. Then Hillsboro and driving through Dallas on I-35, which is either warehouses, strip clubs, tile shops, or enormous chain restaurants with enormous portions. Then there's Oklahoma, which the less said about the better.

I snapped my laptop shut and turned in my seat to face Marja. "I'm not sure you're completely aware of what my job is right now since, you know, we haven't spoken in three years, but I'm the chief content officer for a growing website. That means that not only do I have to write my own share of articles, I have to read pitches from freelancers, edit what they turn in, hope that they are easy to work with and go along with my edits. I deal with contracts, make sure that the freelancers are paid in a timely matter, work with social media to make sure our content is being marketed correctly, track click-through rates, watch trends in the industry to make sure we're not lagging, and I'm always trying to find the next trend before someone else. I'm the cohost of a weekly podcast, I write a weekly newsletter, and I manage two people directly underneath me, plus everyone else because Chloe and I are the bosses."

"Sounds impressive."

"It is fu—" I glanced into the back seat; Helen was asleep. Still, better safe than sorry. "Ducking impressive."

"Sounds exhausting, too."

"It can be. I'm not afraid of hard work."

Marja looked at me and grinned. "I wouldn't expect so."

I looked out the window. It was easy to let my mind wander back to my childhood, to watching Marja work six days a week to make ends meet for the two of us, to going along with her during the summer because Marja couldn't afford child-care when I was too young to help, then pitching in when I got older, to finally running my own crew my senior year in high school. I remember playing quietly in the middle of a living room—coloring, reading, playing with my one, cherished Beanie Baby panda bear with enormous blue eyes—while Momma cleaned. Mrs. Briggs walking in and balking at me being there, the hushed conversation in the other room that still carried to my four-year-old ears.

It's wrong for you to bring that child into my home.
She knows to play quiet and stay out of the way.
She can't come again.
I need this job and I can't afford a sitter. Please.
You should have thought of that before you...

Marja didn't clean that house again, and I learned that being quiet and staying out of the way wasn't good enough. I had to disappear. I became so good at it that once Marja forgot me. She came screeching around the corner and slammed on the brakes in front of Mrs. Nichols's house. I sat on the curb, my book on my knees. I got quietly into the car, clicked my seat belt, and looked out the window. I could hear Marja's breaths coming in gasps, but I couldn't look at her. I'd long since stopped crying but I was sure if I looked at Momma I would cry and I needed to be strong. Momma took pride in being a strong woman, and I wanted Momma to be proud of me.

"I was in the zone, thinking of...the next house and you're so quiet. I'm sorry, Darcy."

"It's okay, Momma."

And it had been. When my tears had dried, pride swelled in my chest. I'd done such a good job of disappearing that Momma had forgotten me. I thought maybe, just maybe, this would work in school, too, and the teasing and bullying would stop. If only I had somewhere to disappear to.

I shook my head free of the past. In the end I had disappeared from Frio, Texas, and into another life, a better life. I hadn't intended to disappear from Marja's life, but Marja had apparently had other plans.

Until a month ago when Marja'd called out of the blue to congratulate me on my upcoming marriage. She'd spoken to Eloise and told me she was planning on coming. I didn't speak for a while, shocked not only that Marja had received an invitation but that Marja was going to come. Before I knew what was happening, I'd agreed to fly down and drive to Chicago with Marja and her dog (when did she get a dog?). The trip really couldn't have come at a worse time, personally or professionally.

I hadn't been trying to impress Marja with my list of tasks. That really was what I had to get done this week before the wedding and before Michael and I left on a fourteen-day vacation to Bali. With the money from Athena Capital, my workload would increase, but I would be able to afford an assistant and shift my thinking from day-to-day to a more global view of the website. Chloe and I believed our little website was on the cusp of something great, and it was killing me to be away from the office for even a day. I wasn't sure how I was going to survive the trip to Bali. Lots of sunscreen, but that was another issue altogether.

"How are the wedding plans going?" Marja asked.

"Eloise says everything's right on track."

"She's planning everything?"

"Yep. That was the deal. I give them the huge wedding I didn't want but they do, they plan the whole thing."

"That doesn't bother you?"

"I could give a sht—"

Bark.

"Hey, not fair. That's not a cuss word," I said.

Marja laughed. "Good ole Granny Evans. She'd be glad

64

you're carrying on the tradition. She knew full well that leaving out the *i* in *shit* never fooled anyone."

Bark.

"That's gotten really old really fast."

"You'll stop hearing it eventually."

"You could just stop cussing, you know."

"Where's the fun in that?"

I looked away so Marja wouldn't see me grin. I rolled my eyes, too.

"Why did you let Eloise and Michael bully you into a big wedding?"

"They didn't 'bully' me. It meant a lot to them and it didn't to me. It's not like I've been dreaming of marriage my whole life."

There was a long pause. "I guess I'm to blame for that."

I looked at Marja, trying to figure if the comment was an accusation. Marja had a better poker face than I did. There were lots of responses I could give. *I never had a good example of a happy couple* or *it's not like you had much good to say about men* or *your taste in men has always been shitty.* Instead, I said, "I never counted on a man, or any other person, to make me happy."

"I'm glad I at least taught you that."

"Oh yes. You taught me not to count on anyone but myself."

"Miss Independent."

"Yeah."

"Hmm. So, Michael makes you happy?"

"Why would you ask that?"

Marja side-eyed me "I'm just making conversation."

"Yes, Michael makes me insanely happy."

"Insanely. Hmm."

"Why are you saying it like that?"

"Well, for someone who makes you insanely happy, you haven't mentioned him once."

"Yes, I have." *Holy sht, I haven't. I haven't even thought of him since I'd gotten into the car.*

"Hmm."

"Stop with the hmms."

"How's Michael doing, by the way?"

I opened my text messages and saw that he sent me a thumbs-up reply to my last message and nothing else. I'm busy, he's busy. He understands. He gets me. Always has.

"I talked to him this morning. He's fine. We're fine." It's a white lie. Sue me.

Marja looked over, waiting. When I didn't continue, she said, "That's it? Fine?"

"Amazing. He's insanely handsome. Kind. Intelligent. Spectacular in bed." None of that was a lie.

"Oh, now it's getting interesting."

"I'm not going to tell you about my sex life."

"Why not? We have to talk about something for the next thousand miles."

"You know what I want to talk about."

"What?"

I scoffed. "God, you can be such a bitch."

Bark.

"Shut up, Helen."

"That's the second time you've called me that. The next time I'm going to put you out of this car," Marja said.

"Don't tempt me. Why did you even want to go on this stupid road trip if not to talk through the last three years? We've been together six hours and you haven't even apologized," I said.

"I'm sorry."

I waited. And waited. "That's it?"

"That's it."

I laughed. "Still don't like explaining yourself to anyone, not even me. The only family you have."

Marja's eyes were glued to the road. "That's right."

"Unbelievable."

"Can't we just pick up from here? Have a nice road trip for a couple of days, go eat some Chicago-style pizza before you get your dress fitted, get you married off to Michael the Sex God? Doesn't that sound like more fun than fighting?"

"No. I'm quite enjoying myself."

"You're having to work very hard to stay mad at me."

"No, that's insanely easy, Momma."

"What does Chloe think of you marrying her brother?"

"What? Why would you ask that?"

Marja shrugged. "You're best friends. It's gotta be weird that you're marrying her brother."

"We're going to be sisters. She's thrilled." Oh my God, even *I* didn't believe that.

"That's great," Marja said. "I thought it would be tough for her, considering."

"Considering what?"

Marja glanced at me. "I always thought she was a little in love with you."

How in the hell did my mother pick up on Chloe's feelings and I never did?

"I'm sorry, you what?"

"Baby girl, I love you, but you've always been incredibly obtuse when it comes to how beautiful you are."

"You're being ridiculous."

"About Chloe's feelings or your beauty?"

"Both."

"I know I'm biased, but you're the total package, Darcy, and always have been. Intelligent, attractive, funny, and so kind. It's no wonder people are drawn to you."

I knew I was blushing, so I stared out the window. "People aren't drawn to me, Momma."

"Is Chloe really happy for you?"

I did not want to have that conversation. I turned in my seat to face Marja. "Do you remember our last conversation?"

"You're changing the subject."

"Yes, Chloe is happy for me. Do you remember our last conversation?"

For the first time that day Marja looked uncomfortable. "Of course, I do."

"Really? Because I don't. Not a word. I've wracked my brain trying to remember if you'd said something, given a clue that it would be our last conversation. Or if I said something that pissed you off."

"No."

Between the road noise and me being inside myself, inside my memories, I sensed that Marja answered more than heard it.

"I didn't realize we hadn't talked for six weeks. By then, I'd forgotten everything. I felt so guilty. For months, blaming myself for being so busy I hadn't reached out. I thought maybe that was what had made you angry, that I had forgotten about you. I hadn't. I think about you every day. When I did reply, I didn't even have time to be worried that you hadn't replied to me. My life was insane right then. Trips and my freelance articles, the podcast and blog and turning it into a website. When you didn't send me a text about my book becoming a bestseller is when I knew something was wrong. So, I called Paz. I wanted to make sure you weren't dead. Do you know what she told me?"

Marja's eyes were on the road, and she didn't respond.

I scoffed to myself. "Paz told me you were alive and that

if you wanted to talk to me, you would. *Paz*. Who lives and breathes family. How much did you pay her to run interference for you? It must have cost you a lot." My voice broke and I turned my head away so Marja wouldn't see the tears flooding my eyes.

Silence. Marja might as well have been carved out of stone for the emotion she showed. Why did I even care about our relationship? She obviously didn't. After three years I'd thought I'd finally gotten over the hurt of her abandonment, but my skin felt like one big, exposed nerve. Any hope I had that this would be an apology tour and that we could repair our relationship was gone. All I needed to do now was survive it. To push all these emotions down and rebuild the shell I'd painstakingly constructed. Once in Chicago, I'd put her in a hotel and ignore her for a week, see her at the wedding, then we could go right back to being estranged. Fine by me. I don't need Marja, I have Eloise.

"Pull over," I said.

"What?"

I pointed to an exit. "Pull over. I need some air and I want to get some kolaches."

"Might as well top off, too," Marja said.

I decided I would not ask her one more question about the last three years. There was no point. Act like everything was normal to keep her happy so we could get to Chicago as soon as possible. It was time to focus on the future and put the past, and my mother, behind me for good.

SIX

We got out of the car at the West Czech Stop, my back popping even though it had only been a couple of hours since we'd been on the road. I leashed Helen, who looked a little miffed at having her nap interrupted and took her behind the bakery to a little square of parched grass to pee. Finished, Helen wiped her feet, little blades of grass and puffs of dirt flying into the air.

"That's a little dramatic for a three-second pee."

Helen didn't look apologetic. Instead, she sat down and licked herself. I watched the dog for a moment, and my stomach roiled at the smacking sounds. "Have some class, Helen. Come on. I feel like a voyeur."

We rounded the building and saw Marja talking to a man gassing up a black Suburban at the next pump. As we got closer Marja saw us, and he turned away, replaced the nozzle into the pump, and walked into the store.

Helen jumped into the car and I hooked her up to the doggie seat belt. "Who was that?"

"Some man making small talk."

"Hmm."

Marja shot me a look and I crossed my arms over my chest.

Two could play at the disbelieving hmm game. "Speaking of, how's your love life? Still sleeping with Tommy Baldwin?"

"We weren't speaking of my love life, but the answer is no."

"Was Tommy a sex god?"

"He sure thought so."

"Well, that tracks," I said. "What do you want?"

"Surprise me."

I got in line behind the mystery man. He was dressed like a farmer, but he was the cleanest farmer I'd ever seen. His hands had clean cuticles and nails, long tapered fingers (no wedding ring), and not a callous to be seen. He was handsome, for an older man, but there was no way in hell he was a farmer. He smiled at me. "What do you recommend?"

"You aren't from around here, huh?" I asked, pointedly looking at his pristine trucker hat.

"No, we're passing through," the woman in front of the man said with a little half smile. She had dark hair, olive skin, and a heart-shaped face with a pointed chin. She reminded me of someone, but I couldn't place who. No way could she think I was flirting with Farmer Ted.

"It's been a while since I've been here, but you can't go wrong with peach or the cream cheese."

"Not a sausage kolache?" the man asked.

"Technically those aren't kolaches, they're klobasnek."

"Why's that?"

"Kolaches are sweet. Klobasnek are savory. There's a place in Frisco that makes brisket klobasnek. They're amazing. If you're heading that way you should stop in."

"How do you know so much about roadside food?" the woman asked.

Penelope Cruz. That's who she looked like. She was way out of Farmer Ted's league.

"I'm a travel writer. One of the first articles I sold was about kolaches and klobasnek and the Czech influence in Central Texas."

"You from around here?"

"No."

One corner of her mouth lifted when she realized I wasn't going to elaborate. "Your momma taught you well," she said.

What an odd comment. Why were people being so weird today? Maybe I was just done with people. After the previous night's party and being stuck in the car with Marja, I'd had my fill of being social. I needed alone time, and I didn't see that happening for weeks. I groaned and hoped that no one could hear it over the din in the busy convenience store.

Farmer Ted ordered two sausage klobasnek and Penelope ordered a cherry and a cream cheese. The man paid, and with a touch to his spotless John Deere cap, told me to have a safe trip.

I ordered my mixed dozen (I know, I know), paid, and turned to leave and was stopped short when I saw Penelope standing there. She held a coffee cup in one hand and a white paper bag in the other. "It was nice talking to you." She grimaced, as if she finally realized how weird she was being.

Ah. I'd been hit on by all kinds of men and women in my travels, and the safest thing to do was to ignore it and extract yourself from the situation.

"You, too," I replied with my thanks for the compliment, but I'm not interested smile.

She walked out the door and held it open for me. I nodded a thanks, and walked to the car. Marja glowered at me from the driver's seat.

I closed the passenger door behind me. "What's that look for?"

"What look?"

"Um, the expression on your face that would murder me if

it had the chance. I got you a kolache, even though I'm pissed at you."

"Why were you talking to that woman?"

"You mean Penelope Cruz?"

Marja laughed.

"You have to admit there's a passing resemblance."

"I didn't get a good look at her."

"She's beautiful, though a little old for me."

Marja's head jerked back. "What do you mean?"

"She was hitting on me. It's flattering—she looks like Penelope Cruz after all—but a little creepy."

"Stay away from her."

I stopped what I was doing and stared at Marja. Her face was red, her lips pressed together in a thin line.

"Are you okay?"

"I'm fine. You shouldn't talk to strange people."

I laughed. "Marja, talking to strangers is what I do for a living. Jesus (bark) I'm not a child. Besides, she was harmless."

"Why do you say that?"

"She wasn't a very good flirt. Though I imagine looking like that she doesn't have to be."

I held out a cherry kolache to Marja. She relaxed a bit and took it. "How many did you get?"

"Assorted dozen."

"That seems like a lot for someone who needs to fit into a wedding dress in a few days."

I took a huge bite of a cream cheese kolache. "Haven't been fitted yet."

Marja grinned. "I hope there's plenty of give in those seams." She ripped her kolache in half and gave one part to Helen.

I watched the dog eat it from Marja's hands, her long pink tongue licking the remnants off Marja's fingers. "Do you know where her tongue has been?"

"She's a dog, so I have a pretty good idea."

"Please tell me you have wet wipes."

"Glove box."

I removed the thick packet of wipes and went still. The glove box was practically a self-defense arsenal. A gun, a hunting knife in a scabbard, a box of bullets, a can of pepper spray, and brass knuckles. "What the fuck, Momma?"

Bark.

"Two women traveling alone can't be too safe."

"A gun? You hate guns."

"People change."

"Is it loaded?"

"What good is an unloaded gun? 'Hang on, attacker, while I load my gun to shoot you.' That would never work."

I slammed the glove box closed. It popped back open, and I recoiled into the seat.

"Don't worry. The safety's on. If you're uncomfortable, just don't touch it. It won't shoot you by itself, you know." She leaned over and snapped the glove compartment closed.

"People kill people," I said.

"Exactly."

"With guns, Momma."

Marja focused on getting us out of the parking lot and back onto the highway. "I can't wait until we get to the back roads. Interstates are soulless, don't you think?"

I stared at my mother in disbelief. That was it? Why am I surprised anymore?

"Why do you have gun, Momma?"

Marja looked over at me and back at the road. She shrugged. "Protection."

"From what?"

"Why is this so surprising? You wrote an article about women protecting themselves when traveling."

"I didn't mention a gun."

"Look, forget you saw it. It's not like we'll have to use it."

"Well, you just cursed us."

Marja laughed. "It's not Chekov's gun, Darcy."

"Jesus Christ."

Bark. Bark.

"Just drop it, Darcy, okay? The gun's staying, and that's that."

SEVEN

Keep going.

It was midnight, somewhere in Oklahoma. I stood on the side of the road holding Helen's leash while she did her business, and Marja was on the phone with AAA requesting a tow truck.

"Are we in a safe location?" Marja said into the phone. "Well, we're in the middle of nowhere, so I guess so. Right. That long? Okay. What's the towing company name again? Tow the Line. Clever." Marja chuckled. "Thanks."

"How long?" I asked.

"An hour. They're coming from Tulsa."

"God."

Bark.

"At least."

"If we'd stayed on the interstate this wouldn't have happened," I said.

"If we'd stopped for the night in Dallas, it wouldn't have either."

"Here's your dog." I tossed the end of the leash in Marja's direction and started walking.

"Where are you going?"

"Away from you."

"Wanna take my gun for protection?"

I flipped Marja off as I walked away.

Remember how I said I loved Marja's car? I lied. The novelty had worn off riding in the Mustang not long after our pit stop in West, Texas. The car might have been pristinely restored, but it wasn't modern or comfortable. It rattled and shook when an 18-wheeler rumbled past and the noise, oh my God the noise; a constant hum from rubber hitting the road and a slight whistle where the wind snuck inside between the window and the frame.

We'd gotten stuck in Dallas rush hour traffic, just like I expected. Inching along in a fifty-year-old car with standard transmission brought my nausea back. I was *not* going to ask Marja to pull over. It had taken all my willpower and concentration to not throw up all over Marja's new carpet. The only reason I didn't is because I didn't want to smell vomit for the next ten hours.

When Marja signaled to pull off in Dallas for the night, my contrariness reared its ugly head. I told her to keep going, that we needed to make up the time we lost at Enchanted Rock. Marja agreed, but said she was getting off the interstate.

Now, here we were. Somewhere in Oklahoma with no cell reception. I needed to call someone and vent, but who? I didn't particularly feel like talking to Michael, or Chloe. Ella would lend a sympathetic ear, but everyone went to Ella. It had to be exhausting to listen to everyone's problems. Jess would be perfect. She would ask about the trip, be jazzed about the Mustang and probably pepper me with a million questions I couldn't answer, want to know all about Enchanted Rock, and talk about work. Jess wouldn't get personal. Jess would listen, if I wanted to share. But she wasn't one to give advice or try to solve people's problems. Or judge.

I wonder if Jess and Ella knew about Chloe's truth bomb? Have they known for years how Chloe feels about me? Am I really that obtuse? Magic 8 Ball says signs point to yes.

I held my phone up in the air, searching for a signal. Instead, I saw the white Apple logo before the black screen of death. *Of course.* I tried a hard reboot, but nothing happened. The phone had been plugged in since Paris, Texas. Or so I thought. Great.

I inhaled a long slow breath and let it out. I wanted to scream in frustration, but I didn't. I'd handled dozens of setbacks on my travels over the last decade. I could handle being stranded in BFE Oklahoma with my mother and an evangelical dog.

Solve the problem, Evans. It's your brand, after all.

Two flat tires, with only one spare, and that one a donut. All we could really do is to wait on the tow truck. Thank God Marja had Triple A. I didn't know how to change a tire, and I had no idea if my mother did. Probably. It was just the sort of thing Marja would teach herself.

Books had been our nighttime entertainment when I was growing up. We had a TV, with an antenna, but rarely turned it on. If I didn't have my head in a classic novel, I was reading a travel memoir or an out-of-date guidebook borrowed from the Frio Carnegie Library. Marja borrowed mostly historical nonfiction, you know, the books that could double as thick doorstops. She hated self-help books but checked out how-to books that could teach her usable skills—electrical, plumbing, Spanish, cooking, and baking are the ones I remembered best. We went to the library every Saturday to return books and check out more. Marja was an incredibly fast reader to get through the books she borrowed with the little free time she had. It wasn't until years later I heard the word *autodidact* and realized that it described my mother perfectly.

So, yeah. I was pretty sure Marja could change a tire. She

probably restored the Mustang by herself, too. Or most of it, anyway.

Marja turned the headlights on so I could find my way back. Did I want to go back? I heard a snuffling sound and looked toward the pasture next to me. A horse stood at the barbed wire fence. I went over and held my hand out for the horse to smell. When it didn't bolt, I moved closer and stroked the horse's cheek. "Did we wake you up, huh?" The whiskers on his, or her, muzzle tickled my palm. The horse stared at me with large, soulful brown eyes. It wasn't Jess, but she would do very nicely as a sounding board.

"You think I'm being too hard on Marja? Well, you're wrong." I leaned forward and stage-whispered, "I haven't talked to her in three years and she expects me to just be all happy and hunky-dory with a one thousand mile road trip?"

The horse turned one ear back. "I did try to get in touch with her. She ghosted me. My own mother."

The horse nodded his head up and down and snorted.

"You don't think I know she's the only family I have? Why do you think I'm so pissed at her?"

The horse pawed her back foot against the ground.

"I want her to beg me for forgiveness, though I think that ship has fucking sailed." I lifted my head and listened for Helen's bark. I wouldn't put it past the mutt to have Superman hearing. Silence, thank God.

The horse stared at me. "You think I should talk to her again? Nope. Not gonna happen. She's impossible and stubborn and I hate confrontation. Confronting and alienating people was Marja's favorite hobby. Probably still is." I absently stroked the horse's cheek and inhaled its horsey scent. It was strangely calming. "I'm a bit of a people pleaser. I know, I know. Don't start. There's nothing wrong with wanting to be liked. Loved." I whispered the last word. "I'd rather have friends than prove that I'm right all the time. Marja doesn't care about what anyone thinks of her. Which is why she doesn't have friends. Maybe she's made friends in the last few years. Friends I wouldn't approve of." Huh. "Could that be why she hadn't gotten in touch with me? She was ashamed of the people she was running around with. That's ridiculous. She's an adult. What I think about her friends doesn't matter. Like Marja would care what anyone thought."

The horse didn't answer, as if she had no idea if Marja'd made friends or not. "I wish I knew your name." The horse flicked her ears back and forth, settling on perking them forward, giving me all her attention. "I can't believe I'm talking to a horse about this. I must admit, you're one of the best listeners I've ever had. Even if you are a bit judgy."

The horse nodded again. "Fine, fine. I'm going. You're a pushy little thing. I think I like you."

Marja was leaned against the car smoking a cigarette. I settled next to her. She held out her cigarette, and I took it. We stared out at the dark pasture and shared a smoke.

"I thought you quit," I said.

"I didn't know you started."

"Only when I'm stressed. Or in France."

"Well, this ain't France. Guess I'm stressing you out."

"Yes." I dropped the end of the cigarette on the edge of the road and ground it into the loose gravel. I turned to Marja, butterflies fluttering in my stomach. "Are we not going to talk about it? Ever?"

"I'd kinda hoped so."

"Nonconfrontational. That's not like you."

"I've mellowed with age. I'm going to be fifty soon, you know."

"Stop changing the subject. Why did you ghost me three years ago?"

Marja got another cigarette out of the pack and lit it. She exhaled and stared up at the sky. I followed her gaze, reveling for the first time this trip in the star-studded sky. There were some benefits to being in the middle of nowhere.

Marja sighed. "Darcy…"

I stared at my mother, waiting, hoping, expecting her to elaborate. Marja didn't.

"I know you. I know how much you love me." My throat thickened, but I pushed on. "You wouldn't ghost me like that without a reason, and it must be a doozy."

"I can't explain it, you won't understand it, you won't like the reason. There are lots of reasons, not the least of which is that I don't have to fucking explain anything to you."

Bark.

"There she is," I said. I walked a bit away from the car and started pacing. "I wondered how long it would take for the Marja I grew up with to show up." I mock looked at my wrist. "You lasted a whole twelve hours as the go along to get along, happy-go-lucky road tripper. Mellowing with age, my ass. You're never going to change."

"Neither are you. It took every bit of courage you had to confront me in the car earlier, didn't it?" I lifted my chin defiantly. Marja pointed the two fingers holding the cigarette at me. "I can see it all over your face. I can't believe I raised such a coward."

"I'm not a coward!"

"Really?"

"Yes, really."

Marja took another drag and studied me. She blew the smoke out the side of her mouth. She looked back toward the pasture, drumming her fingers on her leg. She said *fuck* under her breath, but Helen still heard her.

Bark.

Marja squeezed her eyes tight and in a rush said, "I cut off contact with you to protect you," as if she didn't do it quickly she wouldn't do it at all.

"Protect me? From what? I needed you, Momma. We launched the website and I needed to talk to you, to hear your voice, to hear your pep talks, to hear the fucking pride in your voice. When I got engaged you, ignored my voice mail. Do you know what that did to me? Not having you there for all of that? You're the only family I have."

"I knew you had Chloe and Michael. The Parsons."

"It's not the same."

"You're right. It's better, having a nuclear family for the first time."

I jerked my head back as if I'd been slapped. I held my hand up as headlights from the back of the car blinded me. Marja turned to face the truck, moving a little in front of me. She held one arm out to keep me behind her. "I'm not a child," I hissed.

"Shut up, Darcy."

I looked at Marja. Her entire body was rigid, and her eyes were fixed on the tow truck. Or I guessed it was the tow truck. It was hard to see with the lights so bright.

"You ladies need some help?"

The voice was deep, with an ever so slight accent. When the man moved in front of the lights, we saw how big he was. I half expected The Rock to be our tow truck driver.

When Marja didn't answer, I inhaled to speak. Marja's arm pushed me farther behind her. "Who's asking?" Marja said.

The man looked at the two flat tires. "You called for help. Here I am."

"Oh, thank goodness," I said.

"Are you Big Tow?"

The man laughed and I inhaled to correct her. Marja pressed her hand against my hip, and almost imperceptibly shook her head. Her body tightened like a coiled spring and for the first time in my life I was afraid for my mother.

"Our tow truck," Marja said. "That's who AAA said was coming. Joe with Big Tow."

"That's exactly right, Marja. Joe with Big Tow. Here to take care of you and Darcy."

The man moved his hand from behind his leg. He held a tire iron. Marja shifted, putting her hand behind her and between our bodies, and shielded my eyes from the bright headlights.

That wasn't a tow truck.

"Wrong name, asshole," Marja said.

I would remember very little of what happened next. But I would never forget the ear-shattering sound of a gunshot and the sight of my mother standing over the body of a dead man, pointing her smoking gun at him.

"This Darcy. This is what I was protecting you from."

PART TWO

My name is Marja Evans and you're probably wondering how I got here. Standing over a hit man with a smoking gun, a frantic dog, and a daughter who is about to lose her shit in three…two…one.

Yep. There it is.

What the fuck kind of book is this, you ask. You're expecting a nice mother-daughter road trip story, we bond, bury the hatchet, have some zany adventures along the way, and there's a nice big wedding at the end.

Yeah, this ain't that book. Sorry.

Oh, don't get me wrong. I wanted it to be that kind of book. Who doesn't want to read a zany road trip book? After the last few years I've had, I'd love to read a fucking wild and crazy story. I'm a wild and crazy gal. Man, Steve Martin in his prime was awesome. *The Jerk* is one of the best comedies ever made.

I'm digressing here because I don't really want to tell you this story. But you've invested your hard-earned money in this story and by God, I'm going to give it to you.

Here it goes.

The first thing you need to know is this: I'm a criminal.

I'm not going to try to gloss over what I've done—I'm not *that bad* of a criminal—or even ask for forgiveness. I'm a big one on taking responsibility, and I'm not about to change now that responsibility has higher stakes than going hungry so my kid can eat or having palms the consistency of sandpaper from hard work.

Everything I did, every decision I made, is mine and mine alone.

Here's the thing about decisions, they never just affect the one making them. Their consequences, good and bad, ripple out like a goddamn pebble thrown into a pond.

I've just had the shitty luck to have more bad ripple out from the pebble than good.

EIGHT

I could start this story with the day ten years ago that I decided to launder some money for my then boyfriend, Tommy Baldwin. But, to understand that decision, you need to know how I got there, in my forties, living in the same trailer house I'd lived in for over twenty years, cleaning the same houses I'd cleaned for about as long, Saturday trips to the library, Saturday nights at the dance hall to the west of town, Sunday a hazy hangover until I dragged my ass out of bed to have my weekly call with Darcy. It wasn't a bad life, but it wasn't exciting either.

The two life-changing decisions I've made have been down to immaturity and stubbornness, and boredom. Not the best way to make life-changing decisions, is it? I've never been one for self-help or self-reflection, so I should be thankful that I've kept the questionable life-changing decisions to two.

Frio, Texas, isn't much of a town. Barely two thousand people, no quaint downtown that's been turned into a tourist trap full of antique stores selling junk that the vendors buy for pennies at garage sales. It's one of those towns you drive through, and you wonder, how do people make a living here? Most people work in the larger towns down the road. Me, I cleaned houses. I made a pretty good living at it, too. Raised Darcy with the bare minimum help from the government. Don't get me wrong, I'm not against welfare. But no one *wants* to be on welfare. It's a stopgap until things get better. Sad thing is that the government makes it damn hard to get benefits. Turns out it's expensive and time-consuming to be poor. Texas sure doesn't do anything to lift people out of poverty these days, and the churches that try usually have strings attached to the help; no sex, no drinking, no dancing, and actually going to church. Basically, they want to take away all of the fun things that make living in Frio bearable and replace it with something unbearable. Thank God I was able to have steady work and manage my money well enough that Darcy and I didn't starve. Well, I starved more days than not early on, but thems the sacrifices.

It wasn't easy in Frio, but we had one local business that managed to keep the town afloat for a good few years: a call center for supplemental prescription insurance that had thought the best idea to cut costs was to outsource customer calls to India. I hope they fired the idiot who thought making half-deaf senior citizens try to problem solve with a person in India was the recipe for success. The cost savings were sweet, though, so when they decided to move the call center back to the States the board got together and wondered, Hmm. Where could we put a call center and pay people the bare minimum and they'll be thrilled for the work? Frio, Texas, that's where. That was 2005. I got the cleaning contract. Darcy was at UT on a full ride, so I was able to stop thrifting and going to Walmart and shop at Target for a change. I also started saving money for the first time in my life.

Then, the economy tanked. One of the first things that goes are the indulgences. The good citizens of Frio couldn't cut out lattes, since not one restaurant in town made them, and forget asking them to give up their weekends drinking Lone Star at the Pedernales Dance Hall. No, the first thing to go was a maid. Me. That thirty, forty, fifty dollars a week for me to clean their house was needed now to buy food and pay bills. Of course, if you could drop your price, Marja, I might could swing it.

I'd lived in Frio my entire life. I knew who needed to tighten the belt and who didn't, so I let some clients go. I had the contract for the call center. I was doing good. So good, I caught Tommy Baldwin's eye. Finally.

Tommy Baldwin peaked in high school. Star running back, point guard with the prettiest fade away you'd ever seen, grades good enough to pass. Playing in college never crossed his mind. This was the eighties and select sports wasn't a thing, especially in small town South Texas. Tommy graduated, went to work for his carpenter father, drank on the weekends, but by some miracle managed to not get mixed up with drugs. He also managed to keep his Brad Pitt in *Thelma and Louise* body much, much longer than any of our other classmates so by the time we did start sleeping together, he was just a little soft in the stomach. He still had those arms, though, the arms I spent all of sophomore year geometry staring out.

We'd never dated in high school, never being single at the same time, but we'd circled each other for sure. When Darcy left for college and Tommy was getting his second divorce, there wasn't anything that was going to keep us out of each other's pants.

He was worth the wait. Well, I thought he was. I'd learn later that he wasn't, but I'd been abstinent for eighteen years, and only had one (terrible) time to compare him to.

Then one night, Tommy casually tossed a stack of bills toward me and said launder that for me.

What the fuck, Tommy?

It's nothing illegal.

Laundering money is illegal.

Well, it's not from anything immoral.

Really?

I'm just doing a favor for a friend, and thought I'd help you out. That's a thousand dollars. You'd get twenty points.

He explained how it would work and I agreed. Two hundred dollars for depositing some money and moving it to another account. It was a temporary thing, anyway.

Until it wasn't.

That's not really the beginning of my story. Don't worry, I'm not going to go all the way back to my birth. Your time is more precious than that. Just imagine a stereotypical white trash upbringing and you're probably close to the mark.

Small town is all I've ever known, and small towns slot you into groups when you're young. Popular kids, athletic kids, poor kids from good families, and white trash (me). The Blacks and the Mexicans were even lower than I was, but we didn't mix because this was Texas—in the eighties the racist stereotypes were out in the open instead of politely tucked beneath a veneer of benevolence, like now. Well, not like right now. It's out in the open again, but I'm older and smarter and see that racist bullshit for what it is.

I was from a family of sharecroppers who, out of pride and stubbornness, were determined not to dress up their ancestors by calling them "tenant farmers." My grandad was drafted in World War II, but never made it past the lowliest private even after surviving Omaha Beach and the Battle of the Bulge. The Evanses aren't known for taking orders all that well. A trait that was passed on to me. It's also in the running for the understatement of the century.

My daddy died when I was young and my mama didn't take

the opportunity to marry up in the world, instead marrying down (which was difficult to do, mind you). Ed was a good stepdad, mainly because he didn't try to parent me. He left that to Mama, and she lost interest pretty quick. I was what you'd call these days a free-range kid. But it was the late seventies, early eighties. Everyone was free range back then. It was just I ranged around on my feet while the popular kids did it on hot pink bikes with banana seats and tassels hanging out of the handlebars.

I envied those bikes. I wanted one more than anything in the world. This is where you expect me to tell you about how I pulled myself up by my bootstraps and earned money to buy one. No. That's not what happened. I was dirt poor, and the only way I could get that bike was to take it. And I had the chance coming out of the library one hot July Tuesday. Laurie Dodd's bike, just propped up against the library wall, begging to be taken for a joy ride. I'd seen Laurie inside, but she hadn't seen me, or if she had she'd ignored me pretty well. She and I both went to the library regularly, so I knew her pattern and that she'd be in there for a while. She'd never know. I reached my hand out and let the tassels flow like water through my small, sweaty hands. I looked left and right. No one around. There was even a basket on the front I could put my library books in. I stared at that bike a long time, imagining the wind flowing through my hair, my legs pumping the pedals, my hands releasing the handlebars and floating out to the side. The sense of freedom, of flying, was so real I felt my heart soaring, lifting me off my feet and far, far away from Frio, Texas.

You wanna ride it?

My eyes had been closed, and I hadn't seen Laurie come outside. I jerked away, expecting a shove and maybe being called a name. She ran with the popular crowd and they tended to take pleasure in teasing me, at least until I'd shoved Alisha

Hamilton to the ground at recess in third grade. The flinch away from Laurie had been a reflex, and I was ashamed of it. My cheeks flamed, and I did what I always did.

I don't want to ride your stupid bike.

I don't mind. Go on. Take it around the block. I'll stay here and watch your books.

I didn't know what to think of this...kindness. I was immediately suspicious.

Why are you being nice to me?

It was about time someone popped Alisha.

It was a good summer, the one between fourth and fifth grade. Laurie and I would meet at the library every day, talk about books, and read. She taught me how to ride a bike. She found, and stole, her older sister's well-worn copy of *Forever* by Judy Blume, and we went to the football stadium and hid beneath the bleachers to read it. Tried to figure out what it all meant. I had other friends, but no one who shared my love of books and learning. For the first time in my life, I looked forward to the new school year.

The first day of school, Laurie snubbed me. She was back with the popular group, and when I tried to catch her eye before the morning bell rang, she turned her back and whispered in Alisha's ear. Then, they looked my way and laughed.

Here I am, going on about stuff that doesn't matter, even after I promised you I wouldn't. Sorry about that.

I got pregnant with Darcy when I was sixteen. Somehow, I'd managed to beat the Evanses' odds and be almost pretty in the face. I had a "body like a brick outhouse" according to the men of the town (again, this was the eighties; old men could be creepy out loud and in public, even in front of their wives) and was catching everyone's eye, old, young, Black, white, Mexican. The only one who caught my eye was a twenty-eight-year-old man named Russell Clarke, descendant of the town founders, the same descendants who owned the land my family sharecropped. I babysat his two-year-old son while he and his wife, Chelly, went to the dance hall. They were nice to me. Chelly was an outsider, being from Houston, and didn't have preconceived notions about me. She just knew her son adored me and the kitchen was spotless when she got home, I mistook Russell not leering at me for disinterest. I was flattered when he treated me like an adult.

Turned out, he was just a very good groomer.

It's hard to remember now, nearly thirty-four years on, if I had any big plans or dreams for my life. Sure, I wanted to get out of Frio, but how I planned to do it has escaped me. It wasn't like I had anyone encouraging me to make something better of myself. This may shock you, or maybe not, but there's a certain strain of poor people who don't want others to pull themselves up, to better themselves. It makes them look bad because they haven't managed it, you see. This type of poor people take comfort in blaming everyone else for their plight, usually brown people. I believe these days these complainers are labeled "economically anxious." Well, whatever their label, that pretty much describes my mom.

I expected a bit of sympathy when I told my mom I was pregnant. She had me at fifteen, after all.

Ed and I can't afford another mouth to feed.

I ain't gonna be your babysitter.

I ain't got the money for an abortion, either. Didn't have it when I got pregnant with you, don't have it now. Ask the daddy because take it from me, you don't want to be saddled with a baby at seventeen.

Fuck you, too, Momma.

She was right. I didn't want to have a baby at seventeen. I didn't want to turn into my mother, a bitter, mean woman who blamed everyone else for her terrible life. Especially me. Motherly love? I didn't even know that phrase existed.

No surprise then that when I decided to keep the baby, Momma threw me out. My dad's mom took me in, said she'd look after the baby while I worked. Granny Evans couldn't afford us, either. Her disability and social security checks were barely enough to make ends meet for herself, but she was a kindhearted old woman and taught me everything I know about unconditional love. So, I finished out my sophomore year in high school and went to work. The $500 Russell gave me for an abortion didn't go very far. I was working two jobs, then I started cleaning a few houses on the weekends, cash only. It was better than going on welfare. No one wants to get on welfare; it's usually a stopgap until things get better. And they did. Eventually.

No one was with me when I had Darcy. Granny was pretty much housebound. Momma and Ed hadn't spoken to me in months. Goes without saying that Russell wasn't involved. I hadn't had the time to go to childbirth classes so I'd checked *What to Expect When You're Expecting* out of the library, read it cover to cover, and practiced breathing on my own. Frio didn't have a hospital, so I went to Boerne. Drove myself. When the ER nurse realized I was alone, she got a candy striper to stay with me until she got off her shift. Her name was Mary Bailey and she held my hand, helped me through my breathing all through childbirth. All twelve hours of it. By the end, she knew my whole story, and I don't think you could have dragged her away from my bedside with an F150 and a tractor chain. Mary taught me how to breastfeed, how to change Darcy's diaper, helped me give Darcy her first bath.

The night before I was supposed to leave the hospital, Darcy latched on easily, and I'd settled back against the pillows, the stress of will she or won't she latch, the doubts about my being able to take care of this beautiful little girl were banished, at least briefly. I watched her little mouth suckle my breast, her eyes open and I swear to God they were focused intently on mine, her little fist laid against my swollen breast as if afraid it was going to run off. In that moment, when the lights were dimmed and Darcy's dark eyes looked up into mine with such innocence and trust, I knew what it was to be completely, irrevocably, totally in love. And I knew, no matter what the cost to me, I would do everything in my power to protect Darcy.

I never expected it to lead to murder.

NINE

Darcy

The silence of the Oklahoma countryside was shattered by the gunshot, then the shit hit the fan. Helen barked her head off before launching herself out of the back seat and running off into the darkness. Marja paced, her hands to her head (including the gun) saying, *"Shit, shit, shit."* The man on the ground held his stomach, coughed up blood, and went still.

"This Darcy. This is what I was protecting you from."

I stood there, too stunned to move, to speak, to think. Then adrenaline kicked in.

"What the fuck, Momma? Why did you shoot our tow truck driver?"

Marja pointed at the truck with her gun hand. "That ain't a tow truck, Darcy, and he ain't a tow truck driver. He had a gun!"

Sure enough, a handgun lay next to the dead man.

"Oh my God," I said. "Why was he trying to kill us?"

Marja's eyes went wide, and she swung her gun toward me. I ducked, covering my head with my arms.

"Momma!"

I heard a shotgun being cocked and saw Marja do her best Olivia Benson stance. Then everyone started yelling.

"FBI, put the gun down!"

"Marja, get down! Darcy, stay there."

I didn't have to be told twice.

"Who the fuck are all you people? I'm here to tow a car!"

"FBI. Drop the gun, now!"

"Easy there. Don't get trigger happy. I'm puttin' it down," the man said.

"What is HAPPENING?" I asked.

"Down on the ground!"

"Marja, put the gun down. Now," a woman said in a steely voice.

"Okay, okay," Marja said.

"Hands behind your head," a third man said. I think. It all happened so fast and, honestly, it felt like being in the middle of a CBS crime drama. Surreal. Out of body experience.

"Hey man, you don't need to cuff me. I heard the gunshot and came to help."

I heard handcuffs, and the rustle of the agent pulling the man to standing. I kept my face into the ground, my hands over my head, thinking maybe if I closed my eyes tight enough, all of this would disappear. I would be talking to my mom, waiting for the tow truck driver, worrying about where we might find a decent motel in the middle of nowhere Oklahoma. I heard gravel crunch beneath someone's feet.

A gentle female voice said, "You can get up now, Darcy."

I looked up, and through my watery eyes I saw the kind face of a woman smiling encouragingly down at me. She held out her hand. I took her hand and stood. My knees immediately buckled. She put her arm around my waist to steady me. "Here. Lean against the car. That better?"

I tried to nod, but my entire body shook so badly that I couldn't. "It's adrenaline," the woman said, taking off her windbreaker and putting it around my shoulders. "It'll pass in a bit."

"Th-thank you."

"You're welcome. I'm Agent Elena González. You're safe now."

"What-t-t is go-going on?"

"Where the hell were you?" Marja shouted.

"What are you doing with a gun?" González shouted back.

"I didn't trust you to protect me, obviously, and I was right."

"God, you're a stubborn pain in the ass," González said. "We've got bigger fish to fry here, Marja," she said, jerking her head toward the dead man on the ground. "Jesus Christ you killed him."

Marja handed the gun to the male agent. He ejected the magazine and the bullet in the chamber.

"Where were you, Cooper?"

"Parked on a side road a quarter mile away. Waiting for the tow truck, just like you," the man said.

"Yet somehow this meathead managed to get past you and nearly kill me."

"As soon as we saw him stop, we came. You shot him pretty fast," Cooper said.

"He was aiming a gun at Darcy."

I looked at the male agent full-on for the first time. It was the man from the gas station. "You," I said. My fear was replaced with indignation and vindication. "You're from the Czech Stop. I knew you were suspicious."

"I'm not suspicious. I'm a Fed."

"You don't even see the humor in that, do you?" González said.

"And you," I said. "You're the woman who hit on me."

100

The agent's face blanched. "I wasn't hitting on you."

"I'm going to find my dog," Marja said.

"You need to stay here," Agent González said. Marja ignored her. I would have gone after her, but I didn't think my legs would work. The woman cursed under her breath, and I waited in vain for Helen to bark.

"Do you guys need a tow, or what?"

I looked at the tow truck driver. He was a scrawny young man with long dark hair and a pathetic excuse for a goatee. He wore oil-stained coveralls with an embroidered name patch on one side that read "Earl" and Tow the Line on the other. He didn't look like an Earl. He stood patiently, his hands still cuffed behind him. He'd driven up on two women holding a gun on a dead man and he looked as bored as if was waiting in line at the grocery store checkout.

Agent Cooper grabbed Earl by the arm and put him in the back of the Suburban.

"Hey, man, I didn't do anything. I've got rights," was the last thing Earl said before Agent Cooper slammed the door in his face.

Cooper and González moved a little bit away, but not so far that I couldn't hear. I put my head on my knees and did my best disappearing act. It worked.

Agent Cooper was obviously pissed and not listening to whatever argument González was trying to make. "We tried it your way, González, and now I have a dead cartel hit man to deal with."

I lifted my head. "I'm sorry, a cartel what?"

The agents turned their heads to me.

"You shouldn't be eavesdropping," Cooper said.

"Then you should have walked farther away," I countered. "How did a cartel hit man know our names?"

The agents shared a look but didn't comment.

"When Marja was making sure he was the tow truck driver he said *Marja and Darcy* and we hadn't told him our names."

"Does this look like a tow truck to you?" Agent Cooper waved his hand at the truck.

My brain fog was clearing, and I was taking a dislike to this man who wanted to pin this on Marja as something other than self-defense. "The lights were in our eyes and it's a diesel, right? A fucking huge truck that is obviously overcompensating for Tiny there. I didn't realize it wasn't a tow truck until Marja started shooting."

Cooper dialed his phone and gave me a sour look.

"This is falling on you, González. You know that, right?"

"Yes, Agent Cooper. I'm well aware."

He walked off to talk on his phone.

González went to the Mustang's trunk, hit it lightly with her fist, and it popped open. She pulled a water bottle out of the cooler, opened it, and handed it to me.

I lifted the bottle to my lips, but I was shaking so badly water spilled out onto my hand. I pulled the water down. "Will someone tell me what's going on?"

"Your mom hasn't told you anything?"

"I haven't talked to my mom in three years."

"You've been in a car for eight hours."

"Have you ever tried to get my mom to tell you something she doesn't want to?"

"As a matter of fact, I have."

"Then it's not a surprise she didn't say anything. We were finally getting somewhere when he showed up." The dead man was still dead. I looked away.

"He can't hurt you anymore," Agent González said.

"No, but his friends might."

"I won't let that happen. I swear."

I looked at the agent closely for the first time. Her expression was strong. Determined. She had dark hair pulled back into a severe bun at the nape of her neck. She wore little makeup but she didn't need it. Dark eyes, long lashes, a pointed chin with a dimple in the middle of it. González looked like the most beautiful badass in the world.

González looked behind me, and her expression changed to one of exasperation? Relief? Her faced morphed so quickly from one emotion to the other that I couldn't be sure I hadn't imagined the softening of the woman's features.

"How's Helen?" González asked. She reached out and scratched Helen behind the ear.

"Shaking like a leaf," Marja said, holding Helen close.

"Does she need some water?" González asked.

"I can take care of my dog, thank you. Is Cooper cutting this short?"

"You killed a man, Marja."

"In self-defense!"

"It's a tranq gun," González said. "He wasn't trying to kill you."

"Oh, just tranquilize me and Darcy, kidnap us, and *then* kill us. That would have been so much better."

Agent González inhaled and stood straight, showing off her considerable height. Agent Cooper called her over, and she left, but not without giving Marja a withering look.

I looked between the agent and my mother, whose expression was just as withering as González's. "How well do you two know each other?"

"Shh. I'm trying to listen."

Marja tried to move past me, but I stepped in front of my mother. "Don't fucking shush me." Marja looked irritated and glanced over my shoulder. I followed her gaze. González and Cooper were talking low, with González occasionally looking over at the two of us and nodding. Marja tried to move again, and I cut her off.

"I think I deserve a goddamn explanation after watching you shoot a man, and then the Feds show up? What the fuck is going on, Mom? "Why would anyone want to kill us?" I asked.

"Hold Helen." She shoved the dog into my arms and walked around me. I struggled to not drop the dog, and finally got Helen cradled on my shoulder like a baby. The poor dog was trembling worse than I was. Helen hid her face in my neck. "Shh, shh, shh. It's all over now. You're just fine, Helen." The dog licked my neck, and my heart melted a little bit.

I watched Marja, Cooper, and González argue in low voices. Marja apparently lost. She stalked over to me and tried to take Helen.

"No. She's not going to calm down with you wound up like that."

Marja huffed, stalked off toward the pasture by the road. She screamed, and the horse ran off into the night.

TEN

Darcy

Agent González—Lena, she told me to call her—Marja, and I drove in tense silence for fifty miles, through two small towns, until we found a motel on a side road the other side of Tulsa. It was almost dawn when Lena left us in the car, taking the keys with her, and went into the lobby to get a room.

Helen lay in the middle of the back seat between me and Marja. I had stroked Helen until she eventually stopped trembling and fell into an uneasy sleep. Lena drove, occasionally catching my eye in the rearview mirror and smiling encouragingly. Marja stared out the window for fifty miles. After witnessing Marja's breakdown, I knew better than to broach the subject of what was going on again.

My phone buzzed with messages from Michael, Chloe, Jess, Ella, and Eloise.

Chloe: what the hell are you doing in the middle of Oklahoma at this time of night?

I smiled. Guess Chloe got home from partying and checked Life 360.

Michael: Text me when you wake up.

Ella: Have you talked to Chloe?

Jess: Girl, how was Enchanted Rock? Bring back good memories?

Eloise: Hi Darcy. Call me when you get the chance. We need to finalize the seating chart for dinner. I hope you and your mother are having a wonderful time! Be careful and tell Marja I can't wait to see her!

I glanced at Marja. Still brooding. Yeah, that's not gonna happen.

"Does your face hurt?" I said.

"What?"

"Your face? From holding that pissed off expression all night."

"You don't know what you're talking about."

"Probably not, because no one has fucking told me what's going on."

Helen couldn't find the indignation to bark. She kept her eyes closed and grunted.

"I don't remember you cursing this much," Marja said.

"I don't. You bring it out in me."

"Nice."

I sighed. "Fine. Don't tell me. Change the subject. I'll get it out of Lena." My eyes shifted to the agent who was walking back to the car. Lena popped open the back of the Suburban.

"Come on. I got us a room." She grabbed my duffel and Marja's suitcase, closed the back and started walking away. I got out of the car and followed. Marja waited just long enough to show her displeasure but came along with Helen.

"Sorry it's not nicer," Lena said. "We'll stay here for a bit. Let you guys get some sleep. Cooper will be along later after he's finished at the scene."

It wasn't the biggest dump I'd ever stayed in, but at least the other dump had been in Colombia and not in Oklahoma. Location really did make a difference. I collapsed facedown on the bed farthest from the door.

"I need to run an errand," Lena said. "Can I trust you not to take off?"

"Trust. That's an interesting concept coming from you."

Lena's voice lowered, but I could still hear if I kept really still and held my breath. "Can we not do this, Marja?"

"Do what? Not trust each other?"

There was a long silence. I turned my head toward the two women and caught them in a stare down. Poor Lena, she didn't know who she was up against. As the stare down lengthened and Lena didn't budge, I thought, *Maybe she does.*

"Come on, Helen," Lena said, patting her leg twice. Suddenly energized, Helen jumped off the bed and stood at Lena's feet, wagging her tail.

"Stealing my dog. Nice."

They walked to the door. "I'll bring her back. Along with breakfast. Maybe getting some food in you will improve your mood."

"Not fucking likely."

Bark.

"Well, it'll improve my mood, at least."

The door closed, and Marja collapsed backward on the other bed. I watched her in silence; it was as if Marja had forgotten I was even in the room. She stared at the ceiling for a long time. Eventually, she rubbed her eyes with her palms, turned away, and curled into a fetal position. Sooner than I expected, her breathing evened out.

Now it was my turn to stare at the ceiling. I didn't want to let my imagination run away with me, but Jesus Christ how could I not? A cartel assassin had been sent to kill my mother. My mother. Who'd never so much as gotten a speeding ticket and spent the first eighteen years of my life drumming into my head that the surest way to ruin my life was to do drugs and to trust a man. The doing drugs part had been easy to avoid. I didn't want to do anything to fuck up my chance of getting a full ride to UT and get out of Frio once and for all. As far as staying away from boys, that had been easy, too. Much to my disappointment, though not Marja's.

Marja hadn't dated, had steered clear of men altogether, until I left Frio. She said it was to protect me, that she wasn't about to bring a man into their life and all the drama and risk that went along with it. I didn't understand what "risk" Marja was talking about until sophomore year in high school when a friend had told me through angry tears why she wasn't fucking sad in the least that her uncle was dead. When I got home, I'd hugged my mother tightly and said thank you.

Though Marja never slipped up and said "getting pregnant" would ruin my life, I'd always wondered if Marja didn't think having me, being a single mother in a judgmental small town, had been a huge mistake. Plenty of cruel kids had said as much to me over the years, taunted me about being a bastard and being poor. Maddie Clarke had always been the worst, of course. The only other redhead in their grade. When I'd seen Maddie in kindergarten, I'd thought it would give us a bond, that we would be fast friends. (There are challenges to being redheaded and pale skinned that other kids just don't have to think about. Sunscreen for one thing. Copious amounts of sunscreen. Frizzy hair, too.) But out of all the kids in the school,

Maddie had been the cruelest. Since she was from the richest family in town, the other kids followed her lead. My friends were the other poor kids and the Mexicans. The truth was, I was alone most of the time, so I learned to fade into the background, to observe, listen, and pay attention to the subtext. I'd worked out why Maddie hated me when I saw her dad in the hallway outside of Principal Verne's office when I punched Maddie. My tormenter.

My half sister.

I would figure out what Marja was hiding now, and it wouldn't even be that hard. I had a pretty good suspicion of at least half of it already. It was a crazy idea, but I'd read a lot of fucking subtext already, and Marja didn't have as good of a poker face as she thought. Especially where I was concerned. I had spent eighteen years studying my mother. I was an expert.

My phone vibrated. Chloe. Relief washed through me. I got up off the bed, went into the bathroom, and shut the door.

"Hey," I whispered.

"What is going on? Why are you in… Vinita, Oklahoma?"

"Driving Route 66 with Marja."

"Have you told her it's shit?"

"Yes. She won't listen."

"She hasn't changed."

"Not much, no."

"So, has she explained herself?"

"No."

There was a beat of silence. "Our plan didn't work, did it?"

"Not at first," I replied. "She was about to tell me something when the hit man showed up."

The pause was longer. "Wait, what?"

I started laughing. It was all so absurd, I had to. And, I suspected there was still a bit of adrenaline running through my blood. I was physically exhausted, but my mind was going a mile a minute.

"Are you fucking with me?" Chloe sounded a little impatient.

"Actually, I'm not. We had a flat tire, two flat tires, in BFE Oklahoma. We were waiting on AAA and this guy drives up. Huge truck that I thought was the tow truck. He talked to Marja. I thought he had a tire iron, but it was a gun, actually a tranq gun which just raises all kinds of other questions and scenarios that I really don't want to think about."

My nose itched and tears pricked my eyes. No. I can't break down. Chloe would be here immediately. I wanted her here, but I refused to put her in danger.

"And a *what*, Fitz?" Chloe's voice had taken on her "quit the bullshit I'm your friend talk to me" tone. I might have heard it a couple of times before. Or dozens.

"Fitz, by God if you don't tell me what's going on, I'm going to do something drastic."

I laughed. I couldn't help it. We'd watched *Rear Window* so many times the phrase had become our go to drama queen inside joke.

"Shut up," she said, "and don't change the subject! You can't just casually mention a hit man and not give more details."

"Jesus, read between the lines, Chlo. I probably shouldn't have said anything."

"You have to tell me the rest."

"Marja shot the hit man."

"Holy mother of God. Is he dead?" Chloe squeaked out the last word.

"Yes. The cartel assassin is dead and Marja killed him. With a gun she had stashed in the glove box"

"A cartel assassin? How do you know? Did he look like those brothers from *Breaking Bad*?"

I thought about it. "Yeah, he did a bit, actually. The Feds said he's a cartel man so I guess he is."

"The FEDS? Darcy."

"Chloe."

"How do you sound so calm?"

"I'm exhausted. Probably still in shock. I don't know."

"I'm on my way."

"No, you're not."

"Darcy, you're obviously in trouble. You need me."

I didn't reply. Everything that happened between us Friday night—forgotten in the excitement of these crazy past few hours—came roaring back. For fifteen years, since Chloe had walked into my dorm room with a bright smile and mischief in her eyes, Chloe had been my best friend. Protector. Biggest champion. Shoulder to cry on. Ear to bend. Everyone at Wander Women called us Momma and Mom as a joke though honestly, the only thing missing from our relationship was sex. We were partners through and through, which is why Michael was jealous.

When I met Michael, Chloe's older brother, I'd been completely lovestruck. But Michael was eight years older, a successful, high flying Wall Street broker, getting married, and hadn't taken a second look at me. Until two years ago at Thanksgiving when I was trying to understand my mother's silence, and Michael was trying to get over losing his wife to a much richer, much older man. Commiseration had turned into friendship and eventually into love and an engagement. Naively, I didn't think my relationship with Michael would change anything between Chloe and me. Officially becoming sisters would tie us together even more tightly. I thought I was going to have the perfect life, then Michael dropped the bombshell. He'd already had a wife who hadn't put him first; he expected that from me. Our relationship should take precedence over my friendship with Chloe, and it should be private as well. Sharing our problems with Chloe, or any friends, would weaken our bond. And it would make things too awkward, put a wedge in the Parsons family. People would have to take sides. No, Michael and I were getting married, and each of us would be—should be—the most important person in the other's life. That extended to my relationship with Chloe.

It was a ridiculous request, and we had a huge fight about it.

"You seriously expect me to not talk to anyone about our relationship?"

"Yes," Michael said.

"Ever?" I laughed.

"Yes."

"I can't talk to my friends about us at all. There's going to be an entire part of my life I can't talk to anyone about."

"You can talk about the good things."

"Oh, but not the problems? I'll just have to stew in anger and figure it out on my own."

"No, you talk to me about it, and we resolve whatever problems we have like adults."

I crossed my arms over my chest. "You mean we talk until you wear me down and I give in to what you want."

"That's not what we do."

"Isn't it? When was the last time you admitted you were wrong? The last time you said you were sorry?"

Michael had put his hands in his pockets and jingled his keys, a sure sign he was uneasy. "When was the last time you admitted you were wrong?"

"We're talking about you, not me."

"Why can't I ask you a question? You're asking me questions."

"I asked first."

"Darcy."

"Michael."

"What are we even fighting about?"

I sighed and gave up. It ended just like it always did. I said *fine* and went to work.

I never told Chloe about Michael's demand, but I complained less to her about Michael, which she noticed. Nothing else about our relationship changed. She tried to pry a few times, but I deflected her questions and she moved on.

Chloe was my best friend, and I wasn't going to give up that relationship, that platonic intimacy, for anyone. Even my husband. Chloe knew me better than anyone except Marja, and that would never change.

"Have you told Michael?" she said.

The question shook me back to the present with a stab of guilt, or was it dread?

"I was about to call him," I lied.

The truth was, I didn't want to tell Michael any of this. He loved to tell his business associates about my rags to riches story, the way I pulled myself out of poverty, how Marja had grown her one woman cleaning business to a thriving small business with twenty-five employees, neatly fitting us into his capitalistic bootstrap narrative even though it was complete bullshit. I'd never had the courage to tell him, or anyone, that welfare had kept food on the table during the lean times. I couldn't imagine what Michael would say about Marja being mixed up in a cartel and killing a man, for God's sake. Frankly, I didn't want it to be a story he told his golf buddies.

"Sure, you were," Chloe said. "You know, Fitz, I think you need to really interrogate yourself as to why you had no problem sharing this with me, but the idea of sharing it with Mike scares you to death."

"It doesn't scare me to death."

"Doesn't it?"

"Just don't say anything. I need to know more about what's going on. You know he'll pepper me with a million questions."

"You're going to marry him in six days. Doesn't he have that right?"

"Fine. I'll call this afternoon. Right now, I need to sleep."

I hung up the phone and powered it down. In the bedroom, I pulled back the covers, crawled underneath, and didn't fall asleep.

ELEVEN

Darcy

I woke up with a warm wet tongue licking my face. I opened my eyes and squinted against the shaft of sunlight streaming through the drapes. Helen sat on the bed next to me, tongue hanging out, looking at me with bright, expectant eyes.

"You're a morning person, aren't you?" I said.

Helen barked and grinned. It made her look demented.

"I hate morning people." I turned over. Helen jumped across my body and snuggled next to me, putting her nose right up to my face.

"I think she likes you."

Lena leaned against the dresser, holding a to-go cup of coffee. A traveler with two other cups sat next to her.

"Surviving *High Noon* together will do that to you," I said.

Lena chuckled. "Hardly *High Noon*."

"It might as well have been."

"Yeah, sorry you had to see all that. Want some coffee?"

"Please."

Lena handed me a cup. I removed the lid and blew on it, taking the opportunity to observe the agent over the rim. She had dark circles under her eyes, her clothes looked rumpled, and soft tendrils of her hair and fallen out of her bun and framed her face. It takes real skill to look tired and stressed and beautiful at the same time.

"You don't look like an FBI agent."

She smiled and rolled her eyes. "I get that a lot."

"Did you get any sleep last night? Or this morning, I guess."

"A little."

I looked around the room. I'd been taking up the whole bed, and only one side of Marja's bed had been disturbed. "Where?"

Lena pointed to the chair by the window with the hand that held the coffee cup.

"Keeping watch?"

"Yep."

"I was joking."

She smiled. "There's a bag of donut holes if you want a snack, but there's a diner down the street that probably has better food."

"We can dream."

Lena laughed. "Good point. I've eaten at some pretty shitty diners."

"Same."

"I know. I've read your stuff."

"Have you?"

"Sure." She raised her hand. "Solo traveler here, at least when I can get away from my family."

"Oh, are you married?"

She chuckled. "With a job like this? No. My extended family. They all seem to think since I don't have a husband that I should want to spend all of my vacation time in their tiny house with a TV blaring eighteen hours a day."

"Sounds relaxing."

"It's nice at holidays. I love my family, but I need my alone time."

"Truth," I said. I sipped my coffee. "How long have you been in the FBI?"

"Fifteen years."

I laughed. "Did you start when you were ten?"

Lena smiled and shook her head. She'd heard this before. "I'm older than I look. Good genes, I guess. I'm not going to tell you how old I am."

"She's forty," Marja said. She walked out of the bathroom in nothing but a towel. Her hair was wet, spiky, making her look like a punk rocker. I still hadn't gotten used to Marja's new hair. I missed her long dark blond hair. It had always softened Momma a bit, this incredibly feminine aspect of her. Now, with short ash blond hair contrasting with her pale skin, all softness was gone, replaced with someone who might as well have been a stranger.

Lena's smile faded.

"Sorry, Lena. My mom can be a real bitch when she wants to."

"Oh, I know."

Her back to me and Lena, Marja removed her towel and started getting dressed. Lena looked down and away and blushed.

When Marja was dressed, Lena stepped up to her and looked down. For the first time I could ever remember, Marja looked small. Vulnerable. "You can keep pouting—"

"I'm not pouting."

"Yes, you are," I said.

"—and being a bitch if you want," Lena continued. "But it's going to make the next eight hundred miles pretty miserable if you do."

"What do you mean?"

"I'm coming with you. For protection."

"We don—"

"It's not your decision to make. They sent a hit man for you, Marja. You're lucky Cooper hasn't swept you off into protective custody already. We're doing you a favor here."

Marja's jaw pulsed with the effort to stay silent.

"What favor?" I asked.

"Your mom can tell you." Lena looked pointedly at Marja. "I'm not doing it for you, you coward." To me she said, "How quick can you get ready?"

"Twenty minutes?"

"Make it fifteen. We've already lost a lot of daylight. And we have a deadline."

"What?" Marja said.

"Yeah. Two days." Lena opened the door.

"You promised."

"Cooper promised. Not me. I want to be rid of you as much as you want to be rid of me," Lena said, and the door closed behind her.

Marja stared at the door, and I expected her to find the nearest shoe and throw it. Instead, her shoulders slowly fell from her tense, combative stance. She turned to look at me, with an expression of complete defeat. This was the moment to push her. By the expression on Marja's face, she was waiting for it. Ready for it. The Question.

I disentangled myself from Helen. "I guess I better get a move on."

"That's it? No third degree?"

I shrugged. "Nope," I said, and closed the bathroom door on my mother's slack-jawed astonishment.

The diner was a greasy spoon inside a gas station that had surprisingly good buttermilk pancakes and perfectly crisp bacon. I silently ate the center of my pancakes, soft and rich with butter and syrup, listened to Marja argue with Cooper in harsh whispers, and tried to be invisible. Lena was doing much the same with her two-egg breakfast. I would occasionally glance at the agent, who sat across from me in the booth. Lena ate steadily, not reacting to anything that was said.

"I don't understand why it can't be you," Marja said.

"Three reasons. One, I'm the lead on the case so I can delegate. Two, I've got to clean up the mess you made last night."

"Which was not my fault."

Cooper ignored the statement. "If you'll remember, I thought this was all a terrible idea. If it were up to me, I would have handed you off to WITSEC and been done with you a week ago. You have Lena here to thank for you getting to see your daughter at all."

Lena picked up her napkin and wiped her mouth, and briefly caught my eye. She determinedly didn't look at Marja and went back to her hash browns.

"So, third reason. You killed a man—" Cooper said.

"Who was going to kill Darcy."

"—and if you do anything else stupid, it's all falling in Agent González's lap. She convinced our bosses this was the best way to get you to cooperate, and that's proved to be a major miscalculation. She'll be lucky if the worst thing that happens to her is being sent to Alaska and forgotten about. You are her responsibility for the next twenty-four hours. Not a week, and there is absolutely no discussion about it. She's going to deliver you to the Chicago office, you're going to give us everything you know, on the record, and the access code to where you have the evidence parked, and then you can start your new life. If you don't, you're going to jail."

My fork stopped halfway to my mouth and my entire body turned to ice. "I'm sorry, twenty-four hours until what now?"

Cooper stared at Marja with raised eyebrows. "You haven't told her?"

"I was getting around to it."

"Would y'all stop beating around the bush and tell me what's going on?"

Marja sat back in the booth and looked down at her hands. "I got mixed up with the wrong people, and now I'm paying for it."

I waited for more. It didn't come, so I put my fork down. "I'd figured that out for myself, you know. You worked for a cartel? Doing what? Selling drugs?"

"Of course not."

"A contract killer, then."

"Don't be ridiculous. I laundered money."

"Like Skyler in *Breaking Bad*?"

"Yeah. I did a better fucking job at it than she did."

"And now you're turning state's evidence?"

"Only because she got caught," Lena mumbled.

Marja glared at her. "I turned myself in."

Lena raised her eyebrows. "Because you were about to get caught."

Marja blushed and turned her angry gaze back to Cooper. "You're really going to stick me with her for the next twenty-four hours."

"Say goodbye to your daughter and I'll take you now."

"No."

"Then grow up, Marja, and be thankful for what you got. You aren't the fucking victim here. You're a criminal, and frankly I hate giving you a deal at all. Lena was doing her job or trying to at least."

Lena glared at Cooper.

Marja threw her napkin down on her plate. "I've lost my

appetite." She stalked out of the diner. An agent sitting at the next table got up and followed her.

Cooper took the check. "I'm going to pay."

I picked up my fork and stared at the last good bite of my pancakes and suddenly felt nauseous.

My mother is a money launderer for a drug cartel. What is Michael going to think? If this ever comes out, it might hurt his career. Oh my God, the website. What would the association do to the website? Would the VC money dry up when this comes out?

"You okay?" Lena said softly.

"What?" I looked into the woman's eyes and found compassion and tenderness. My well-being was incredibly important to Lena González, and I didn't understand why, though I had a suspicion or two.

"I know it's a lot to take in," Lena said.

"I'm thinking about how my fiancé is going to react. What it will mean for my business."

Lena's brows furrowed, and she smiled ever so slightly. "What about you?"

"What do you mean?"

"Aren't you worried about what it will mean for you?"

"Oh. I guess, yeah. If the website goes under, I'll be out of a job. I've been a freelancer before. I know the hustle."

"And if your fiancé doesn't react well?"

I stilled. What if Michael didn't react well? "I don't know."

Lena started scooting out of the booth. I grabbed her hand. "What's between you and my mother?"

"I was undercover in one of Marja's companies."

"Companies? Multiple?"

"Yes, she was very good at her job. That's why the cartel is after her. We became friends. I got too close and my judgment was questioned. I got pulled from the case. She came to the FBI not long after for a deal. They sent me to talk to her with Cooper."

"Well, now it makes sense. When someone crosses my mom, then it's all over. She doesn't forgive or forget."

"Yes, I know."

I narrowed my eyes. "You were doing your job, and you'll be rid of her in twenty-four hours."

"Right. In less than a week, I'll never see her again." Lena got up from the booth. I watched her go, unsurprised that the idea seemed to upset Agent González so much.

TWELVE

Marja

I guess my biggest splurge was the Mustang. It was easy enough paying cash to have it refurbished. Motorheads don't ask a lot of questions when a pretty woman in tight jeans and a wad of cash brings in a '69 Mustang and says, "Do it right, boys. Get it done in six weeks and I'll double it."

It was done in four weeks.

The first weekend I took the Mustang out for a drive with the top down…man, oh, man, that felt like freedom. I drove up north to San Angelo just because I'd never been there. I stayed the night, wandered around town a little bit and decided I hadn't missed much. The next day I took my time going home, drove back down through Llano and had some BBQ, stopped off in Lynchfield and browsed the antique shops. Picked up some kolaches for breakfast the next morning and drove to Tivydale and parked my car in the abandoned barn on a piece of land I'd bought (real estate; the best money laundering scheme the world over) and was home by dusk. To an empty house.

I didn't miss having friends when Darcy was growing up. I was too busy working, taking care of Darcy, spending time with Darcy. She was an amazing child, so intelligent and fun to be with. And she loved me so much. Unconditionally, same way I loved her. Darcy is the longest, most stable relationship of my life. Of course, I had to go fuck that up.

But we're not to that part of the story, yet.

After she went to UT, I tried to reconnect with some friends from high school, and for a while was having a good time hanging out with them. I joined a book club—a wine club really but who's gonna complain about getting together and drinking wine once a month?—volunteered to read to the local nursing home residents on Sunday afternoons, and even went back to church for a month. I couldn't stomach seeing all those people whose houses I cleaned, whose secrets I knew, being pious and hypocritical once a week.

Things were going pretty well, so I should have known that Chelly Clarke would find out and ruin it for me. The nursing home suddenly didn't need me. Chelly Clarke's donation made sure of that. I mean, what kind of blazing bitch thinks it's an accomplishment to keep a middle-aged maid from reading *Gone with the Wind* to a bunch of deaf old people?

Look, I get it. My mere presence in Frio with Darcy—Chelly's husband's unacknowledged bastard—has been a life-long humiliation for her. Should I have taken the money Russell gave me for an abortion and left town, started over in San Antonio or Austin? Hell, no. First off, he only gave me $500. I'd have to spend half of that for one month's rent in a shithole apartment in Frio. It might have covered the deposit for a place in San Antonio, if I was lucky.

Second, and most importantly, I was sixteen years old. I didn't have a high school degree, and I knew I sure as hell wouldn't be able to get one unless I had help. Thank God for my Granny Evans who let me live in the trailer with her, took me to my doctor's appointments, made sure I ate right, gave me a shoulder to cry on when my own momma would say something particularly vile to me. It's not like my momma had any room to be judgmental; she had me at sixteen. At least I'd be seventeen when I had my baby. I guess Momma was trying to harden me, to toughen me up, give me a taste of all the shit I'd receive from the rest of the town for…well, for-fucking-ever, as it turned out.

Wow, this is getting to be a pity party. Sorry about that. Back to that bitch, Chelly. She's pretty much done everything she can to make my life miserable and, if I wasn't so fucking stubborn, she would have succeeded. The final straw, though, was book club.

Books had been a solace my entire life, and I'd used books for the last twenty years to fill in my gaps of knowledge from not going to college. I've always had this ability to retain information, even the tiniest detail. I don't have a perfect memory (that'd be so cool if I did) or a photographic memory (same), but I did have the ability to remember useless information. I kicked ass at Trivial Pursuit. I'd just hadn't had anyone to play it with for a decade or more.

I showed up to the *The Husband's Secret* meeting, a bottle of expensive Chardonnay (wine is a good way to spend money without raising suspicions), looking forward to the discussion when who opens the door but my nemesis. In a flash I knew what she was doing. Chelly was not a reader. She was a numbers person. She'd tutored me in Algebra when I sat for them all those years ago. Somehow she found out that I was joining this book club and set out to ruin it for me. I decided, fuck that, then and there. I smiled and said hello and breezed right past her.

For four months, you couldn't melt butter in my mouth. A

cross word never left my lips. I didn't ignore Chelly, but I didn't go out of my way to talk to her, either. Chelly, on the other hand, tried to include me in every one of her conversations, usually concerning things I wouldn't know anything about, be able to participate in, fucking *This Is Us* in particular. Everyone watched that show. Buying the expensive television with all the apps was the dumbest purchase I made. After a couple of weeks searching through Netflix, Amazon, and Hulu for an hour a night without finding something I wanted to watch I turned the TV off, threw the controller away, opened a book and never looked back. I'd made the mistake of mentioning I didn't watch TV, so that became the new topic of conversation each month. The main topic. "Have you given this one a try, Marja? I think you'd like it," Chelly would say, knowing I'd hate it.

I held on for three more months (did I mention I was stubborn?) but Jesus Christ, I couldn't take it anymore. When I texted the organizer I was dropping out, she said she thought that was best. Any hope I had of those friendships surviving outside the fourth Tuesday of every month was dashed when I tried to reach out to a few people and was always met with excuses of why they couldn't get together.

All the while this was going on the amount of money I was laundering was increasing pretty dramatically. I couldn't launder so much money through my small, but growing, cleaning business without raising red flags. I either had to expand, diversify, or both. When the school board decided it would be cheaper to contract the district's cleaning out, I bid, and I bid low, to get the work. Darcy had been gone long enough that my temerity of flaunting Russell Clarke's bastard around town had faded. Now I was small town success story. Pulled myself up by my bootstraps and all that shit. I leaned into it, trust me.

I didn't think twice about the morality of laundering money through a school district contract.

The last thing I needed was for Chelly Clarke, or anyone, to be focused on me. So, I retreated back into solitude. It was the best thing for everyone.

I had a number in mind. Once I reached it, I'd get out. Move to Chicago or nearby to be close to Darcy. Go to college and get a degree. Maybe, just maybe, meet someone and fall in love. But, really, it was the being close to Darcy part that I ached for. We'd talked about it multiple times, Darcy and I, and she loved the idea. For the first time in my life, I allowed myself to dream.

Big mistake.

The bigger mistake was telling Tommy my plan.

You'd think I would have learned my lesson there, about pillow talk.

And yet.

Eva Molinares was good, I'll give her that. Or maybe I was just distracted. I bought her story without giving it a second thought. Eva'd left Dallas after her boyfriend hit her one too many times and came to Lynchfield, a couple of towns north, to stay with her cousin. She was tired of watching her cousin's kids, and needed a job so she could get her own place. Being a couple of towns away from family was fine by her. That's why she'd answered the ad.

Her résumé spoke of hard work—cleaner, cook, gardener—and low wages, but there was something about Eva that struck me as different. Maybe it was because her clothes fit so well, though they were definitely old and well-worn. Her jet-black hair was pulled back into a ponytail, and her bronze skin was unlined. Eva Molinares was fresh-faced. I'd met a lot of hard-working Mexican women (there were no other kind in my experience) over the years, and not one of them could be described as fresh-faced. Hell, I could relate. I long ago left fresh-faced behind.

I looked at Eva's application. "You're thirty-nine?" No fucking way was this woman thirty-nine.

"Yes. I have good genes."

I couldn't help myself, my eyes scanned down her body. "They look pretty old to me."

"Funny."

"Let me see your hands."

"I'm sorry?"

"Your hands."

Eva hesitated, balling her hands into fists, before stepping forward and holding them out over my desk. I took her hands and turned them over. Callouses at the base of her fingers, nails bitten down to the quick. Long, bony fingers. Hands attached to lean but muscular arms by an impossibly thin wrist. I looked up at Eva. She was watching me with a strange expression. When she caught my gaze, she shuddered and stepped back.

I picked up my pen and clicked the end a few times while I looked at the application. "I'll call your references and let you know."

"When?"

"After I check your references."

"I'd prefer to wait."

"I'm not going to get to it today."

"I really need this job."

"So do a dozen other women. With families. Referred by people I know. Why should I give it to you?"

"I'll be able to cover their work when they call in with a sick kid."

"Rarely happens."

"I need this job."

"I'll get back to you." I motioned toward the door.

"Because I have nobody."

I stopped pretending to ignore her and looked up. There was defiance in her expression, as if daring me to feel sorry for her. She knew exactly how to win me over.

Like I said. She was good.

I never suspected a thing.

I didn't see Eva for three weeks. I'd spread the new hires around with my experienced crews, and put Eva on Paz's crew, my fastest and hardest working. Barring any cleaning emergencies, they could do eight houses a day. If Eva could hang with Paz and her girls, she was worth keeping.

Paz is—was—my right-hand woman. She was the first person I hired when I expanded into other nearby towns, years before I started laundering. Considering she is related to almost every Mexican in a twenty-five-mile radius, I had no problem filling up positions and continuing to grow. You'd think having a bunch of relatives work together would be a recipe for disaster—personality conflicts, grudges, etcetera—but not with the Dela Cruz family. They have a good-natured competition going on, which crew does the best and fastest job. I mean, I sure didn't complain about it. It's down to Paz and her family that Evans House Cleaning has the stellar reputation it does.

Hey, don't ding me for a boring company name. It's tough to find something quippy to go with Evans, let alone Marja. Plus I need everything in my life to be as plain Jane as possible.

After a few months, Paz and I came to an agreement. She manages the crews, I manage the business. I bumped up her hourly rate to fifteen an hour (everyone starts at ten, which is good money for small town Texas) and added $500 to her monthly bonus. I'd like to think she'd walk over fire for me because I'm a good boss, almost a friend, but it's probably just the money, and that's okay.

Paz followed me around while I spot-checked the house. I saw Eva upstairs on her hands and knees, cleaning a kid's bathroom. One of the worst jobs. She caught my eye, smiled, and said hi, her soapy yellow gloved hands scrubbing the pink off of the white grout. I ignored her. When I got Paz into another room, I asked what she thought of Eva.

"Good worker. Keeps mostly to herself."

"She speak Spanish?"

"Yeah. Not from South Texas."

"How did you know?"

Paz shrugs. "Different dialect."

"Any weird questions about me or the business?"

"Not a one."

"What do the girls think?"

"They say she's pretty funny when they can get her to talk."

"So, she's a listener," I said.

"Uh-huh. Which may just be worse."

"Drop some lies."

"You got it, boss."

No, I didn't trust Eva Molinares. Sure, her references checked out okay. But there's a reason I use women from the same family: trust. Eva walking in off the street was a pretty big red flag, and she had no idea. Why did I hire her? Good question.

I'll tell you later.

The next time I saw Eva was at the library. She sat at the communal table between nonfiction and sci-fi. She was hunched over a book laid out flat on the table. Her dark hair was down, and she was absently chewing on a strand. She wore a tank top (it was summer in South Texas, after all) that showed off thin but well-defined arms. It was biting cold in the library. I watched as Eva put the strand of hair between her upper lip and nose like a mustache, squinch her mouth to hold it in place, and put on a thin hoodie, all the while never taking her eyes off her book. She zipped up the hoodie and readjusted herself in the chair and looked up straight at me. Her eyes widened, and her mouth relaxed, dropping the strand of hair down to meet the rest. She blushed and gave me a brief wave.

If she hadn't caught me staring, I wouldn't have spoken to her, but it would be rude not to now. A smile lit up her face when she saw me coming over.

"Hi, um, Ms. Evans."

"I thought you lived in Lynchfield."

Her smile dipped, and I don't blame her. It came out brusque. Accusatory. I could really be a bitch sometimes, even when I didn't mean to. I couldn't take it back or risk looking weak.

"Um, I got a place here so I don't have the drive. I was ready to get out of my cousin's house, anyway. Too many kids asking too many questions."

"They'll do that all right. What are you reading?"

"Oh." She shrugged and showed me the title.

"'*Midnight Assassin: Panic, Scandal, and the Hunt for America's First Serial Killer,*'" I read aloud. My eyebrows rose.

"I kinda have a thing for true crime ever since I read *Helter Skelter* in middle school."

"You read that in middle school?"

"Yeah. My dad liked true crime. He tried to hide them from me, but I cleaned the house every Saturday. I knew all the hiding places."

"Did he ever catch you?"

"Nope."

"Sneaky. I like it."

She smiled again. "Are you here for books?"

131

"Just dropped off some. About to check out some more."

"What do you like to read."

"Everything."

"It's a pretty big library. You better get jiggy wit it."

I raised an eyebrow, and Eva rolled her eyes. "I make terrible jokes when I'm nervous."

"Why are you nervous?"

"You're pretty intimidating."

"No, I'm not."

Eva dropped her chin and lowered her voice. "I thought you lived in Lynchfield."

I tried to suppress a grin. It was a good imitation, I'm not gonna lie.

"I do not sound like that."

A librarian at the desk shushed me. I rolled my eyes but sat down next to Eva. "She hates me."

"That nice old lady?"

"Her name is Mrs. Mabry and she's a dragon. She's been shushing me for forty years."

"Maybe you should be quiet, then," she whispered.

"I'm usually here alone," I stage-whispered back. "She just likes to pick on me."

"Why?"

"Long story." I nodded toward the book. "You know you could take that home and read it."

"I'd rather be somewhere I need to wear a jacket to stay warm than walk around in my underwear to stay cool."

I felt my face flame, horrified at the visual that popped into my head. Or maybe horrified isn't the right word. I changed the subject. "Where are you staying?"

"One half of a house on Oak Street with a window unit that struggles to keep up."

"Do you have a fan?"

"Yep. It does a great job of moving hot air around. I feel like I'm living in a convection oven."

"Get an empty gallon jug, fill it with water and freeze it. Put that in front of the box fan and voilà! White trash AC."

Eva had pushed her book a little away and was leaning on her arm, watching me with a slight smile and furrowed brows. It was disconcerting.

"What?"

"All of your workers love you."

I felt myself blush. "Do they?"

"You can't tell?"

"They work hard for me, I know that."

"Why do you think they do that?"

"Well, for one thing, Mexicans are the hardest workers I know, and it's not even close. So, there's that. Two, I pay them well, they know it, and they don't want to lose their job. Three, I guess you'd call it an unspoken contract between us all. I know I have a good thing, with my crew. I'm not going to do anything to fuck it up. They know they have a good boss in me, and they aren't going to fuck it up. Mutually assured success."

"Wouldn't it be nice if all bosses thought like this?"

"Had some bad ones?"

"Oh, yeah. Haven't you?"

"I've been my own boss since I was seventeen years old."

"So, for ten years."

"Ha ha. I have a thirty-two-year-old daughter."

"There's no way."

"I had her when I was seventeen. I can see you doing the math. I'm forty-eight."

"I don't believe it."

"I appreciate you lying to me, but it's really not necessary."

"Has no one ever told you you look like Jennifer Aniston?"

I barked out a laugh and covered my mouth quickly. I looked

at Mrs. Mabry and sure enough, she was coming around the desk to scold me in person.

"I know, I know. I'm sorry, Mrs. Mabry," I whispered.

"It's my fault," Eva said.

The old woman glared at us, and I knew the insults that were going through her mind. She was opening her mouth to speak, but I interrupted her. "I'm glad you came over, Mrs. Mabry. It's time for my quarterly donation to the Friends of the Library. I was wondering if you could look at your budget, see what the shortfall is this quarter, so I can make up the difference. I believe you're wanting to expand your digital catalog?"

She pursed her lips. "Yes. I'll get that number for you." After a moment, her face relaxed into a smile. "I can't thank you enough for your support. There's just never enough money."

"I've loved the library my entire life. Library books were mine and Darcy's entertainment for years. Remember how we would come here every Saturday?"

"I do. How's Darcy doing? She was always such a sweet little girl."

"Amazing. She and her best friend started a travel website."

"You don't say."

"Yep. Wander Women dot com. You should check it out. It focuses on women travelers, especially solo travelers."

"Oh, I would never have the courage to do that. And Ed wouldn't like it."

I smiled at her. "Well, let me know about the donation."

"Sure thing. Will you be here for a bit?"

"Yeah."

I watched Mrs. Mabry go and turned back to Eva. She had a strange expression on her face. "What?"

"You glow when you talk about Darcy."

"I'm just sweaty."

Eva's gaze traveled over my face. "Hardly." Our eyes met, and we both looked away.

Eva looked at her watch and straightened. "I better get going. Leave you to reading all the books." She stood.

"Only a few left."

She chuckled. "Somehow I think you're not kidding."

I watched her leave with an appreciative grin.

I hadn't been kidding.

I haven't had great luck with friends, as you've seen. But, if someone were to put a gun to my head and force me to tell them the name of someone I considered a friend, I would have to say Paz Dela Cruz.

There are some people who are just born leaders, and Paz Dela Cruz is a born leader. From the beginning, all my workers deferred to her even though she wasn't the oldest. It's quite a gift to be able to order people around all day and not sound bossy, but somehow Paz pulls it off. Paz is short and plump, with a round smiling face and a propensity to hug. I'm not a hugger, and I had to set some boundaries with Paz pretty early on. She just grinned, and said with her adorable accent, "You just tell me when you need a hug, Lupe. I'll be there to give it to you."

"Why are you calling me Lupe?"

She fluttered her hand. "It's your name, just accept it."

So, Paz called me Lupe, though I still don't know why.

It pained her, a woman surrounded by her family all day every day, that I was alone. Every week, she asked me to join their family on Sunday at the park, every week I declined. Until one Sunday about a year after my visit with Russell Clarke I received a text from Darcy telling me fine, she'd gotten the message, my silence was deafening, and she wouldn't bother me anymore. Oh, and by the way she and Chloe had started a travel website for women. Not that I would care. I cried for an hour, then decided it was time to take Paz up on her offer of a hug.

Sundays are family days in the Mexican community and they are sacrosanct. The Dela Cruz family meets out at the park by the river. A few get there early to stake their claim, while the others go to Mass. Around midday, they all gather and stay for the entire day. Swimming in the river, eating lunch, visiting, playing soccer, napping, and doing it all again until the sun starts to set behind the hills.

I'll be honest; one of the reasons I never went before was because I was jealous. My family hadn't done anything remotely like this, save the holidays when everyone got drunk and yelled at each other and Uncle Carl would try to grope me in the laundry room. I'd tried to make holidays special for Darcy, creating traditions and rituals like eating Green Chile Chicken Enchiladas on Thanksgiving because neither of us liked turkey; drinking hot chocolate and singing "O Christmas Tree" with the lights off after we decorated the Christmas tree; going to San Antonio to see *A Christmas Carol* on stage; driving around Alamo Heights, and looking at Christmas lights; opening a book and pajamas on Christmas Eve and spending the evening reading together on the couch. Ringing in the new year with Dick Clark. Black-eyed peas and cornbread on New Year's Day. I think Darcy has fond memories of our holidays, but when she got older I was too afraid to ask. Does she remember the fun things we did, or does she remember it being just the two of us eating our holiday dinners on our two-top Formica table with mismatched chairs?

I never missed my family enough to try to include them. I didn't want their lowlife, small-time criminal ways to influence her. Of course, I was accused of being stuck up, above my station. I was only a fucking maid, after all. No better than the other Evanses, no matter what I thought. Sometimes I do regret not giving Darcy a family, though. Getting married, having more children. I want that for her, a family. Michael's not the type of man I would have chosen for her to have a family with, but I'm happy she's going to have the opportunity I didn't.

Wow, I'm getting way off course here.

Paz was so thrilled to see me that Sunday that she forgot my boundaries and threw her arms around me. I didn't care. This way I didn't have to ask her for a hug. It would just worry her, that need, and she'd make it her mission to find out what was wrong.

Soon enough, I'd been introduced to all the adults I didn't know (which was more than I expected) and was so lost with all the faces and names and rapid-fire Spanish that I could just about keep up with but not quite, that when a nice man named Miguel handed me a cold beer, I took it thankfully and downed half of it.

Kids from toddlers to teens were a little ways off playing soccer and right in the middle of them was Eva, running and laughing. Paz sidled up to me.

"I guess she passed the test," I said.

"She's gotten chattier, but if you pay attention, she asks questions and listens."

"What kind of questions?"

"About our families. Our lives. She remembers everything. Asks about sick kids, or relatives."

"Does she ask too many questions?"

"No. She's too good."

"You think she's a plant?"

Paz shrugged one shoulder. "She didn't grow up poor or on the border, that I know."

"How?"

"Everyone has a story about ICE or the police and fear of

deportation. She's been pulled over, but that's about it." Paz sighed. "All the same, I like her."

"Obviously if you invited her here."

Eva saw us and waved. We waved back.

"Oh, she's hiding something, but—" Paz pointed to her heart "—I think it has to do with this, not your business."

"A man?"

Paz shrugged.

"You have a minute?" I asked.

Paz furrowed her brows. "Sí, Lupe. Always for you."

I jerked my head, and we started walking away from the crowd. "I want you to start learning the business side of things. Working with me in the office."

She stared at me in astonishment, and a little fear.

"No," I said. "Not that side."

Her shoulders dropped in relief. "I'm coming up on fifty and I want to retire," I said. "Travel. I've got as big of a nest egg as I need, and it'll keep growing if I only pull 3 percent out a year."

Paz shook her head. "If you say so."

We stopped and faced each other. "This is all stuff I'm going to teach you, Paz. I want to know when I'm gone that you aren't living paycheck to paycheck. That you know how to save and invest and have plenty of money so you can retire sooner rather than later. Put those kids through college, too."

Paz looked at her large extended family, shook her head, and smiled. "It's a pretty big family."

"Don't you worry about that. I've got you. I'll sell you the business, for a very, very low price, and you'll just keep doing what you're doing. Our clients won't even know the difference, because you've got such a handle on the operations."

"What if I can't understand the numbers and figures and do something wrong with the taxes?"

"Taxes are what accountants are for. If you have trouble with the day-to-day stuff, which I don't think you will, I bet there's someone in your family who can help you."

"I have a niece who got a business degree at UTSA and could only find a job at a call center."

I waved my hand. "There you go."

I could see Paz's eyes brightening as she warmed up to the idea. She looked up at me, a smile pulling at the corners of her mouth. "Lupe, you are too good to me."

"I'm not nearly good enough. Do me a favor though and keep this under wraps. Tell Enrique, of course, but only if you think he will keep his mouth shut."

"Well, that's never a sure thing when he's drinking."

"Then let's just keep this between us for now. I don't want my plans getting around town, you know?"

The light in Paz's eyes dimmed slightly. "You promise none of the other stuff will be part of the price?"

"I swear. None of that will ever come near you or your family. As far as anyone knows, you know nothing about it. You keep saying that to anyone who asks, and I mean anyone, you'll be fine."

A family member called out to Paz and she waved at them, telling them she would be there in a minute in Spanish. "Entiendo. Gracias, Lupe."

"Lo siento. Now go feed your family."

I drank my beer and sauntered back over to the group to get another. I watched as Eva and a lanky teen boy cleared a path for a three-year-old girl to dribble the ball inexpertly down the field and kick it in the makeshift goal. Everyone clapped and yelled and Eva lifted the little girl up in the air and put her on her shoulder. The girl's grin was so big it split her face. The adults noticed and started cheering, too. The girl was too excited to be still and wiggled off of Eva's shoulder. Eva came over to me.

"Hey, boss. Good to see you."

"I didn't know you played soccer."

Eva furrowed her brows and tilted her head to the side. "Why do you do that?"

"Do what?"

"It's like you can't just say, 'Hi, how are you doing, Eva? Good to see you, too.' Why is that?"

Paz's words echoed in my head. She's hiding something. I figgered as much myself, and part of me knew I shouldn't trust her. The truth was, I'd been thinking about Eva a lot since I saw her at the library.

Do you ever meet those people you just know you'll be friends with? Until I met Eva, I never had. I'd read about it. Eva was my experience with friendship at first sight, if that's what you want to call it. It wasn't until I lost it that I realized Chelly and I had been friends, of a sort. Chelly was one of the only adults who didn't talk down to me so of course I admired her. She was also gorgeous and kind and a great mother. And, she helped me get a solid B in Algebra. I'm sure Chelly realized I had an innocent crush on her, which is why what happened later was so devastating for her, and for me.

I saw in Eva Molinares a potential friend, a woman alone on the lower end of the social scale, like me, or at least on this end temporarily. She was a hard worker, funny, and she liked to read. I wanted to be her friend, I wanted her to want to be my friend, and it made me feel weak. So I was brusque.

It sounds so ruthless to say it, but the more distance I kept between me and Eva, the less I would have to worry about Chelly Clarke doing something to torpedo it, or Tommy threatening her. Goddammit, I was lonely. Without Darcy…

I truly had no one I cared about. The hug with Paz was the first human contact I'd had in months.

Beside Paz, Eva was the only person who even attempted to be my friend. I would be an idiot to reject it. I didn't want to reject it.

"You're right. I'm sorry."

"Apology accepted." Eva took my beer and finished it off. She handed me the empty bottle with a cheeky grin.

"That's not the best way to make friends, drinking someone's beer."

"Is that what we're doing? Making friends?" She raised her eyebrows.

"I hope so."

Eva grinned. "Good. That's what I've been trying to do. I guess I'm out of practice."

"Same. Why are you out of practice?"

Eva sighed. "Oh, you know. Working too much, having a partner who's the jealous type."

"I can relate to the working too much. Jealous partner, not so much."

"You're lucky then. Why are you out of practice?"

"Oh, I'm just a bitch. No one likes me. Except Paz and the girls and I pay them so they don't count."

Eva studied me. "I don't believe that."

"Which part?"

"That no one likes you." Eva's mouth twitched while she tried to suppress a grin.

I pushed her shoulder playfully and went to ask Paz if there was anything I could do to help. Eva offered, too. Paz said no, we were guests, put two more beers in our hands and shooed us away. We sat down on a spare bit of grass out of the way of others and watched the kids play soccer.

"That little one, the one who scored? She's gonna be a star," Eva said.

"How can you tell?"

"I can't. She's only three. It's more wishful thinking."

We drank in companionable silence for a minute, when Eva said the worst thing she could say that day, especially after my conversation with Paz. "So, tell me about Darcy."

Red flags waved in my head, but two could play at her game. If I wanted to figure out what she was up to, I had to give her a little of what she wanted, too. I swallowed the lump in my throat. "She lives in Chicago. She's a travel writer."

"That sounds like a fun job."

"She says it is."

"Like, what does she write?"

"All kinds of stuff. Lists of travel tips, product reviews, and of course articles about places she's been. She specializes in off the beaten path destinations, and budget travel. Problem-solving on the road."

"Is her name Evans, like yours?"

"Why wouldn't it be?"

Eva leaned away from me.

"Sorry," I said. "Yes, Darcy Evans. She started a website called Wander Women with her best friend, Chloe. It's for women who travel. Obviously."

"Do you get to go on a lot of trips with her?"

"No. When she travels she's working. We always go on a road trip together each summer. Or these days whenever she can get off. Growing up we went on road trips around here. That was all I could afford. And we just kept up the tradition. We've been able to go farther afield the last few years, which has been nice."

"Oh, yeah? Where?"

"Grand Canyon. Smokey Mountains. Yellowstone."

"Where did you go this year?"

"We haven't. We aren't."

"Oh. Why not?"

I glared at Eva. "None of your business."

She held my gaze, then said, "I'm sorry. That was too personal."

"It was. What's with the twenty questions, anyway?"

"I'm trying to get to know you. So, fair play. Ask me something personal."

"Okay, who are you? Really?"

Eva furrowed her brows. They were thick and smooth and perfectly plucked and created a V when she drew them together. "I'm a second-generation Mexican American woman who's about to be forty years old with nothing to show for it but a bad taste in partners and a job as a maid in a shitty South Texas town."

"You don't look like a maid."

"Yet, I am."

"Who are you really?"

"Why don't you believe me?"

I scoffed and drank my beer. "Honestly? With a face like that there are lots of other jobs that can earn you a lot more money than scrubbing toilets in this two-bit South Texas town."

"I could say the same for you."

"You better believe if I had other options earlier in life I wouldn't have made cleaning up other people's shit my career."

"Maybe I tried the better jobs you're talking about and decided the safety of working with a bunch of women like me, in a little out of the way town, was the better option."

She faced the soccer game and drank her beer. I stared at her profile, which was set in a determined expression. She was pissed and hurt and I felt like a total heel.

"Did someone hurt you?" I said softly.

She turned her gaze to mine. "People have been hurting me one way or another my entire life."

In that moment we recognized in each other two damaged souls searching for safety. Understanding. Friendship. Vulnerability. Eva looked away first.

I exhaled. I didn't give a shit who she was. A Fed, a Texas Ranger, an East Coast reporter slumming undercover for a story. I liked her more than I distrusted her, and I knew she liked me. I'd never realized how desperate I was for a friend until that moment.

"But seriously though. How do you have skin like that? It's like an angel's wing," I said.

Eva nearly choked on her beer. "What kind of experience do you have with angel's wings?"

"Well, what I imagine an angel's wing would look like."

"You're crazy."

"Do you drink the blood of virgins on the full moon?"

"That's exactly what I do."

"Can I come to the next sacrifice? Or am I too old to benefit from the treatment?"

Eva took my chin and moved my face back and forth in the light. "It's a close call, but not yet. Once you hit fifty, you have to drink a puppy's blood."

"Too far."

"Yeah. You're right." She still had a hold of my chin. "I told you you look like Jennifer Aniston. I should be asking you for tips."

"Tip number one, live a clean life."

Eva rolled her eyes and swigged her beer. "Try again."

"Stay away from men."

She laughed so hard beer shot out of her nose. "Ow, that kinda hurt," she said, still laughing.

I got a paper towel from the table, handed it to her, and sat back down. "You're a mess."

"God, don't I know it." She wiped the beer from her face and swiped ineffectively at the front of her shirt. "Thank you."

"Lo siento."

"Oh, I can't believe I forgot. I have something else to thank you for."

"What's that?"

"The air conditioner," Eva said.

"I don't know what you're talking about."

"Please. It wasn't two hours after I talked to you that someone came to fix my air conditioner. Actually, he replaced it, and on Monday when I got home he was waiting with a new unit to put in the other room."

"Your landlord must have realized."

"Chelly Clarke didn't know what I was talking about when I called to thank her."

"Strange."

"You really don't know how to take a thank you or a compliment."

"Have you given me a compliment?"

"Maybe not yet, but I know you won't take it well."

"You're right. I won't."

"Are you always this ornery?"

"God, I'm usually so much worse."

Eva laughed and warmth spread through my body.

"Marja, I think this is the start of a beautiful friendship."

Eva's house was dark when we drove up. She was in the passenger seat of my Accord, her eyes closed and her head leaned back against the headrest, exposing her long neck and why was I admiring her neck? Thinking about her neck? My eyes traveled down her body to her long, toned legs. Something foreign stirred in me, and I didn't like it.

"Wake up," I said, and pushed her shoulder hard enough that her head slid off of the headrest and against the window.

"Ow, shit," she said. "That hurt."

"We're here. Don't you know to leave lights on for safety?"

"I didn't think I'd be gone till dark."

"Can you walk?"

"Pfft. Of course, I can. You didn't need to drive me, you know. I'm not drunk."

"Uh-huh. I saw Enrique pour a double shot of cheap tequila into your margarita. You're gonna feel that tomorrow."

"I'm a Latina. I can hold my tequila."

I got out of the car and went around to help Eva out. It took two tries for her to heave herself up and out of the Accord. "Too low to the ground."

"Uh-huh." I grabbed her purse off the floorboard and held it open for her. "Grab your keys."

"You get them."

"I'm not digging through your purse."

"Why? I trust you."

"Just get your fucking keys, Eva."

She leaned forward and bent her head. Her hair smelled like peppermint. She felt around in her purse for what felt like forever before saying, "Gotcha!" and lifting her head with a triumphant smile. Her face was so close to mine our noses were almost touching, which meant she was a blur to me without my readers. It was just as well, because seeing the change in her expression through unfocused eyes did weird things to me. It would be easy, later, to pretend I'd misread her expression.

I took the keys and walked up the front steps, assuming she would follow. I opened the old-fashioned screen door and was amazingly able to insert the key into the lock on the first try.

Eva leaned against the doorjamb and watched me. A frigid blast of air hit us when I opened the door.

"The AC works all right," I said.

"Thanks to you."

"You're welcome," I said. I dropped her keys in her purse and put it inside the door. "Do you need help inside?"

"No."

"Well, here you are. Safe and sound. Be sure to take an ibuprofen and drink a bunch of water before bed."

"Have a lot of experience avoiding hangovers?" Eva said softly.

"No. I read about it somewhere."

"Right. You read a lot."

"It passes the time. Good night."

Eva grasped my hand before I could leave. "I'm sorry you had to bring me home. I don't usually drink so much."

"You didn't, really. Blame Enrique's cheap tequila."

"I'm going to be mortified when I wake up in the morning."

"You probably won't even remember this."

Eva scoffed. "Yeah, I will." She released my hand. "I didn't expect you to be so nice."

I looked at her then. "What do you mean?"

"That first day, um, you were pretty harsh."

"I didn't trust you."

She raised her eyebrows. "Why?"

I couldn't tell her the real reason. "I don't trust anyone."

"Then why did you hire me?"

I couldn't tell her that reason, either.

"Pity. Good night."

I made myself saunter back to my car when what I really wanted to do was run.

THIRTEEN

Darcy

Lena laughed when Marja said she was driving.

"Not on your life, Marja. Get in." Lena pointed at the passenger door as she walked around to the driver's side. "Front seat."

"Why?"

Lena stopped, looked up to the sky, and sighed. She turned and walked right up to Marja, into her personal space. Lena was taller than Marja, fit, and a little intimidating. Marja did her best to look unphased, but she flushed. Lena shifted from foot to foot and moved closer. You could possibly put a sheet of paper between them, but it would be a tight fit. Lena stared down at her for a few uncomfortable moments. Marja lifted her chin, trying to brazen it out. I almost bought it, too.

"Are you going to argue with me just to argue for the next eight hours?"

Marja shrugged. "Seems like a good way to pass the time."

"No, it doesn't," I said.

"No, it doesn't," agreed Lena. "I want you in the front because you should never turn your back on your adversary."

"Oh, I'm your adversary."

"You seem determined to be, yes." They stared at each other for another long moment. "Get in the car, Marja," Lena said in a voice that brooked no opposition. She walked off and got in the car. Marja crossed her arms and stood her ground.

"Jesus Christ, Momma. Get in the car," I said. I looked down at Helen, who stared up at me with a can-you-believe-this-shit expression. "Even Helen's tired of your shenanigans." I opened the back door of the Suburban and Helen jumped in. I followed her.

Marja got in and buckled up. Lena pulled onto the road without a word. Marja started right back in, though.

"Where's my car, by the way," Marja asked.

"No idea. Tulsa probably," Lena said.

"I want it back."

"You know that's not going to happen."

"For Darcy. It's her wedding present."

"You should have thought of that before."

"Before what?"

"Good Lord, where to start?"

"My God would you two kiss or fuck (bark) or something? All this bickering is making me car sick."

"Watch your mouth," Marja said.

"I don't know what went on between you two, but I have a pretty good idea it was more than friends. Work that out later, I don't really give a shit (bark). It's time one of you tell me what's going on. All of it. No more bullshit (bark, bark, bark). Oh, give it a rest, Helen," I snapped. She whimpered, got in my lap. She walked around in three circles and settled down on my legs. "Good girl," I said, and absently rubbed her back.

"I'm waiting" I said.

"Do you want to tell her or should I?" Lena said.

"You don't know everything," Marja said, her voice dripping with disdain.

"Momma," I warned.

"Turn here, Lena," Marja said.

Lena glared at her.

"Please?"

Lena turned her signal on and took the turn harder and faster than she should have. We passed a Route 66 sign.

"Thank you."

"You're welcome."

Marja blew out a huge breath. "About a decade ago—

"A decade!"

Marja gave me the "mom look" and I shut up.

"Tommy gave me some money and asked me to run it through my business. Keep 20 percent, transfer the rest to another account. Simple."

"Fucking Tommy Baldwin," I said.

"Yes, I was fucking Tommy Baldwin. There aren't a lot of options in Frio, Darcy, as you know. Besides, he's a friend and I've known him all my life."

I glanced at Lena, caught her eye in the rearview mirror. She returned her attention to the road and remained silent.

"Did he tell you where it came from?"

"He said it was dogfighting."

"Dogfighting? Really, Momma?"

"I'm not proud of it. So, I gave a little bit of my cut to PETA every month. Still do."

"To soothe your conscience?"

"Yep. That's exactly right. It wasn't a lot of money to start, a couple of thousand a month. Some would be bigger than others, but that was about the average. Worked just fine for a year or so. I was able to pay off credit cards, my car and was totally debt free. I put money aside for myself for the first time in my life, so maybe I wouldn't have to work until I dropped dead. Business was good, I'd saved enough I had a cushion, so I told Tommy thanks for the help but I didn't need it anymore. He said, cool, and that was it.

"I'd hired Paz by this time, and we kept getting more and more referrals. So, I decided to expand. Hired some of her relatives, started a crew. It kinda snowballed from there. I mean, you know this part."

"I was so proud of you," I said. "Finally doing something with your life."

Marja jerked her head toward me. "What the fuck does that mean? Doing something with my life."

"Momma, I—"

"What I'd been fucking doing with my life was working my ass off raising you, protecting you from all the shitty people in Frio."

"Protecting me? That's what you were doing?"

"Yeah."

"That's not how I remember it."

"I was fucking celibate for eighteen years to protect you, Darcy. I didn't want you to be stuck—" Marja clapped her mouth shut. A small muscle pulsed in her cheek.

I leaned back against the door of the car and crossed my arms, feigning cool outrage but my stomach was churning with fear. Here it was finally. The Truth. "Go on. Finish it."

"Darcy, I—"

"Fucking finish what you were saying!"

Marja swallowed. "I didn't want you to get stuck in Frio like I did."

I nodded jerkily and swallowed the thickness in my throat. "You didn't want me to get pregnant like you did, right? Stuck with a redheaded bastard you never wanted."

"That's a fucking lie."

Bark.

Helen trembled and licked my hand for comfort, hers and mine, I suspected.

"I wanted you. You're the one good decision I've made in my life."

"Right. No one made you stay in Frio. You chose that. You could have left."

"It's not that simple, Darcy."

"I think it is. Sometimes I wonder how much better my life would have been if you had. I wouldn't have had your mistake hanging over my head every day for eighteen years. I wouldn't have had adults stop conversations when I got too close or been bullied and ostracized by kids in school. Hell, maybe I would have had a friend before Chloe, who knows!" I turned away. I couldn't look at her for another minute.

"Your life has turned out pretty well for all your hardships," Marja said.

"No thanks to you."

Marja was silent, but I could feel her anger building, getting ready to blow. I glanced over and saw Lena put her hand on Marja's left knee, give it a small squeeze. Marja stiffened. I half expected the blow to come then, and be directed toward the Fed. Instead, after a long moment Marja relaxed, swallowed down all that stubbornness and anger and her fucking need to be right and not be challenged. She touched Lena's hand, and removed it quickly. With another light squeeze, Lena released my mother's leg.

Holding Lena's gaze, I said to Marja, "Where does the cartel come in."

"A couple of years after I stopped laundering for Tommy, he came back to me with the same offer, but significantly more money. I knew it wasn't dogfighting money, and I suspected it was drug related. Tommy assured me I was laundering his cut and no one else's, that no one above him knew who I was."

"And you believed him?"

"For the amount of money I'd be earning I wanted to, so I did."

"And you never stopped to think whether or not it was right or moral?"

"I enjoyed the challenge of learning something new, refining my methods, getting better and better at it. Fooling the government was pretty nice, too." Lena shook her head but didn't comment. Marja continued. "What I enjoyed most, though, was watching my bank accounts grow. Compound interest is a beautiful thing. I've worked my ass off my entire life and scraped by. It was nice not having to worry about money for a change. So no, right or wrong, morality didn't come into it."

"Where does Lena come in?"

Lena spoke. "I got a job with the cleaning company. Undercover for the FBI."

"She lied to me from the start, became my friend and just kept on lying."

"It was my job, Marja."

"It's a dirty job, is all I can say."

"Your mom has a unique ability to cast everyone else as the bad guy, even though she was the one committing a felony."

"Oh, yeah. She's great at not taking responsibility," I said.

"That's just bullshit," Marja said. "All I've had since I was seventeen years old is responsibilities, and I've met them all."

"She's also stubborn," I said.

"Not always a bad thing, unless that stubbornness is directed at you," Lena said.

"True. You know, in all the time I lived in Frio, my momma didn't have friends. How did you do it?"

Lena's gaze settled on me in the rearview mirror. "We just

153

clicked." Marja angled herself away from us and stared out the window. "You ever have a friend like that? As soon as you met them you knew you'd be friends?"

"Yeah." I thought of Chloe and my stomach clenched with pleasure. What the fuck?

"That's what I felt when I met your mom. She hated me on sight."

"Not true," Marja said.

"Well, you didn't trust me."

"And my intuition was right."

"Not in the end."

"What do you mean?" Marja said.

"Your mom was so good I couldn't get a thing on her. I tried for a year before they pulled me off the case and sent me back to Dallas."

Lena continued. "I couldn't say goodbye, not properly. I sent a text about a sick relative—"

"A lie," Marja said.

"It wasn't actually," Lena said. "I turned my phone in, protocol, and never texted back."

"You ghosted my Mom?"

"Yes," Lena and Marja said in unison.

"Six months later, Marja got in touch with the FBI," Lena said. "She gave us a treasure trove of financial information. She'd been planning this from the moment Russell Clarke threatened you."

My entire body went cold. "I'm sorry, did you say Russell Clarke? As in my asshole father, Russell Clarke?"

"Yes," Lena said.

"Shut up, Lena," Marja said.

"She needs to know the story, the whole story, Marja."

"It's my story to tell."

"Well, you're doing a shit job of it."

Bark.

"Sorry, baby girl," Lena said. "Tell the story, Marja."

Marja sighed. "He didn't actually threaten you, but he might as well have. That's why I distanced myself from you. I wanted him to think we didn't have much of a relationship, so he wouldn't go after you."

"Russell Clarke. Who lets his wife steamroll him on everything? He's a criminal mastermind?"

"God no. He's a middleman. He's probably being threatened by the really dangerous people above him. If I had to guess, and I've thought a lot about this, I'd say he had gambling debts or borrowed money from the wrong people and this is how he's paying them off."

"And you turning on him is signing his death warrant?"

"Probably."

"Not if your mom would stop dragging it out and give us Russell. We could protect him and his family like we're protecting you."

If this was a normal story about a normal family, I'd be bothered that my mother was setting my father up for a fall. But Momma and I'd suffered for years because I was Russell Clarke's unacknowledged bastard. All I felt was a twisted sense of satisfaction that Momma would finally get her revenge. I'd definitely have to talk to my therapist about that next week.

I looked out the window at the passing scenery. It was all too much. Cartels, dead boyfriends, money laundering, my deadbeat father, an undercover FBI agent who may have laid a honeypot trap for my mother. This was the week before I was going to marry the man of my dreams, and I hadn't given him, or the wedding, a thought in the last eighteen hours.

"We need to pull over," I said.

"Why?" Lena and Marja said in unison.

"I need to puke. And make a call."

"To whom?" Lena said.

"That's none of your business."

"Getting you and your mother safely to Chicago is my business."

"How does me calling my fiancé put us in danger?"

Lena inhaled. "Just trust me."

"Ha," Marja said.

"Shut up, Marja."

"I'm calling Michael."

"No, you're not."

"Why can't she?" Marja asked.

"Because the more people who know about you, the more people we have to put in WITSEC."

"Hang on a second. My mother is going into witness protection?" I said.

"Not only her."

It took a moment for me to comprehend what Lena was saying.

"Do you mean that I...?"

Lena held my gaze. "Yes. For your and your mother's safety, you're going to have to go into witness protection, too."

FOURTEEN

Marja

We didn't make it to the rest stop in time, and Darcy puked all over the back seat of the Suburban. Luckily for us, the Fed Mobile we were riding in had cleaning supplies in the back, along with an arsenal of guns. Never know when you might have to clean up a crime scene, I guess. I took Helen and went with Darcy to make sure she was okay. Truth of it is I didn't want to clean up the puke.

Calling this turnout a rest stop was being generous. It was a stop leftover from the mid-twentieth century when travelers would take homemade lunches and eat along the new interstate road system. A couple of picnic tables and a trash can and a restroom chained closed long ago. Eighteen-wheelers barreled down I-40 toward St. Louis, cutting through the frigid wind and leaving the smell of diesel fuel in their wakes.

"I guess a cold front is moving in," I said.

"There's a snowstorm coming down from Canada," Darcy said. "I can't believe you haven't checked the weather." Helen pulled at the leash, eager to smell the pee mail left by hundreds of dogs that came before her. She found a spot and left her message for the future.

"Darcy, I didn't know you would have to go into WITSEC. I never intended for that to happen."

"Sure."

"I swear to you I'm going to do whatever's necessary to not let that happen."

Darcy put her head down on the picnic table. "Just leave me alone, okay?"

"I'll go get you a coat," I said.

I hoped Lena had one because I definitely hadn't packed for the cold. My future plans don't include Aran sweaters and hooded parkas.

Helen jumped back into the Suburban as soon as we got back to the car. Lena was bent over, wiping down the rubber floor mats. Thank God the car wouldn't smell like vomit for the rest of the drive. Lena straightened, a can of Lysol in one gloved hand and paper towels in the other.

"Sorry about that."

Lena looked over my shoulder at Darcy. "How's she doing?"

"Not great. Do you have an extra coat?"

Lena went to the back of the Suburban. I followed. She took off her gloves and put everything in a trash bag before taking off her black waterproof bomber jacket. Her gun was holstered on her left hip, her FBI shield clipped to her belt on the right. She wore a white Henley and dark jeans, and I was a little taken aback by how looking at her made me feel inside. She draped the coat over my shoulders, pulled the front together at the collar, and said, "How's that?"

The jacket was warm, and the scent took me back to the last time we stood this close to each other. By the look in Lena's eyes, she remembered, too. "It smells like dryer sheets,"

I said, my hoarse voice betraying the sensations ricocheting around my body.

Lena's eyes soften when she smiles. I love her smile. I love making her smile.

"I'm still not sure if that's a compliment."

"It's a compliment."

We stared at each other for a long moment. Helen barked, and broke the trance.

"What?" I said. "No one cursed."

Helen barked again, and I remembered Darcy.

"Do you have an extra coat for Darcy?" Call me a bad mother if you want but there was no way I was giving up Lena's coat.

"Yeah, let me see."

Lena pulled a blanket out of the back of the car and walked to Darcy and draped it over her shoulder. Darcy raised her head and gave her a wan smile. Lena said something to my daughter, who shook her head, and came back. Helen and I got in the car, and Lena followed. Helen jumped onto her lap. Lena bent down and let the dog lick her mouth.

"I don't know how you let her do that," I said.

"Aw, has Marja not given you kisses the entire time I've been gone?" Lena said to Helen in a baby voice. "Poor little girl, not getting any love."

"She gets plenty of love, and she can lick my face as much as she wants. Just not the lips."

Lena picked Helen up and put the dog's face next to her own. "Look at this little face, Marja. How can you deny her?"

I swear to God Helen was giving her best puppy dog expression, as was Lena. They were both so fucking cute it almost pissed me off. We had important stuff to talk about here.

"Since when is Darcy going into WITSEC?"

Lena sighed and settled Helen back on her lap and stroked

her back. "Since you walked into the Austin office and turned yourself in."

"Not because killed a cartel man?"

"No. The threat of hurting Darcy can be used against you up to and during the trial that you will have to testify at."

"You've been lying to me."

"No, Cooper has. I'm not on your case anymore."

"You haven't told me what's going on."

"I can't, Marja."

"Can't? Present tense?"

"I don't know very much. I'm on a very short leash with you."

"Why's that?"

"Cooper doesn't trust me."

"Why not?"

"Because I got too close. He thinks my judgment is compromised."

"Is it?"

She paused, looked me straight in the eyes. "Yes."

That shut me up. The expression on her face made me want to run and jump off the nearest cliff and it made me want to stay, which was more of a mountain than a cliff.

I turned away.

I was on a road trip with my favorite people in the world, something I'd daydreamed about more than I will admit to anyone, and so far it had turned out to be the shittiest road trip ever. But every time I looked over and saw Lena there, or smelled her perfume, a little bubble of happiness burst in my chest. I'd missed her almost as much as I'd missed my daughter.

Now, the bombshell. Darcy would have to go into WIT-SEC, too. I know, what did I expect? There was no way I would have been able to get through this road trip without

Darcy grilling me on the last three years. None at all. She is my daughter, after all.

I'll only admit this to you and I'll call you a liar if you tell Darcy, but part of me was thrilled at the idea we would be on the run together. In hiding, I mean. We would be free of Frio and the judgments that had followed us around. I'd lived through it as much as she had, but she'd been a child who didn't understand why people didn't like her. I did my best to protect Darcy, and when I couldn't I told myself that she would be a stronger person for all of it.

I'd been right. Well, mostly right. She'd made a success of herself. She had a loyal friend in Chloe, and a future husband who would make her secure financially for the rest of her life. She was at the pinnacle of her career, and Wander Women was taking off.

Now, she was going to have to give it all up. Because of me. I couldn't let that happen. I turned back to Lena.

"Whatever you're about to ask," Lena said, crossing her arms, "the answer is no."

"You haven't heard the question."

"Marja."

"Lena."

She lowered her voice even though we were alone in the car. "My hands are tied, Marja. This is Cooper's case now. You'll have to appeal to him."

"I'm appealing to you."

"Marja, I don't think you understand…"

I waited. Lena didn't finish the sentence. "I don't understand what?"

It seemed like it was a struggle for Lena to keep her eyes on mine. I didn't have that problem. Lena had deep brown eyes with a thin copper band around the iris, and they were framed by the longest eyelashes I'd ever seen. And, her eye-

161

brows. I'd never given my eyebrows much thought, probably because they were thin and blond and almost invisible. Lena's eyebrows were epic; dark, straight, and thick.

"Cooper is already going to rip me a new one for telling you about Darcy's WITSEC," Lena said.

She looked in the rearview mirror. I turned and followed her gaze. A black Suburban parked behind us.

"Another Fed Mobile?" I asked.

"Maybe."

Two men got out of the vehicle. The driver walked toward our car and the other one walked toward Darcy.

I heard a snap. "Stay in the car, Marja. That's an order," she said. She opened the door and got out.

"Fuck that," I said, and got out. I jogged over to Darcy, barely reaching her before the agent did. He was bullnecked and bald, with a swagger I associated more with police officers high on power instead of the Feds I'd come across. I glanced at Lena who was talking to the other man, who from what I could tell was cut from the same cloth as this one.

The man reached into his jacket and I instinctively moved in front of Darcy, who'd stood from the picnic table. The man smirked and pulled out a leather wallet. He opened it and said, "DEA. You need to come with me."

"No fucking way," I said.

"It wasn't a request, Miss Evans."

"She's not going anywhere with you," Darcy said.

"You're both going with me," he said. He reached out to grab Darcy's arm and I moved back, pushing Darcy along behind me.

"Don't touch her."

"It's okay, Marja." Lena walked toward us with a smile on

her face. "Cooper's orders. Come on, let's get your bags out of the car."

She stopped next to us and smiled at the DEA agent. "We'll just be a second."

We walked off, Lena between us. "Do exactly as I say. No questions, no talk back. I'm going to the back of the car. You two act like you're getting your purses out of the car. Front and back seat. Get in but leave the door open, lean down like you're searching for your purse. Stay down. No matter what happens."

Lena went to the back of the Suburban and Darcy and I went to the front.

"Momma?" Darcy said, her voice shaking.

"Just do as she said," I told her, glad that my voice wasn't shaking.

I got in the front seat and opened the glove box, hoping against hope there would be some sort of weapon stashed there. Nope. I heard latches opening in the back. Helen started barking. Darcy was trying to shush her. I looked out the open door and saw Meathead with a gun in his hand. A shot reverberated through the car and Meathand's hand disintegrated, his gun falling to the ground.

Meathead roared. Lena came into view, walking calmly away from the Suburban, a gun in each hand pointed at the two DEA agents. The other agent had started toward Lena. She put a bullet in his left knee and the man fell to the ground. Meathead, hand dripping with blood, had recovered enough and was now stalking toward Lena, face red with fury or pain or both. She put a bullet in his right knee, and he dropped to the ground.

I got out of the car and walked toward Meathead. Lena shouted at me to get back in the car, but it was little more than white noise. This bastard needed to know there were consequences to threatening my daughter, goddamnit. I jogged the last few steps to the man, pulled my leg back and kicked him in the face like it was a Super Bowl winning field goal. His bones crunched against my foot, and blood flew out of his mouth as he fell back to the ground, unconscious.

"Nice form," Lena said, guns still drawn. "Get his gun, phone, ID, wallet, and get in the car. I fucking mean it, Marja."

The other agent was still writhing on the ground, holding his knee. Lena put a gun in her holster as she walked over to him, relieving him of his gun. She stepped on his wounded knee. The man screamed. "Talk."

"Fuck you."

"That's not what I call interagency cooperation," Lena said. She pressed down on his knee again. "Who are you working for?"

"The DEA, you stupid bitch. I pulled my gun when I saw Agent Charles pull his. I was trying to help you. Cooper sent us."

"You know how I know you're lying? Because Cooper would rather eat shit than let the DEA in on this case."

The man's face froze, then turned into a smirk. "You're dead, you know that, right?"

"Well, I'm not dead yet." She kicked him in the ribs, then the face for good measure, knocking him out cold. She took his phone, badge, and ID, put a bullet in two tires and two more in the grille of the car as she walked by.

Lena got into the car and closed the door. "Turn your phones off," she said over Helen's frantic barking. Lena tossed the agent's phone in my lap. "Turn both phones off and take out the SIM cards." She opened the console and released a gun magazine into it. She pulled the action back and caught the chambered bullet as it flew out into the air and did the same for the gun in my lap.

She looked at us for the first time. Darcy and I were both wide-eyed and speechless. Helen had stopped barking but was shaking like a leaf in Darcy's lap.

"Those weren't tranq guns. We need a new plan."

FIFTEEN

Marja

"How long do you think she's going to be in there?"

Darcy and I sat against the headboard of a queen bed at the Boots Court Motel in Carthage, Missouri. We'd driven around back roads for two hours before Lena stopped to make a call. When she returned to the car, she took photos of the SIM cards.

"You didn't call Cooper, did you?" I asked. I didn't think Cooper was dirty, but what did I know?

Lena didn't respond. "Are both of your phones off?" she asked.

"Yes."

"Keep them off until I say otherwise."

The ride to the motel was silent, though I was bursting at the seams with questions and I'm sure Darcy was, too. We could tell from the set of Lena's jaw that it was best to keep our questions to ourselves for the time being.

After we checked in, Lena made a beeline for the shower in the adjoining room. Darcy and I were on the bed, our backs propped up against the headboard, Helen curled up into an impossibly small ball and fast asleep between us.

"What the hell is taking so long?" Darcy asked, gently stroking Helen's back.

"She does her best thinking in the shower," I said.

Darcy raised her eyebrows.

"We were friends, you know. She's trying to figure out how to help us. To keep you from having to go into WIT-SEC," I said.

"I'm just not going to go," Darcy said. "I can't, Momma. I've worked so hard to get where I am. Chloe texted—"

"You didn't tell her anything, did you?"

"No, of course not," she said, but her voice was higher than normal.

Shit. Chloe knows. "Whatever you do, don't tell Lena you've talked to anyone, okay?"

Darcy nodded emphatically. She whispered, "When I get back from my honeymoon, we will have $10 million to expand our website, hire more people, improve benefits, pay freelancers more. That's all me. I'm the COO. I can't just disappear into witness protection and become a what? Secretary at the electric co-op in the middle of nowhere Wyoming? And, leave Mi—my life? It's not going to happen."

"I know, baby girl. I'm not going to let that happen. I swear on my life."

"Don't you dare swear on your life. You're going to speak it into being or something. They've sent people after you *twice*. Chekov's gun *came true*."

"We aren't in a thriller, Darcy. This is real life. Nothing ever wraps up in a neat bow in real life."

"Yeah, no sht." She rubbed her stomach.

"Are you sick?"

She dipped her chin and looked at me. "Is it any wonder that I've been nauseous all day?"

"I guess not." We sat in silence for a moment. "Your boobs don't hurt, do they?" I blurted.

"No. Why would my boobs hurt?"

"Mine did when I was pregnant with you. Sick as a dog every morning and my boobs hurt."

"I'm not pregnant," she snapped. "I've been in two gunfights in two days. I'm stressed and worried and afraid. Anyway, I'm never having kids."

"What?"

"I don't want kids, like at all."

"Does Michael?"

"We've agreed not to have them. He got a vasectomy a few months ago."

"Oh. Wow. That's a big step. What did Eloise and Robert think of that?"

"I have no idea. It was none of their business, anyway."

"Michael just agreed to it?"

"Why are you giving me the third degree about this?"

"Asking a few questions about a major life decision my daughter and her fiancé have made is not the third degree."

"Are you about to guilt me about not giving you grandchildren?"

"No, of course not. Though I doubt Eloise would be so accepting."

"What made you think I was pregnant?"

"Sick in the morning, fine in the afternoon."

"Yesterday I was hungover, today I was almost kidnapped. This road trip beats the boat orgy story, and I didn't think that was possible."

"Boat orgy?" I asked.

"One of my crazier travel experiences."

"Did you…?"

"No, of course not."

"Did you want to?"

Darcy cut her eyes at me, a sly smile on her face. "Maybe a little. Being a voyeur was fun, though."

"Darcy, oh my god." I laughed, though. "Have I told you lately how proud I am of you?"

"Not in three years, no."

"Touché. I am proud of you. You're everything I'd wished—"

I stopped, knowing the fine line I walked with Darcy about voicing my choices as regret. One day, she would understand what it was like to look back on your life and wish you'd done things differently, without resenting the life you made.

"I'm not going to let you lose your life. And neither is Lena."

"Why?"

"I just told you."

"No, why is Lena helping me? Helping you?"

"It's her job. And she feels guilty about the way she treated me."

Darcy nodded slowly and studied me. "Guilt, huh?"

"What else?"

Darcy smiled at me. "You're so sheltered."

My stomach tensed. "Please don't make fun of me," I whispered.

Darcy's face fell. "Oh, Momma, I'm not." She pulled me into her arms and hugged me. I settled into her embrace and hugged her back with all the strength I had. The last time Darcy had comforted me like this had been in the middle of the Dairy Queen when she was seven years old. It was strange, the role reversal, but such a relief to finally lean on someone else for a change.

The shower cut off. I released Darcy and sniffed loudly. I couldn't meet her eyes. "I guess Lena's finally done."

Darcy held my hand, stroked the back of it. "Momma, do you really not know why Lena's helping you?"

I looked at our joined hands. I wasn't quite as dense as Darcy thought, but I couldn't let myself think Lena's offer was from anything other than professionalism or well-earned guilt. But part of me wondered. Hoped?

I looked up at Darcy. "Do you?"

Darcy's mouth crooked up into a mischievous smile. "She's totally into you."

It felt like someone was tap dancing on my stomach. "Don't be ridiculous."

"I've been around enough lesbians in love to know it when I see it."

"Really, Darcy. You're being ridiculous."

"How would you feel if she was? Into you?"

"Out of my depth?"

She leaned close and whispered. "Kissing a woman is nice."

I jerked away. "You've done it before?"

"Sure. With all your talk about how men were shit and untrustworthy, is it any surprise I experimented with women? I think you'd be hard-pressed to find a drunk millennial college girl who hasn't kissed a friend or two."

"Chloe?"

"Yeah. Once. It was nice. Very nice." Darcy focused on our joined hands but her neck was splotching, a sure sign of embarrassment. "I've only slept with men. Momma, stop avoiding talking about you and Lena."

"I want to talk about you."

"I don't. You and Lena…"

"There is no—"

"Jesus, Momma. You're clearly into her, too."

"What?"

"Oh, you're trying to deny it, hide it, and I'm pretty sure Lena is too terrified to hope."

"How in the hell have you gotten all of that after being around us for a day?"

"The bickering, for one. I have the gift of discernment, didn't you know?"

"No. Since when?"

"Well, I had a lot of practice trying to be invisible and watching people growing up."

I pulled Darcy to me in a fierce hug, the pain in my heart almost too much to bear. How could I ever apologize enough for her childhood? For the shit she'd endured. I couldn't, I *knew* I couldn't, so I'd always refused to admit there was anything to apologize for, that I'd made the only decisions I could. It was all a lie, though. I don't deserve to be happy.

Darcy pulled away. "Of course, you do, Momma."

I furrowed my brows. "What?"

"You deserve to be happy. Why do you think you don't?"

"Oh, baby girl. I didn't mean to say that out loud."

"Well, you did and its bullshit. If anyone deserves a little happiness, a little lovin', it's you." Darcy wiggled her eyes and I laughed.

"Nothing's happened, Darcy."

"You want it too."

"I wouldn't know what to do."

"Trust me, you will. Start by asking her if she wants to kiss you."

"Just straight out like that? I couldn't!"

"Sure you could. Consent is very trendy, and she's not going to make the first move. You're pretty terrifying, you know."

"No, I'm not."

"Sure, Mom. Whatever you say. How could you not want to kiss her? She looks like Penelope Cruz."

"That's exactly what I thought. I love her eyebrows. They're very expressive," I said.

"That's a new one," Lena said.

Darcy and I looked up. Lena leaned against the adjoining doorjamb. Her hair was partially dry. I swallowed the lump in my throat.

"Oh, hey," I said, wishing there was a hole I could crawl into and die. "Um, how much of that did you hear?"

"No one's ever complimented my eyebrows before."

"Um… They haven't?" My voice went up three octaves. I was doomed.

"I'm going to take Helen to do her business," Darcy said.

"Outside and back in only," Lena said. "We need to stay off the streets."

"Okay. Sure."

We watched Darcy clip the leash on and close the adjoining room door with a solid thud, and a loud click of the lock. We were alone, and she knew I liked her. What was I thinking, complimenting her eyebrows? A dead giveaway that I'd spent way more time than platonically necessary studying her face and every expression she'd ever made. For God's sake, Marja.

"So, you think I look like Penelope Cruz."

"How much of our conversation did you hear?"

"Enough. Do you really think I look like Penelope Cruz?"

"Surely you've heard that before."

She laid her towel over the back of a chair and walked toward me. How had I never noticed how her hips swayed when she walked? Too busy studying her eyebrows, I guess.

"Yeah. Along with Eva Longoria, America Ferrera, Gina Torres, Rosario Dawson. None of whom remotely resemble each other." Lena sat on the edge of the bed next to me. "We all look alike, you know."

Lena smelled like Dove soap, pure and clean. The urge to touch her damp hair was almost overwhelming. When my eyes finally met hers, she raised her eyebrows. Completely unfair, I know.

"I have a plan," Lena said.

"Do you?" My voice was higher than normal.

"Are you okay?" Lena said.

"Not really, no. Do you want to kiss me?"

I can't believe I said it, either. I just blurted it out. Without thinking. I immediately wanted to take it back. I also wanted to kiss her more than anything I've ever wanted to do in the world.

"What?"

Shit. She thinks I'm ridiculous. Of course, I'm ridiculous. Who just comes out and asks a question like that? Idiots like me, that's who. "You know what. Forget I said that." I stood up. "I'm going to catch Darcy." I tried to get out the door as soon as possible. What the fuck was I thinking?

My hand was on the doorknob and opening the door when Lena put her hand out, closing it gently.

I felt her body against mine, her breasts on my back, her breath in my ear. "What did you say?"

I pressed myself against the door to try to put some space between us. I didn't want to scorch her when I exploded with the desire coursing through me. She pressed closer. Holy mother of God.

"Um…"

She turned me around. She towered over me, and I can't say that I minded. One hand on the door, the other touching my jaw, I felt safe, protected, but also very vulnerable, especially with the way Lena's gaze lingered on my lips, the way her tongue licked her own, the way her eyebrows raised slightly, maybe as surprised as I was that you couldn't put a Post-it note between us, and that I was tilting my head back, lifting my lips to meet her slowly descending mouth. A beautiful, lush mouth that I had daydreamed about kissing.

I'm an unreliable narrator, what can I say? I wanted to kiss Lena from the moment she walked into my office.

But this next part? This is the God's honest truth.

My bones melted. If Lena hadn't been pressing me against that door, if I hadn't felt every inch of her, I would have dissolved into the ground. Her lips were soft and gentle. She gave me a few tentative kisses, giving me the opportunity to pull away, to say no. I slid my hand behind her neck and pulled her closer, kept her lips on mine, somehow got the courage to run my tongue along her lips. She opened her mouth to me and moaned when my tongue met hers. My body exploded with sensations I'd never felt before. I felt her in every part of my body. Her leg between my thighs, rubbing against me, one hand on my ass, pulling me close, the other on my breast, gently kneading and oh my God what the hell was happening to my insides? There was a fire building inside me that needed release. Oh my God, did it need to be released.

I pulled away abruptly. Lena was as breathless as I was. Her eyes were hooded, her lips plump and wet, her expression faraway, befuddled, then it cleared.

She stepped back, and my body felt cold and barren without her next to it.

"I'm sorry. I should have explicitly asked if I could kiss you. It's just you asked, and then your—" she groaned again "—tongue and God I've wanted to do that for so long I should have taken it slower instead of acting like you're some sort of gold star lesbian and now I've fucked things up. Well, even more than things were."

I grabbed her hand before she could turn away. "Eva." I squeezed my eyes shut and shook my head. "*Lena*. Please stop talking." I stepped closer to her, all of the uncertainty from earlier a faint memory. I felt the heat from her body, smelled her perfume, could still taste her on my lips. I reached up and touched her face, skimming my thumb over her bottom lip. It quivered. I leaned in and bit it gently and was rewarded with another long groan.

Darcy had been right; I did know what to do.

"My God, Marja. You're killing me."

"How?"

Lena leveled her dark eyes at me. "I want you so much right now," she whispered. "This is definitely not the right time."

"Are we going to get another chance?"

Lena was silent.

"I didn't think so. Whatever your plan is, it doesn't end with our happily-ever-after. How could it? I'm a criminal who has to disappear and you're a cop with a career and family and a bright future. This is it. Our only chance. No one knows where we are at the moment. Once they do, we won't have another chance like this. I want you. I think I've wanted you since the day you walked into my office."

"Don't say that unless you mean it."

I felt a surge of power like I've never known just then. Sexual power mixed with fear of the unknown. "No one's ever kissed me like you did. With so much feeling"

She caressed my cheek. "You deserve that and so much more."

I turned my head and kissed the palm of her hand. She took the opportunity to lean forward and kiss my jaw gently, trailing butterfly kisses along to my ear. She nipped at my earlobe and sighed, sending shivers down my entire body.

"Oh my God, Eva." I tensed. "I mean, Lena."

She pulled away and looked at me with an amused expression on her face. "Have you been fantasizing about me as Eva?"

"No," I said, too quickly and too defensively.

"Uh-huh." One of Lena's hands was at my waist, pulling up the hem of my shirt, resting her warm palm against my bare side. "You can call me whatever you like," she whispered. "Eva. Lena." She raised an eyebrow. "Mistress."

"Now I'm really nervous."

"You don't ever need to be nervous with me, *mi alma*. I know being with a woman is new to you. We'll do as much or as little as you want."

I suddenly didn't want to tell Lena how inexperienced I was, that I'd only been with two men in my entire life. That the only way I'd ever had an orgasm was by reading romance novels and masturbating furiously after reading the sexy parts. That I'd dreamed about her often, but they'd been more impressionistic than instructive, that I'd been too confused and embarrassed to admit my attraction to her, even to myself, that I couldn't bring myself to watch lesbian porn to give shape to what I felt at night, to the need I felt every morning. I didn't want to waste time talking. In twenty-four hours I'd never see her again. But, right then, all I wanted to do was to kiss her and see what happened next.

"You talk too much," I said, and leaned forward and touched my lips to hers.

SIXTEEN

Darcy

Helen and I stood in the motel parking lot, looking at each other. "I wonder how much time we should give them?" I asked. Helen peed on the sidewalk. "Come on, then. Let's go to the drugstore."

We walked down the road, Helen stopping to sniff every three or four feet, or so it seemed like. It was less than riveting and soon enough my mind was swirling between Michael, Chloe, Marja, Lena, Wander Women and back again to the cartel that was trying to kill my mother and, quite possibly, me.

My breath fogged the air. I shivered and looked at my surroundings. We were on an old portion of Route 66, a two-lane asphalt road that got bypassed when I-44 was built in the mid-twentieth century. A few businesses held on, but everything seemed intent to maintain a "those were the days" aura. I know Lena said I shouldn't be outside, but no one looked suspicious, and I needed a pregnancy test.

I knew what Marja and Lena were doing back at the motel.

Still, I couldn't quite wrap my head around the idea of Marja and Lena. Or Marja with anyone. This wasn't just a case of a child coming to terms with a parent as a sexual being. I'd never seen my mother show a bit of affection to anyone but me. I had no memory of a mother and father giving each other brief hello and goodbye kisses, I didn't have grandparents, or aunts and uncles I was close to. The one grandparent I had, Granny Evans, died when I was five. The memory I have of her is based on an old, sepia-colored photo of me sitting on her lap. In my conjured memory, she's warm and soft and smells like talcum powder. She calls me her little Cricket in a smooth alto voice. I put my head on her shoulder, nestle into her neck, and she sings "Baa, Baa, Black Sheep" as she rocks me to sleep.

It's all a lie. None of that happened. But it made great English essay about my earliest memory. I got an A.

As far as I know, Momma has zero experience with romantic love. She sure as hell didn't wax rhapsodic about men and falling in love when I was growing up. Which is no wonder it took me over ten years to fall in love. Everything I know about falling in love I learned from Nora Roberts and Diana Gabaldon. Not bad teachers, those. Still, I don't trust it. Part of me doesn't believe in it, unconditional love. I think I have it with Michael, but how do I know? The only unconditional love I know is Momma's love for me, and that's not really the same thing, is it?

Would Michael give up his life for me? Would he go into WITSEC if that was the only way to be together? I didn't want to think about the answer.

Would I do it for him?

Would Chloe do it for me?

Yes.

That stopped me in my tracks. I shook my head and kept walking, much preferring to think about Momma and Lena's love story, friends to lovers, with a betrayal in between. Who are we kidding, it could be a Nora Roberts novel. It probably was.

I'd seen the looks that passed between Marja and Lena, the longing gazes when the other wasn't looking, felt the sexual tension like a physical thing in the car. It was Lena putting her hand on Marja's knee and calming her that made it hit home to me: Marja loved her. No one, and I mean no one, had ever been able to calm Marja Evans down with a mere touch like that. Marja probably didn't realize it was love, but—I looked at my watch; how had twenty minutes gone by?—she probably realized it by now.

Oh my God, my mother is having sex right now.

"Ew."

Helen sniffed a metal post, found it appealing, and peed on it. When she finished, she sat down, looked up at me, and barked.

"If you weren't so cute, you'd be annoying." The dog perked her ears. "I bet Marja talks to you like you're a real person." Helen tilted her head. "Yes, I see the irony. Shut up."

I raised my eyes to the darkened sky. "I'm talking to a fucking dog."

Bark.

"That one's legit," I said. "Come on let's keep going."

I had always known Momma was strong, but that she was courageous had never crossed my mind. But what else could I call it when she decided to take on the cartel instead of running like she very well could have. Okay, granted, she'd put me in danger with this stupid road trip, but could I really blame her for wanting to make amends? No, the alternative would have been Marja disappearing without a word. I would have never recovered from that, and Marja knew it as well as I did.

Witness protection. I should probably be researching it. All I had to go on was…what? A TV show on the USA network that I never watched and even now can't remember anything about except the main character was blonde. Witness protection is all Italian Mob guys who ratted out guys with names like Soprano and Corleone and were sent to live in the middle of Idaho with a bunch of Mormons and how in the hell didn't they stand out? Would Marja and I be sent somewhere together? Surely. What in the hell would we do? Live on the government? Would I ever be able to travel freely again? Probably not. I would lose my friends and my career.

Chloe.

My stomach clenched at the idea of never seeing my best friend again, of never resolving what happened Friday night. Between me and Michael's sister.

Shit, *Michael.*

I would probably feel better if I felt guilty about kissing her. But I don't, and that worries me.

I crossed my arms over my chest and squeezed myself for warmth. I winced in pain.

Sore boobs.

Son of a bitch.

Michael had gotten the vasectomy when I was on an extended trip, a month island hopping in Indonesia. When I asked how it went on one of our calls, he said *Without a hitch.* With the type of procedure Michael had, there would have been little to no scarring and when I returned, I hadn't even thought to look or ask about it. I had an IUD, anyway. We were doubly protected.

Or so I thought.

I turned my phone on and dialed Michael's number. He picked up on the first ring.

"Hey."

"Hey. Where are you?"

"At the Vegas airport.Where are you?"

"Carthage, Missouri."

"I don't know where that is."

"Still two whole states from Chicago."

"What time will you be home tomorrow?"

Would I even be home tomorrow? Or ever? I should tell Michael about WITSEC. He has a right to know what's going on. That our lives might be about to be upended. No, not yet. I need to ask Lena more questions, have more answers for Michael when I tell him. Why am I thinking about this as if it's a foregone conclusion? I'm not going into WITSEC. I'm not giving up my life.

I'm still not telling him.

"Late. It's an eight-hour drive, and Helen has to stop and pee every two hours."

"Who's Helen?"

"Marja's dog."

"When did Marja get a dog?"

"No idea. Helen has a tiny bladder, and she barks every time someone curses."

Michael laughed. "Only Marja."

I know he didn't mean it cruelly, but it irritated me, nonetheless. "You've never even met her," I snapped.

After a beat of silence Michael said, "I didn't mean anything by it, Darcy. You and Chloe have talked so much about her I feel like I have."

I shook my head. "I know, I'm sorry. It's just been a stressful couple of days."

Michael's voice softened. "I'm sorry, baby. It's almost over. Text me when you get home, okay?"

"I will." I cleared my throat. "Was your bachelor party fun?"

"Honestly? Not really. I would have rather been with you."

My heart melted a little. "What a sweet talker you are."

"I try. Get some sleep. Drive carefully tomorrow. There's some weather coming in from the north. Have you seen the forecast?"

"No, but it doesn't feel like October."

"Welcome to climate change. Our green energy investments will open tomorrow on an upward swing. Always do when there are weather extremes."

"Actively rooting for natural disasters so you can make money is not a good look, Michael."

"I'm not, of course I'm not. If you don't get to Chicago soon you might get stuck in Missouri. Sleet is forecast, then snow."

"O'Hare will be a nightmare. You'll probably get stuck in Vegas."

"Perish the thought. But don't worry about the wedding. My mom will have contingency plans for the contingency plans. The wedding will go on no matter what."

"Right." I moved on. "Hey, have you been back lately to check your sperm count?"

Michael laughed. "Wow, where did that come from?"

I shrugged, though he couldn't see me. "Just checking to make sure you're making sure the vasectomy took."

Michael paused. "You're not…are you pregnant?"

"I shouldn't be. I have an IUD, and you had the vasectomy."

"Right," he said slowly. "Do you think you're pregnant?"

"Do you want me to be?"

"I know you would think it's the end of the world, but I wouldn't."

"We decided we weren't going to have children."

"I know, I know."

There was something in his voice, a resignation, a disappointment, that I didn't want to hear. I didn't want to talk about it, think about it, interrogate it. "Anyway, I'm cold. I gotta go buy a hoodie. Bye."

I clicked off, trying to ignore the fact that he didn't answer the questions.

Then again, neither did I.

SEVENTEEN

Darcy

Right inside the door of the CVS I was greeted with a display of blue-and-white hoodies, sweatshirts, knit hats, and gloves with Carthage High in varsity block letters. I grabbed an XL zip up hoodie, the only size they had, put a knit hat on my head, and wandered around until I found the pregnancy aisle. I stopped dead.

"Why are they're so many fucking options?"

Helen groaned and lay on the cool linoleum. "I can't believe it. I've broken you down." Helen was so unimpressed or so over me, I wasn't sure which, she let out a huge snore. "God, you're dramatic. I love that about you. I'm not carrying you back, by the way."

Helen opened her eyes and looked up at me from beneath her eyebrows and I knew, without a doubt, that I would indeed be carrying her back.

"Drama queen."

I looked at the array of pregnancy tests again. I longed to be in Europe where the grocery stores were smaller, more efficient. They gave you one option of everything and that's it. That's all anyone needed. Endless choices drove me crazy. I actively avoided the cereal aisle, and the toothpaste aisle made my teeth itch. Endless choices just made you second-guess yourself. A can of beans is a can of beans.

I grabbed an EPT because I remembered those from soap opera commercials when I was a kid. It had been around a long time. Must be good. At the counter, the cashier sat on a stool and glared at Helen. "Is that a service dog?" she growled in a three pack a day voice.

"Yep."

"It ain't wearing a vest."

I pulled a Snickers bar off the display and plunked it down. "It's at the cleaners."

The woman looked from Helen to me. "Uh-huh."

I grabbed three more Snickers and placed them on the counter. "Got a craving for peanuts?" Her name tag said "Fred."

I added a bag of beef jerky. "No, Fred, I'm eating my feelings." I took off my hat and put it on the counter. "Anywhere around here where I can drink them?"

Fred raised her eyebrows and looked at the EPT. "That a good idea?"

"You're awfully judgmental for a woman named Fred."

Fred glowered at me for a good ten seconds. "Grab two king-size," she said. "It's a better deal."

I did so, and Fred rang it and put the food in a bag. I ripped the tags off the hat and hoodie and put them on. She studied me again. "You all right?"

"Not really, no." I sighed and gave her a wan smile. "Thanks for the candy bar tip."

"You're welcome." As I turned to leave, Fred said, "Children are a blessing from God."

"That's what they say," I replied.

"Ice in the forecast, so if you're passing through you best get on the road to beat it."

"Thanks, Fred." The automatic doors opened, and a blast of chilly air hit me. I turned back to the clerk. "Is your name really Fred?"

She nodded. "Mama wanted a boy. My brother's name is Sue."

I narrowed my eyes at her, sure she was putting me on but she was stone-faced.

"In or out, it's getting cold as a witch's tit out there," Fred said.

Outside, the air was more crisp than chilly, and a gentle breeze swirled around me. But Fred wasn't wrong; I'd survived enough Midwest winters to know that this could get very bad, very quickly. I picked Helen up, put her inside my hoodie, and zipped it up. She looked up at me with adoring brown eyes and licked my chin.

I didn't know what to say to that, so I ripped into a candy bar.

I had eaten one king-size candy bar by the time I got back to the motel because the fact was I did crave peanuts and chocolate, goddammit. Why hadn't I gotten something to drink?

I sighed and looked at the Boots Court Motel. A midcentury, flat-roofed stucco building trimmed in green neon in the middle of Missouri. It didn't look like your typical roadside motel, which for Americans pretty much defaulted to a long low string of rooms with an office at the end and an expansive parking lot in front. Oh, and the neon sign blinking Vacancy. Basically, the Bates Motel.

Boots Court was narrow from the street, its main building reaching back into the small corner lot where Route 66 made a dogleg east. What was most unique about the motel were the carports between the rooms. The '69 Mustang would have fit in perfectly with the midcentury aesthetic. But we hadn't seen the Mustang since the night before, and Lena hadn't been forthcoming when we would get it back. My guess was never. Now we were traveling in a black Suburban with blackout windows that would have been less conspicuous if it had THIS IS A GOVERNMENT CAR written in white shoe polish across its back window.

My watch said it had been an hour since I left Momma and Lena. Surely that was enough time. An ear against the door of Marja's room said surely not, and I remembered Jess and her friends talking about how all-night lesbian sex (with multiple orgasms) was the norm, not the exception, then laughing at my and Ella's reactions.

"Well, I'm gonna have to try that," I said, and three of Jess's friends raised their hands to volunteer as tributes. Chloe made it four.

I sat on one of the metal chairs in front of the office, tore open another Snickers ate half of it in one bite.

Don't think about Chloe.

Don't think about Chloe.

Don't think about kissing Chloe.

Watching the seven o'clock Carthage, Missouri, traffic did not take my mind off of kissing Chloe.

I forced myself to think about work, remembering how hopeful I was to get a story or two out of this trip. Not sure almost being murdered twice was exactly the kind of content our investors were looking for.

I looked into my plastic bag. Beef jerky and the pregnancy test I was avoiding. I opened the jerky, found a small morsel, and fed it to Helen. She sniffed at it daintily and gently took it from my fingers. "Aren't you a good girl." I rubbed behind her ears, and Helen closed her eyes and groaned.

"I can't be pregnant. Michael got a vasectomy." I bit off a piece of jerky.

I fed Helen another piece of jerky, and Chloe's smile flashed through my mind. The way her eyes crinkled at the corners.

Don't think about your best friend like that, Darcy.

I thought about Michael, the polar opposite of Chloe. One was professional and slick, the other was natural and carefree. One smelled of Versace and the other smells like citrus and long walks on the beach.

"Christ."

Helen licked my chin again, and I stared down into those soulful brown eyes. Emotions swelled in me, forced their way out of my mouth as a sob. "I don't think I should get married, Helen." She didn't respond, obviously, which was a relief. I blew out a breath. "I said it. The world didn't end."

Would I be able to say it aloud to Michael? How could I? We were too far in. The wedding was in six days. Eloise had done so much work. All that money wasted. I felt physically ill at the thought. There was no way I could pay them back, and I would want to. Need to, or the guilt and shame would weigh me down for the rest of my life.

"No," I said out loud. "I love Michael. He loves me. It's natural to have cold feet. Fantasizing about someone isn't the same as doing something about it, and I would never."

Wouldn't you though? You kinda did on Friday.

An anomaly. Chloe's inopportune confession. Too much to drink. A moment of weakness.

But wow. What a moment it had been.

The wind decided it was done pussyfooting around. Leaves were tumbling down the road, swirling in little tornadoes, before skipping out of sight. The cold cut like a knife through my hoodie. Helen whimpered.

We entered the adjoining motel room and immediately discovered the walls to the Boots Court Motel were indeed paper thin. I dug my headphones out of my backpack and turned up my music. Helen jumped on the farthest bed, curled up, and immediately went to sleep. I took the pregnancy test into the bathroom to discover my fate.

I'd dialed Chloe automatically. Chloe had been the first person I called for everything for so long… Michael had been right.

She answered on the first ring.

"Fitz? Everything okay?"

Tears welled in my eyes and a small sob escaped me.

"No." My voice was high, plaintive. I hated it.

"What is it? What's wrong?" Chloe sounded panicked.

"There's so much, I don't know where to start."

"The beginning, Fitz. Start at—"

The damn broke, and everything came rushing out of my mouth like a waterfall.

"Marja is in the next room having sex with Lena and I'm sitting in the most depressing room ever with a dog who barks every time I say fuck (bark) hear that? I've started to wonder if maybe we shouldn't get married, even before he left for Vegas or we kissed, and I shouldn't be thinking about your smile and crinkly eyes but I am and I've been sick every morning for a week and I took a pregnancy test and I'm a fucking mess and need my best friend." I hiccupped. "I need you."

There was a long, long silence on the other end. I pulled the phone away to make sure we were still connected. "Chloe?" I whispered.

"Have you told Michael?" Her voice was firm.

"I talked to him about an hour ago."

"He knows all of this? What did he say? Is he on his way?"

"No."

"No, what?"

"I didn't tell him, and he's not on his way."

"Why not?"

I swallowed and closed my eyes. Shook my head, ashamed to admit what I knew to be true, what I knew would always be true. "Because he's not my best friend."

"Where are you?"

"Carthage, Missouri. Boots Court Motel."

"I'm on my way."

"Chloe, the weather—" The phone line beeped. She'd hung up. Probably afraid I would hem and haw and try to change her mind. I couldn't blame her, but I was disappointed Chloe didn't hear what I wanted to say.

Hurry.

PART THREE

PART-THREE

EIGHTEEN

Darcy

Three Days Earlier

"Good morning, beautiful."

I stretched and opened my eyes. Michael sat on the edge of the bed in a crisp white shirt, blue necktie tied in a perfect Windsor knot, navy suit pants with a sharp crease down the middle. His short dark hair was gelled into place, his face freshly shaven. Michael was handsome and successful and rich. Despite all of my professional achievements, I was always a bit surprised Michael fell in love with me, an illegitimate small-town girl from Frio, Texas, and every time I was angry for letting that little bit of my old, insecure self seep through, even if it was only in my head.

Michael and I were both early risers, but he was a chipper one. I was not.

"Ugh."

Michael rubbed my bare arms. "Sleep well?"

"I did."

Okay, that was lie. A white one. Maybe gray. Closer to charcoal, if you want to know the truth.

"Or did you toss and turn about seeing your mom?"

"Among other things."

"Don't stress, Darce. You aced your pitch yesterday, everything is on track with the wedding, and in ten days we will be on our honeymoon in Bali. All you have to do is go pick up Marja and be back by Monday."

"That's a ridiculous oversimplification of the next week of my life."

"Is it? The pitch is done and the decision is out of your hands. There is nothing to gain by worrying about it. My mom is planning the wedding, so there's nothing to do there but show up when you're supposed to."

"To all the parties I don't want to go to."

Michael sighed. "It's the least you can do to pay back my parents for planning and paying for everything."

I bristled. "I wanted to elope, remember? The agreement was I would have a big wedding for Eloise as long as I didn't have to plan it. There was no agreement about a party every night for a week leading up to it."

Michael shrugged. "It was implied. That's what everyone does."

I inhaled and counted to five. There was no point in rehashing this or pleading ignorance of the ways of old money Chicago.

"When's your flight?"

"Eleven."

"I guess I'll see you when I get back."

"On Monday."

"I'll get back as soon as I can."

"You shouldn't have agreed to drive up here with her, with everything going on," Michael said.

My temper snapped. Michael and Eloise had gone behind my back, against my wishes, and invited Marja to our wedding. "Well, I didn't fucking invite her, did I?"

I got up, stalked into Michael's bathroom, and turned on the shower. It would be our bathroom in a week. It was sleek and modern, all Carreras marble, black and white with brushed gold accents. It was tasteful and beautiful, but even with the heated tile floors it struck me as cold and impersonal. I kinda hated it.

Michael leaned against the doorjamb. "Can we not have this fight again, Darcy?"

"Are we fighting?"

"You're snapping at me and sounding bitchy."

I inhaled. "You don't get to have it both ways, Michael. You and Eloise invited my mom, but you don't want the inconvenience and uncertainty that comes with it. This is it. This is the inconvenience. Who the fuck knows what Marja has up her sleeve? But I guarantee you she has something, and it's not going to be holding hands and singing 'Kumbaya' and apologizing to me for not speaking to me for years. So, yeah. I'm not looking forward to being in a situation you and your mother put me into. And don't you dare try to guilt trip me about your parents planning and paying for everything. I didn't want *any* of this."

"Jesus, Darcy. Do you even want to get married?"

"Why would you ask that?" I felt myself redden and hoped that Michael thought it was the steam from the shower.

Michael reached up to run his hand through his hair, remembered his grooming, and stopped. "Things have been pretty tense for a while now. I've always thought that once we were through everything that we would go back to normal, but it's getting harder and harder to remember what our normal is."

I looked down. "I know."

"Do you still want this? Us?" Michael asked.

"Of course, I do," I said quickly.

Michael was everything I'd ever wanted in a man. Smart, successful, handsome, kind. I would become part of a wonderful family with in-laws who'd been married for nearly forty years. Chloe would be my sister. I would be crazy to not want this.

"I'm just stressed about the VC funding and seeing Marja and everything I have to do before the wedding. I'll be fine."

Michael smiled and came to me, wrapping his arms around me. "I love you. Everything will work out with your mom, I'm sure of it."

The fight had gone all out of me as soon as it came. "You're probably right."

He kissed me gently on the lips. "Drive safely."

"I doubt Marja will let me drive, to be honest."

"I really can't wait to meet her."

"You say that now."

He kissed me on the nose. "Don't forget to act surprised tonight."

"Uuuuugggggghhhh." I dropped my head on his chest. "Don't remind me."

"It's just a wedding shower with lots of wine and all your favorite foods."

I looked at him suspiciously. "How do you know so much about it?"

"Ella loves me."

"You mean you flirted and charmed Ella until she spilled everything."

Michael got a mischievous grin on his face, the grin and playfulness that made me fall in love with him. "I only use my powers for good, Darcy."

"Uh-huh. Get out of here. Have fun this weekend."

"You, too."

He rolled his suitcase down the hall, and the apartment

door opened and closed. The smile faded from my face and all my anxiety and stress that had been briefly banished came roaring back.

I flopped back onto the bed and threw my arm over my eyes, blocking out the world, or trying to.

The truth is, the closer I got to marrying the man of my childhood dreams, the colder my feet got. But it was too late to turn back.

Chloe knocked on my desk and sat on the corner. "Hey, Fitz. Ready for your surprise shower?"

I looked up from my spreadsheet and saw Chloe holding two coffee mugs from the coworking space kitchen and a full bottle of liquor.

"What do you have there?" Darcy asked.

"Liquid courage." Chloe held up the bottle.

"Fireball? Haven't we graduated to something a little classier by now?"

"Never forget your roots, Fitz."

I scoffed.

"Okay, our roots."

I rolled my eyes. "Do I really need that much courage for a surprise wedding shower?"

"Jess is in charge, so probably."

"True."

I inspected the cleanliness of our mugs and decided they were good enough. Chloe poured a shot in each. I arched an eyebrow. "That's a hefty pour."

"I'm getting you drunk tonight."

"Oh, hey, speaking of." The new guy at the co-op, King—just King, I'm not into being owned by the patriarchy, man—put his messenger bag in his lap and rolled his desk chair over to us. Yes, he is exactly the type of young millennial who works remotely and thinks that taxes are tyranny. He always seemed to be only a few desks away, and always had a toothpaste perfect smile for Chloe, who would rather eat dirt than date a libertarian.

"I'm going to be out of town next week so I want to give this to you now." He opened his messenger bag and pulled out a bottle of Veuve Clicquot. "Sounds like you can put it to good use tonight. Congrats on your marriage."

I took the bottle. "Wow, um, thanks, King."

He held up his hands. "I don't mean to eavesdrop, but you know, word gets around the co-op and all. I like what you two, and your friends, are doing with Wander Women. If you ever need anything tech related, just let me know."

With tiny salute, he rolled back to his desk.

Chloe looked at the bottle with suspicion. "Do you think he spiked it with something?"

"Why would he do that?"

"I don't trust anyone who doesn't pay their taxes."

King rolled back over. "I didn't spike it and I do pay my taxes. I just pay as little as possible, which is perfectly legal." He winked and rolled back to his desk.

"It's not polite to eavesdrop."

"Then talk quieter," he said.

"I think he likes you," I whisper to Chloe.

"Hmm."

"Well, regardless. I'm not getting drunk tonight. I have an early flight tomorrow."

"You can write a 'how to survive a hangover at thirty-five thousand feet article."

"You're so generous."

"I'm a giving friend, what can I say." We lifted our mugs. "Sláinte."

"Cheers," I said.

I gasped after it went down. Chloe wasn't affected at all. "Why do we drink this again?"

"Because you don't like tequila."

"That's all your fault," I said.

"Yes, yes, it is." Chloe poured another shot, but smaller. "Just like all of our college regrets."

I lifted my mug. "To Chloe Parsons, being a bad influence on me since 2006."

"I'll drink to that."

When we finished, Chloe put the lid on the bottle. "You about ready?"

"As I'll ever be. Jess and Ella don't know I know, do they?" I said. As much as I hated surprises and being the center of attention, I hated the thought that I might somehow disappoint my friends' plans.

"I haven't told them. I wish you hadn't told me. Now I don't get to enjoy your fake surprise."

"I'm not really good at faking stuff like that."

"I know. That's why you need to practice."

"What?"

"Practice. On the count of three, I'm going to yell *surprise*, and you're going to show me your shocked but thrilled face. One, two, three…"

I waited. And waited. Chloe stood there, watching me. "You didn…"

Chloe spread her arms and jumped, as if she was going to launch herself over the desk. "SURPRISE!"

I jerked away and nearly fell backward out of her chair. I grabbed the edge of my desk just in time. "Shit, Clo."

"People are trying to work here, Parsons," someone said from across the room.

"Come on, Fitz, before we get put into detention."

I gathered my stuff. "I hate being the center of attention."

199

"You should have thought of that before you agreed to have the wedding of the decade at Holy Name Cathedral in eight days."

I almost said *don't remind me*, but caught myself just in time.

"Hey," Chloe said. "Michael didn't want to tell you this, but I think you should know."

"Know what?"

"The Obamas are coming," Chloe said.

"What the fuck. No, they aren't."

"They are."

"Michael said it was a courtesy invite, that they'd never come," I said.

"Michael lied. My parents have supported Obama since his senate run, and they're big donors of The Obama Foundation. They were always going to come."

I put my head in my hands and took a few deep breaths. Chloe came around the desk, leaned down, and hugged me from behind.

She whispered in my ear. "Hey, you've got this. You have a week to come to terms with that anxiety, but we have ten minutes to get through the surprise party anxiety."

"I'm a mess," I said.

"No, you're a bride one week away from being the center of attention at the wedding of the year."

"You aren't helping here, Chlo." Darcy tapped Chloe's hand. "Rub."

"Laptop neck?" Chloe asked.

"Yes. The shooting pain one."

"You aren't doing your exercises, are you?"

"Why would I when I know you'll rub my shoulders?"

"I feel so used," Chloe said.

"Used and abused."

Chloe dug her thumb into the tender spot where the shooting pain emanated from. "OW."

"Oh, did that hurt?" Chloe said innocently.

"You're mean."

"I'm tough. There's a difference."

"You're a marshmallow," I said.

"Only around you because you're my favorite."

"I better be. I've put up with you for the longest."

"You mean you've loved me for the longest," Chloe said.

"In your dreams."

"Yes, every night I dream about you. Don't you hear me calling out for you?" Chloe said.

"Is that why all of your lovers leave in a huff the next morning?"

"The men think it's hot, and want to invite you in. The women not so much."

I turned around and looked at Chloe, my stomach fluttering. "We're still joking here, right?"

Chloe paused for a second before smiling. "Of course we are, Fitz."

I ignored the stab of…something I always felt when we talked about Chloe's lovers. I shrugged off Chloe's hands, said thanks, and stood.

"Everything is taken care of. Emails answered, away message created. I've reviewed last month's numbers and sent it on to you. Jess is taking over my social media, Ella is going to sit in on the podcast…" I said.

Chloe picked up the bottle of Fireball and her mug and walked toward the door. "We got it, Darcy," she said over her shoulder. "We can survive without you for a week. You just need to focus on enjoying your time with Marja."

Chloe was sulking.

This mood would take over her at the strangest of times, and I hadn't been able to predict when one was coming for a long time. Since around the time I started dating Michael. I'm sure one thing had nothing to do with the other.

It wasn't difficult to figure why these days. Our relationship was eight days away from changing dramatically. That's how it works. The thing is, Chloe has held the number one place in my life for years, Marja aside. It doesn't help the situation that Chloe only occasionally got along with her much older brother.

I'd dreaded telling Chloe that I was dating Michael, that we were sleeping together. I expected a huge fight between us, but Chloe had surprised me by not reacting much at all. By the time Michael and I started talking marriage, Chloe had gotten used to the idea enough she'd been genuinely happy for the two of us, exclaiming how happy she was that I would be her sister as well as her best friend.

Chloe had gone into moods like this since we met fifteen years ago, and I'd long ago learned the best thing to do when she was in one was to let her come out of it on her own.

So, we walked in silence and I thought about what was in store for me with my mother for the next two days. The mother who I hadn't talked to in years. The woman I was flying to Texas and driving back to Chicago for the wedding with because Marja was apparently afraid of flying now, and she had a dog she couldn't leave behind.

The dog was news to me. I'd wanted a dog since I was four years old and Marja had always said no, that she didn't want to clean other people's houses all day to have to come home and clean up after a dog. All my promises to take care of the dog and love it fell on deaf ears. The idea that my mother now had a dog and was attached to it so much she couldn't leave it for a week or two, was pretty rich.

Actually, it was suspicious. Just like everything about Marja these days.

When I gave my guest list to Eloise, Marja's name wasn't on

it, and why should it be? Marja'd cut off all contact with me for no reason that I could see. Sure, we'd drifted apart over the years, but didn't all adult children drift apart from their parents? Daily calls turned into weekly, and eventually turned into mostly texts. Our yearly road trips had dried up when I started travel writing full time. The last thing I wanted to do on vacation was travel. Staycations had become my thing, and there was no way in hell I was going to have a staycation in Frio, Texas. I'd worked too hard to put that town, and every horrible person who lived there, behind me.

Marja had visited me regularly in Chicago (flying), until three years ago. Marja loved Chloe, Jess, and Ella, but hadn't met Michael or his dad. She had only met Eloise the one time. The Parsons had invited us to dinner each time that Marja visited, and Marja had always replied that it was up to me, but she was perfectly happy spending time just the two of us. So, we never went.

If I'm completely honest, I was relieved. I would have hated for her to be uncomfortable or stressed, though despite their wealth, the Parsons are some of the nicest and most down to earth people I knew. They'd welcomed me with open arms first as Chloe's best friend, and now as Michael's fiancée, and I knew they would do the same with Marja. But Marja wasn't interested, which is why it was such a shock when she agreed to come to the wedding, especially after years of silence.

We arrived at our brownstone door and Chloe turned to me. "Can I ask you a question?"

"Of course."

"Why did you flinch?"

"What?"

"Twenty minutes ago. You flinched from me as if, I don't know, you thought I was going to attack you."

"You practically jumped across my desk, Chloe."

She closed her eyes and shook her head. "Not then. When I was rubbing your shoulders."

"No, I didn't."

"Yes, you did. And you've done it before."

"Maybe it's weird that you rub my shoulders," I said, not meeting her eyes.

"You ask me to do it! But, hey. Don't worry. I'll never do it again since you *obviously* think it's some prelude to me trying to seduce you or something," Chloe sneered.

"Trust me, I *never* think you're trying to seduce me," I said, my anger rising along with my embarrassment. "You told me years ago that you didn't think I was pretty so I've never—"

"Wait, what did you just say?"

I forced myself to look Chloe in the eye. I'd wanted to talk about this for years but had never had the courage. Apparently now was the time.

"You really want me to repeat it?"

"I never said you weren't pretty."

"Yes, you did."

"When."

"When you told me you were bisexual. You said I was unattractive so I didn't have to worry."

Chloe chuckled.

"It's not funny! It was devastating to hear someone who I thought was my friend tell me I was ugly to my face, to repeat the same sht I'd been hearing for years in Frio. It took me months to get over it." That's a big ole lie. I still wasn't over it, but I'd learned to forget it, or not think about it, though every time Chloe brought a beautiful woman home, the memory bowled me over like a freight train.

Chloe's laughter died. She stepped forward and took my hands. "Darcy, I don't remember exactly what I said, but I

204

know I never said you were unattractive. I definitely never said you were ugly. I've never thought that. Not once."

"You haven't?"

"No. You're smoking hot, Fitz. I probably said something stupid to put you at ease because I didn't want to lose you as a friend. Coming out to you was terrifying, you know." Chloe cupped my face and wiped my tears away with her thumbs. She cleared her throat and said in a low voice, "The truth is, I've wanted to kiss you since the moment I met you."

My skin where Chloe cupped my face seared from her touch, and my knees went a little weak. I could barely get the next word out. "What?"

Her eyes were as soft as her thumbs caressing my cheeks. "I couldn't very well tell you that, could I?"

"Why are you telling me now?"

"Our relationship is about to change forever. I might as well be completely honest with you. You're the most beautiful woman I've ever known." Her gaze dropped to my mouth, which I am sure was gaping in surprise. She dropped her hands from my face and I fell a little forward, as if her light touch had been the only thing holding me upright. She reached out to open the door.

"One more thing, Fitz. I've been in love with you since the moment I met you, too."

She opened the door and walked in, and twenty of our friends jumped up and said, "Surprise!"

"It looks like the wrapping paper aisle in Walgreens threw up in here," I said.

I was nestled in the corner of the couch, my legs tucked under me, balancing a glass of red wine on the arm.

It was almost eleven o'clock, and the last guests had just left. Jess, Ella, Chloe, and I had collapsed into our favorite spots:

one corner of the couch for me, the other corner for Chloe, the floor for Jess, and Ella curled up in a leather club chair that was big enough for two people. Risqué lingerie and sex toys of all types lay scattered amid the paper bags, tissue paper, wrapping paper, and raunchy cards. A stray paper plate or two crusted with smears of dried flesh-colored icing and plastic forks had been abandoned by guests leaving in a rush when Ella had mentioned in passing that I had an early flight in the morning.

"My grandmother would want to keep it," Ella said. "That is the problem with you youngsters, you think everything and everyone is disposable," Ella said in a perfect imitation of her Desi grandmother's voice.

"My mom would have insisted everything be wrapped in a reusable container. Like a hemp tote bag, or something," Jess said.

"Tote bags are worse for the environment than plastic bags," Chloe said, her eyes on her phone.

"Bullshit," Jess said.

"I read that article, too," I said.

"It was probably written by some plastic bag manufacturer PR guy," Jess countered.

"True," Chloe and I said in unison. Our eyes met for the first time that night, and we both looked away.

I had been too stunned to move, let alone speak, when Chloe had dropped her bombshell and opened the door. Everyone was thrilled with my reaction to the surprise, and I was ushered into the apartment on a wave of raised, laughing voices, a glass of cabernet magically appeared in my hand. All I could do was drink a big gulp and hold on to it like a life raft. The party progressed—eating Ella's delicious red curry chicken, playing a game (I think), opening sex toy after sex toy. No one seemed to notice that I wasn't there in the room, that I was still standing outside the door, hearing Chloe's confession.

I've been in love with you since the moment I met you, too.

Who the hell said something like that to their best friend a week before their wedding? And right before they walked into a room full of people?

I'd barely been present during the party, instead I turned the last fifteen years of friendship with Chloe over and over in my mind. Had I really been so dense as to not notice Chloe's romantic feelings for me? Or had she been that good at disguising them? Between my habit of trying to not be noticed and my complete cluelessness when it came to picking up on signs that men and women were interested in me, it was easy for me to believe that I'd been dense. But no. Chloe had made it clear to me from the moment she told me she was bisexual that she thought of me only as a friend. Why should I suspect it? Why shouldn't I have chalked up Chloe's affection as platonic?

Luckily, my shocked and vacant expression was easily explained away by not only the surprise at the shower, but the discovery that none of the gifts had been purchased off our registry but had been bought at various sex stores across Chicago and online.

Ella, the nurturer of the group and the only one more reserved, possibly repressed, than I am, pulled me aside and said, "I tried to tell them this wasn't a good idea."

"It's okay," I said.

"Are you feeling all right? You look a little pale." She rubbed my arm.

"I'm fine. I haven't been feeling very well today."

"Do you think you're coming down with something?"

"I'm coming down with dreading the road trip with my mother."

"Oh, it won't be that bad."

I crossed my fingers and forced myself to look happier than I felt. I had felt a little queasy most of the day, but what I felt at that moment… I'm not sure what it was. I wasn't sick to my stomach at the idea of Chloe being in love with me. Surprised, stunned, shocked. Yes. Queasy? No. A little turned on?

Maybe?

Probably.

Okay, fine. *Yes.*

This is wrong. I'm getting married to Chloe's brother a week from tomorrow.

The wine tasted bitter, my mouth was dry, and my stomach wouldn't stop churning. When someone gave me the plate of curry, I thought I was going to vomit, and it's my favorite dish.

To watch Chloe, you would have never known that anything weird had happened between us. She was ebullient and chatty, not trying to be the center of attention but inevitably becoming it. Everyone was drawn to Chloe. She's charismatic. Intelligent. Brash, but likable. Attractive. Spontaneous. Fun. My polar opposite. I tempered Chloe's self-destructive impulses with thoughtful caution, and Chloe encouraged me to take risks. She only managed to convince me to take small risks, but then again, I'd only managed to pull Chloe back from the brink a fraction of the times I've tried. I'm the yin, Chloe the yang.

But, there was nothing harmonious about us tonight.

I thought I caught Chloe looking at me a couple of times, but then again, Chloe had caught me doing the same. Still, we sat as far apart as possible when we ate. Chloe sat just out of my peripheral vision as I opened one embarrassing sex toy after another, dutifully writing down what each gift was and who it was from. I was relieved when Ella dropped the hint for everyone to leave. What I wanted more than anything was to go to bed and forget Chloe's confession. Ignore it. Leave in the morning and by the time I returned on Monday everything would be back to normal. Chloe didn't mean it. She'd promised to make sure I looked surprised. Mission accomplished. Though, a part of me thought it was cruel to say something like that, to get my hopes up…

Wait, what? What hopes? That she would kiss me? Or more? No. No. This isn't right. It will ruin my relationship with Chloe, Michael, her parents. God knows what it would do to our relationship with Jess and Ella. And Wander Women. Oh my god. There is too much at stake for anything to happen. At all.

"What's up with you two," Jess said. She tilted her beer back and finished it off.

"Nothing," Chloe and I said in unison.

Jess and Ella looked at each other, clearly not believing a word we said. "Our two moms are fighting," Jess said to Ella.

"Don't be stupid," Chloe said. "I need to get going so I'll start cleaning up."

"What?" I said, still confused and distracted by the direction my thoughts had taken.

"Are you going out?" Ella asked.

"Why not? Shower's over and it's Friday night."

"Take off if you need to." Jess stood to help. "I'll get it."

"Thanks, Jess." Chloe went upstairs to her room.

"You're leaving?" The tone of my voice stopped everyone. Ella and Jess looked at me in surprise, while Chloe merely paused and continued up the stairs.

I put my wineglass down with a click and followed Chloe. Ella said, "Oh shit" and Jess replied with, "Oh yeah, they're fighting." I gave a perfunctory knock and went into Chloe's room, closing the door behind me.

Chloe had taken off her shirt and was standing in front of her armoire looking for another one. The scar on her left shoulder from a childhood accident looked redder than normal, as if all of Chloe's pent-up emotions were forcing themselves to the surface in the only vulnerable spot. Chloe glanced over her shoulder at me and looked away. My stomach clenched.

"Couldn't you at least knock?" Chloe said.

"I did. Where are you going?"

"Out."

"Why?"

"Because I can't stay here."

"Why not?"

Chloe jerked a shirt off the hanger, sending it clattering to the ground. She pulled the garmet roughly over her head before turning around. She released her long, dark hair from the back of the shirt, twisted it, and let it fall over her right shoulder. "Why do you think, Darcy?"

"Is this about what you said outside the door?" My laugh sounded forced and fake. "I know you said that so I would look surprised when they opened the door." This was the only rational explanation, the only way forward. "It worked like a charm. They have no idea I knew."

Chloe studied me for a few seconds before turning away without saying anything. She brushed her hair and pulled it back into a messy bun. I leaned against the door, because the room was starting to spin. That fourth glass of wine probably wasn't a good idea. Luckily, I have a go bag at the ready at all times so no need to worry about packing. My bed was drawing me to it like a magnet.

"That's not why I said it," Chloe said. She applied a bright red lipstick on her full lips. She really was going out.

"What?"

Chloe sighed, clicked the lid on her lipstick and turned around. "I meant it."

"What did you mean?"

Chloe scoffed. "Forget it. You're drunk. With any luck you won't remember any of this in the morning." Chloe grabbed my moto jacket from the bed. "Do you mind?" she asked. We borrowed each other's clothes all the time, and rarely even bothered to ask anymore.

"Of course not."

Chloe put the jacket on with a flourish. She came to the door and tried to get past me. I wouldn't move.

I'd been this close to Chloe thousands of times before, but this was the first time it made me feel like every cell in my body was electrified. The energy coming from Chloe felt primal. Dangerous. Our eyes met.

Fuck all that stuff I said before. I needed to know what this was.

I want this.

The realization almost brought me to my knees. Luckily, I had the door to hold me up. I clasped the doorknob behind me as if it was a life raft and dove headfirst into either the biggest mistake of my life or the best worst decision ever.

"Why did you say it?" I whispered.

"Because it's true."

"But why now?"

Chloe sighed and looked down. "I shouldn't have, and I'm sorry."

"How long have you felt this way?"

"Darcy, just…can we forget it ever happened?"

If she had actually stabbed me in the heart, it would have hurt less than the thought of her wanting to forget it. "No. You don't get to say something like that, say you meant it, and not have to explain it."

"And what good will that do, huh? You're still marrying my brother in a week."

I inhaled. "You're jealous."

"Of course I'm jealous. I'm losing my best friend to the person I hate the most in the world."

"Don't say that."

"Which part? Losing you or that I hate your future hus-band."

"Both. You're my best friend. That's not going to change."

"Not according to Michael."

"What?"

"Nothing."

"God Almighty, Chloe. Stop starting something and not finishing it. What did Michael say to you?"

"Nothing I haven't dreaded since the day you told me you were dating."

"What did he say?"

"That I was going to have to get used to the fact that he was the most important person in your life. Not me."

This I could fix. "Chloe…"

She looked up sharply. "He's right. He should be the most important person in your life." Her hazel eyes met mine. "Is he?"

"You are always going to be my best friend. We will see each other every day at work."

"Everything is going to change, Darcy, and you know it." When I didn't answer, Chloe said, "I need to go," in a stran-gled voice. It gave me hope.

I blocked her way.

"When did you become so fucking tenacious?" Chloe said.

"I don't know. Ten minutes ago I just wanted to go to bed and pretend it never happened."

"Sounds like a plan to me." Chloe tried to get past me again. "People are waiting on me."

"Who?" My heart thudded against my ribcage.

When Chloe didn't answer immediately, I knew she was lying about meeting someone. I moved away from the door, knowing she wouldn't leave. "Okay. Go." I sat on the bed. "I'll be here to talk when you get back."

Chloe sighed again. "What do you want me to say, Darcy?"

"I want you to explain to me how you 'think' you're in love with me."

"I've never been in love, so I don't know what it feels like."

"That's a cop-out," I said.

"Really? Why? I've loved you, as a friend, for almost half of my life. You're the most important person in my life. You're the first person I think about when I have news, or want to talk to someone, or when I need advice. And the last person I think of at night."

"You stole that from When Harry Met Sally," I teased, though my heart was soaring at the words.

"Hey, steal from the best, I always say," Chloe replied. "Fitz, it's been killing me, knowing I'm not that person for you anymore. I started thinking about my life without you and it looked bleak. Colorless. Dull."

"How is that possible? You're the life of the party while I sit in the corner and make sure no one is being overserved."

Chloe stepped forward. "You watch over me, and that…" She cleared her throat, but her voice thickened with emotion. "Knowing you'll catch me if I fall, gives me strength to take risks. Does that mean I'm in love with you?" Chloe shrugged. "I've loved you in one way or another for so long that I have no idea what this really is. I'm confused, and hurt, and dreading like hell watching you marry Michael next week."

"I love you, too," I said. We'd told each other we loved each other for years, but this time felt different for me. But could I blow up everything on this want? This physical need I'd never felt before? Was that fair to anyone?

Chloe sat down next to me. "The worst part is I know myself, and I might just be jealous. I've always been a little jealous when you've made other friends."

"I never knew that."

"Because I reminded myself all the time how ridiculous and unfair it is to keep you to myself, to not let other people know what an awesome person you are. Especially with your upbringing."

I cleared my throat and looked away. Chloe took my hand. "I wanted you to have as many friends as possible so you would start to really believe that you are as amazing as everyone thinks you are. As long as I was still your favorite, of course."

"Of course."

"It's hard to give up that spot."

"But you won't."

"Yes, I will. I have to be completely honest with you." We looked at each other. "The reason I said I think instead of I am is because I'm not sure if these confusing, frustrating feelings that have been keeping me up nights are because I'm losing you to my brother."

I stilled, and the warmth that had spread through my body at Chloe's words about love, and Chloe's touch, turned to ice.

I removed my hand and stood. "It makes perfect sense. You knew me for over a decade and never thought of me in that way but as soon as Michael wants me, your competitiveness kicks in. Right. Got it."

"No." Chloe grasped my hand to keep me from leaving. "That is not it. Even a little." Chloe stood. "I remember what I said to you. Back in college. I said, 'You aren't attracted to every guy you meet, and I'm not attracted to every girl or guy I meet.' I never said you were unattractive. I've never thought that. For a second."

"Okay." I tried to pull away again, but Chloe held fast. My

hand tingled where it met hers. "You don't have to keep on about it."

"I'm not. I'm apologizing for lying to you. I was attracted to you from the beginning, but I knew that if I told you, you probably wouldn't react well."

"Yes, I would have."

"No, you wouldn't. No one did back then. Everyone thought that because I liked men and women I wanted to fuck everyone I met, and I was afraid you would think that, too. So, I lied and I suggested I wasn't attracted to you. It was far from the truth. Very far. I dated other people and it faded, and anytime my gaze would linger on your lips I'd push those thoughts away quick. Our friendship was too important."

"And now?"

"Nothing needs to change. I've gotten good at ignoring my attraction to you, and I don't think now would be a good idea to test it."

"You're probably right." We held each other's gaze. "But here's the thing. Now I know." I leaned forward slightly and whispered, "That you're attracted to me. And I don't have years of experience avoiding it. So, how awkward is it going to be the first time I'm with you and—" I cleared my throat "—Michael together?"

"I guess that depends."

"On what?"

"If you've ever been curious. About kissing me." Chloe's voice turned husky. I thought of all the men and women who had heard this voice of hers before me. Jealously shot through me, hard and fast.

She was so close to me. When did we get so close? My voice was barely above a whisper. "During those dark moments when I wondered why you found me so unattractive, yeah. I did. I am curious. Now."

Chloe's breath caught and her eyes dropped to my lips. I didn't know if it was the wine, or being so close to Chloe, but I felt light-headed and a little dizzy. I swayed toward Chloe and nearly fell forward onto the floor when Chloe backed away.

"This is a bad idea."

There was no way I was letting her leave this room without kissing her.

"Oh, for Christ sakes, it's only a kiss." I stepped forward, cupped Chloe's face and placed my lips gently on hers. Chloe's lips were full and soft, if a little sticky from the lipstick, which was weird. I moved my lips against Chloe's but got no response. I pulled away. Her eyes were open, and she stared at me. My insecurities flooded back. "I'm sorry. You're right. It was a bad idea."

Chloe pulled me close and kissed me, gently but with plenty of feeling. The tip of her warm tongue traced the line between my lips, which opened instinctively. Our tongues met and Chloe tasted like red wine and vanilla icing and her lips softened, lost their stickiness and before long I wasn't thinking about red wine, lipstick, penis cake or Michael or the wedding. I wasn't thinking at all but feeling every inch of my best friend's body hot against mine, everything fitting together in the most natural way imaginable, her hand on my breast. It was heaven, and I never wanted it to stop. I wanted to feel more, to do more, to know every inch of Chloe, inside and out.

I pulled away "Okay then. That was um…well…the best bad idea I've ever had, and I totally don't know what that means or even what I'm saying."

I released a long sigh and searched Chloe's face and an expression I'd never seen before. Lust. Pure unadulterated lust. My heart did a little tango in my chest, and warmth spread through the center of my body. I throbbed with need for her.

My God, when had I felt like this with Michael? With anyone? Holy shit. What have I done?

"I, uh, really should probably go," I said.

"Yeah."

"I really don't want to go, but I'm afraid to stay."

Chloe's hands slid down my arm. Our hands intertwined, and Chloe pulled me closer. Her voice was low, a little hoarse. "I don't want you to go."

"What does that mean?"

"Things just got complicated."

"Yeah. Complicated." I knew that Chloe was right, but I didn't know why. All I knew was that I couldn't take my eyes from Chloe's lips, which were smudged with lipstick and wet from my mouth and tongue. Blood rushed southward and my need intensified. I dragged my gaze to Chloe's eyes. "Why are they complicated?"

Chloe could read me like a book, and now she read the desire on my face and her expression changed to smug amusement. I knew that expression. I'd seen it enough on Michael's face.

Michael. The wedding. Leaving tomorrow for a road trip with my mother. Wanting more than anything to say "fuck it" to everything and everyone and keep kissing Chloe. My best friend. Michael's little sister.

"I think I'm going to be sick." I grabbed my stomach and ran out the door and into the bathroom and threw up the red wine, the curry, the cake, and everything else I'd eaten that day. I hated throwing up, and I was known for being able to avoid it, but this time, I couldn't stop, dry heaving for so long that surely I would be able to purge these strange emotions and confusion and desire I felt for Chloe and flush it all away. Everything would go back to normal, and all I had to dread was seeing my mother for the first time in three years and why couldn't I go back to that small, ridiculous dread instead of now having this mountain of confusion pressing down on me.

When I finally pulled my head out of the toilet, I realized Ella was next to me, her hand on my back. "Oh my God, are you throwing up blood?"

"No. Red wine. Where's Chloe?"

"She left like a bat out of hell. Didn't say goodbye even."

I flushed the toilet and stood on shaky legs. I rinsed out my mouth and looked in the mirror. Chloe's red lipstick was smeared across my lips and chin. When I started to wipe it off, I caught Ella's eyes in the mirror.

"Oh my God. You didn't."

"We did," I said, and burst into tears.

PART FOUR

NINETEEN

Chloe

Getting to Carthage, Missouri, from Chicago is easy most days. Interstate all the way. But doing it in the middle of the first winter storm of the year is another story. In October no one is really prepared for snow and ice and sleet. I'd already been getting alerts from my travel apps that everything out of O'Hare was delayed, more so than a typical day that is, so flying to KC, the nearest airport, was out. So, an eight hour drive it was. That I would find a way to get to Darcy was never in question. My best friend needed me. Winter Storm Amber wasn't going to keep me away.

That bitch Amber wasn't going to keep Jess and Ella away either, though I tried my hardest to talk them out of coming. How could I feed my savior complex if they were there to help?

"First of all, there's no way I'm letting you drive eight hours in this weather by yourself," Ella said, her arms holding every blanket and throw in the house against her chest.

"Out of all of us, I'm the best in an emergency," Jess said. She was hoisting her backpack on her shoulders. I knew there was enough food, water tablets, gadgets, and clothing layers inside to help Jess survive for at least three days.

"You know that's true," Ella said, readjusting the blankets. "You know what? We need a thermos of coffee." She dropped the blankets on the couch and went into the kitchen.

"Jesus Christ, we're just driving down I-55" I said.

"Into a winter storm," Ella called from the kitchen. "Which is bonkers, but Fitz needs us."

Fitz needs me, I thought, but kept my trap shut. I know how unhealthy that train of thought is. I'd been talking to my therapist about it for years. She would be rather proud of me that I was giving in to accepting help so easily, especially when it came to Darcy Evans.

"Fine, let's go. We'll get coffee on the way."

"I've got Stanley," Ella said, holding the olive green thermos aloft.

"She's been hanging out with you too much," I said to Jess.

"She'll be a survivalist yet," Jess said, grinning from ear to ear.

"You know what?" Ella said again. "We need one for hot chocolate, too." She retreated back into the kitchen. "And snacks!"

"Good Lord," I mumbled.

"Let her be," Jess said. "It's her love language, and five minutes isn't going to matter." Jess grabbed the blankets. "I'll go down and start the car."

"Here." I held out my keys.

"Uh-uh. I'm not getting stuck in a blizzard in a fucking Prius. We're taking my Subaru, and I'm driving."

We didn't have time to argue, and she had a good point. Plus she probably had more survival gear in the wayback. And I wouldn't have to drive.

Ten minutes later, we were all piled into the Outback and

driving down I-55. We stopped at a truck stop outside of the city to fill the tank and so Ella could fill the thermos, and were on our way in earnest an hour after I hung up the phone with Fitz.

"So," Jess said, turning down the radio. "Want to tell us what's going on?"

Ella scooted forward and leaned between the front seats to hear better.

Where should I start? What should I tell them? I tried to organize my thoughts, the snippets Fitz had told me in our two conversations but she'd been vague and I'd been wallowing in my own sense of betrayal that I hadn't given her the attention she needed.

"Fitz is having a crisis."

"About getting married?" Ella asked.

"What makes you say that?" I asked

"She told me what happened Friday night."

"Oh," I said. A thousand questions popped into my head. Was she upset? Crying? Did she like it? Is she angry I left in such a rush?

"I'm in the dark here," Jess said. There was no anger in her voice, but she gazed unblinking at Ella in the rearview mirror.

"I wasn't sure if I should share it," Ella said. It was difficult to see her face clearly in the dark of the car, but knowing Ella she was blushing.

"Hmm. Right," Jess said. She inhaled and exhaled slowly, and her grip on the wheel tightened.

"Friday night, before I opened the door for the surprise, I told Darcy I'm in love with her. After the party, she kissed me."

"Thank God it's finally out in the open," Jess said.

My stomach twisted. "I was that obvious, huh?"

"Yeah, a little," Ella said.

"All my lesbian friends caught on being around you two even once," Jess said.

I grimaced. "And here I thought I'd done a spectacular job of hiding my feelings."

"Fitz didn't have any idea, did she?" Jess said.

"No."

"There you go. Are we going to Missouri so you can win the girl?" Jess asked. "Because I am 100 percent on board with that plan."

"Me, too," Ella said.

"No, now isn't the time. Darcy was manic when she called. Everything she said ran together. She said something about a pregnancy test."

Jess's head jerked toward me, and Ella said a Punjabi curse word. "But that's not possible," Jess said.

"No, you wouldn't think so," I replied.

We were quiet for a minute, then Ella said, "I know he's your brother, Chloe, but I never trusted he would do it."

"Me, either," Jess said.

"Why didn't you say something to Fitz? Warn her?"

"Why didn't you?" Jess asked.

"Because he's my brother, and my family would think I was trying to sabotage their relationship."

"Because you're possessive and jealous and in love with your best friend," Jess said.

"Yes, thank you, Jess, for reminding me of all my faults and why I'm in therapy."

Jess looked at me. "Don't give yourself so much credit. Those aren't *all* your faults."

My mouth dropped open in astonishment until Jess's mouth turned up into a crooked grin and I could see the teasing in her eyes.

"Bitch," I laughed.

"You're too hard on yourself," Ella said.

"Maybe. But I'll never forgive myself if she's pregnant."

"You know it's impossible for *you* to get her pregnant," Jess said. "Especially since y'all aren't having sex."

"And you're not a guy," Ella said.

I looked out the window. The Chicago suburbs had given way to farmland. The slate gray sky pressed against the earth. Orange, red, and yellow leaves were being shaken from the trees by a northern wind that buffeted the cars on the interstate.

I'd never truly believed Michael got a vasectomy because a) I know my brother and b) something my mother said in passing, which sounded strikingly like what every gynecologist had replied to Fitz when she asked to have her tubes tied: she might change her mind one day.

They didn't know Darcy Evans.

I'd never asked Michael if he'd gotten snipped directly, and I'd never mentioned my suspicions to Darcy. Our relationship shifted when they got engaged, and I knew that not only would my family think I was coming from a place of jealousy, but Darcy might as well. It wasn't jealousy, or possessiveness. Regardless of my romantic feelings for her, I was Darcy's best friend and it was my job to look out for her, just as she looked out for me. Protecting Darcy was second nature by now. Hell, I'd been doing it ever since I walked into her Jester Hall dorm room at the University of Texas fifteen years ago and saw Darcy sitting cross-legged on her bed, reading a book.

It was move in day, and the building was bustling with parents settling their kids into their freshman dorms. My roommate, a girl from Houston named Bunny (I shit you not), and her mother were busy decorating her half of the dorm room with twinkle lights, a garish pink paisley comforter, and more pillows than a sheikh's harem. More than once they'd looked at my side of the room, all minimalist and modern with bedding of grays and blues, a sleek silver lamp, and a bulletin board of my best photographs; Frank Lloyd Wright architecture (I'm from Chicago, after all), a black-and-white of an Icelandic church, Chicago street scenes, and my best photo to date having pride of place in the center.

Bunny's mom, I think her name was Carol, said, "Is that your grandmother, Chloe?"

I followed her gaze to the close-up black-and-white photo of an old woman with a wide nose, cracked lips, and long, curly gray whiskers dotting her wrinkled face. "No, I don't know her name. She's a homeless woman I met in Grant Park. I won the Under-20 *Chicago Tribune* Street Photography contest with it last year."

"Impressive," Bunny's dad said in a booming voice. I would discover later that he was known as the Quicklime King of Texas. I can't remember his name to save my life.

"Oh," Carol said. "Well, it's...something else."

"Thank you." I studied the photo. I'd been wandering around downtown on a gray, windy day, experimenting with an antique film camera I'd picked up at a flea market. It was amazing how different I looked at subjects when I knew I had only twenty-four shots to use. The woman had been huddled inside a coarse looking blanket, but her eyes sparkled when they met mine. I couldn't help but be drawn to—fascinated by, really—her curly gray whiskers. They were exactly what my mother lamented about each morning as she studied her face from every angle with a pair of tweezers in her hand. I'd given the woman ten dollars and asked if I could take her photo. She shrugged. "For ten dollars you can do anything you want."

I resisted the urge to take more than one, forcing myself to trust my instincts about the lighting, the manual settings I'd used, and I'd been rewarded when I'd developed the photo at the newspaper office. Ernie Knight, the photography editor, had stood behind me as I hung it up. "You should enter it," he said.

"And be accused of nepotism? No, thanks."

He leaned forward. "If you're worried about that, use a professional name. Chloe Knight has a nice ring to it."

I jerked around and looked at the old man. My mentor. One of the best photojournalists of the twentieth century. "Are you serious?"

"I'd be honored."

So, I'd entered the contest under the name C. Knight, and won. My parents had been proud of me, proud of my independence, proud of my talent. They understood why I wanted to use a professional name but were rather disappointed I didn't choose one from the family. Michael congratulated me but said that photography was a hobby, and it would never make me rich.

Yeah, he's always been an asshole. No, I don't see what Darcy has ever seen in him.

My new roommate's voice cut into my memory. "Are you seriously going to keep it on the bulletin board all year?" Bunny said, and I knew that southern twang was going to grate on me.

"I am," I said.

Bunny rolled her eyes and curled her lip. "Great. This is what I get for going potluck."

"Bunny," Carol admonished, "Chloe is obviously very talented."

"Whatever."

I grabbed my camera and left the room without a word.

I headed away from the main elevators, knowing they would be impossible to catch with a twelve-hour window for a thousand students to move into Jester Hall. At the opposite end of the hall the crowd thinned, and I was laser focused on the metal door to the stairwell and my escape when I passed the last room on the left, whose door was open. I stopped in my tracks when I saw a redheaded girl, alone, sitting on her bed, reading. She had pulled a lock of hair across her upper lip and, scrunching her mouth up to hold it in place, had made a mustache. Without thinking, I lifted my camera and pressed the shutter release. Through the viewfinder I saw her turn her head my way, eyes widen, and the hank of hair fall from her mouth when it formed into a perfect "O." I dropped the camera.

"Did you just take my picture?"

"Yeah."

"Why?"

"I'm a photographer." I stepped into the room. "I'm Chloe Parsons."

"Darcy Evans."

"Darcy? Like *Pride and Prejudice*?"

Her eyes lit up and she smiled. "Yes. You're the first person who has ever made the connection."

"Really? I find that hard to believe."

"You didn't grow up in Frio, Texas."

"No. Chicago."

She waved her hand in the air as if that explained it.

I jerked my head toward the empty side of the room. "Your roommate running late?"

"Beats me."

I sat on the bare mattress. "What, your moms haven't been emailing back and forth for the past three months, planning the decorations?"

Darcy blushed. "Hardly."

I felt bad for saying it when I looked at her side of the room. It was more Spartan than mine and looked lived in, as if she'd taken her bedding from home instead of made a run to Bed Bath & Beyond with her mother.

"What's your major?" I said, since Darcy wasn't trying to make conversation.

"English literature. What's—"

"Wait, wait. You're named after Mister Darcy and your major is English Lit?" I couldn't help but grin.

"Yes, I get the irony. I want to be a writer. A travel writer."

"Really? Done much traveling?"

"Nope. That's why I want to be one. What about you? Photography major?"

"No. This is a hobby, according to my brother, who probably heard it from my father. Journalism, minor in business."

"Photojournalist, then?"

"Maybe." It was nice, meeting someone who had no idea who I was, who my family was, what was expected of me.

Darcy waved her fingers in my direction. "Come on, then. Let me see the photos."

She put her book down and I sat next to her. She leaned in close, her unruly red hair tickling my cheek. She smelled like lemon verbena, and up close I could see the array of freckles on her face. She looked up at me with the most amazing hazel eyes; dark blue outer rim, moss green center, and a golden band around the iris. I would discover that they changed from green to blue to sometimes copper depending on what she was wearing.

"What?" she asked.

"Nothing." I scrolled through the photos to the first one I'd taken, when she was completely unaware. Those were always the best ones, and this was no exception. It was the only way to capture someone's true self, their essence, when they were open, vulnerable.

Darcy inhaled. "Wow." She reached out and touched the LED screen. "I look so...vulnerable."

"Exactly." Our eyes met.

"I don't like being the center of attention."

"Do you want me to delete it?"

She stared at the screen for a long time before shaking her head. "Can I have a copy for my mom?"

"Of course."

"And will you keep it between us?"

I smiled. "I'll never share a photo of you without your permission."

Darcy returned my smile. "Will you let me tell you which ones to delete?"

"Let's not go crazy, Fitz."

"Fitz?"

"Come on, it's *right there*."

"Right. Fitzwilliam Darcy. How very original."

"Feel free to come up with a nickname for me."

"Oh, God, the pressure."

"Come on, Fitz. Tell me about yourself while I wander around campus and take photos of unsuspecting people."

"Isn't that rude?"

"Not if they don't catch you."

It didn't matter that Fitz didn't want to be the center of attention, she couldn't help it. Especially once she cut her red hair into a Jean Seberg pixie cut and revealed her swan-like neck. The camera loved her—my camera loved her—and Fitz could have easily quit school and walked the runways, but the mere idea of having so many people looking at her made her break out in hives. I kept my promise to not share her photos, but I had a bulging computer file full of photos of Darcy Evans ready to share with the world whenever she was.

It took less than a week for me to arrange to move into Fitz's room. Her roommate never showed, no idea why, and I moved out of Bunny's room one Saturday night when she was at a frat party. I would see Bunny around but she never looked at me, or acknowledged my existence in any way. It was weird and wonderful, and so far from my everyday life in Chicago where calling my life a fishbowl was putting it too lightly.

Darcy loved The Photo.

Fitz and I sat on her bed, staring at it. She tilted her head back and forth, studying it like a piece of artwork. She narrowed her eyes. "Her name is Olive, and she was a spy in World War II."

"She wasn't that old," I said.

"Your photo tells a different story. Look at those wrinkles. They're deeper than Palo Duro Canyon."

"I have no idea what that is."

"The second largest canyon in the country. It's in West Texas. Amarillo."

"Have you been?"

Fitz shook her head and looked down at her shorts. She picked at the threads of her cutoffs. "No."

"How far is it from here?"

She shrugged. "Seven hours?"

"We should go."

Fitz looked at me. "My car won't make it to Amarillo. I'm lucky if it takes me back to Frio."

I nudged Fitz's shoulder. "Good thing you don't want to go back there, isn't it?"

She looked at me. "Want to get out of here for a while?"

"Always. Where?"

"It's a surprise. Put your tennie shoes on and grab your camera."

"Tennie shoes?"

"Fuck off, City Girl, and do as I say."

I hopped off the bed and went to my closet. "You really suck at nicknames, you know it, Fitz?"

"Oh, I'm good at nicknames if I don't like someone."

I turned around slowly, holding one shoe in my hands. "Do tell."

Fitz was putting a bottle of sunscreen, two water bottles, and a couple of granola bars in a string bag. She pulled her straw hat out of her closet and faced me. "My God you're slow."

"And you are avoiding the subject."

She said, "I'll tell you in the car," and walked out of the room.

I hopped around putting on my shoes, grabbed my safari vest and camera bag and was on my way out the door when she called, "Bring a hat!"

I grabbed my Longhorn cap off the dresser and followed my enigmatic friend.

Fitz's car was a beater, there's no way around it. A 1992 silver Honda Civic, cheap radio, manual windows and an air conditioner that worked sporadically. Luckily, it was the end of October.

"Where are we going?" I asked when we were settled in and driving down.

"Enchanted Rock."

I waited for more, but she was silent.

"How far?"

"Hour and a half."

"Great. Plenty of time to tell me about all those people you hate."

"I never said that."

"But you meant it. In the two months I've known you, you've never said a bad thing about anyone. So, yeah. I'm intrigued."

Darcy kept her eyes on the road, hands at ten and two, drumming her thumbs on the steering wheel. The silence stretched between us. The theory that if you remain quiet after asking a question that the person will eventually be so uncomfortable they will answer didn't work with Darcy. (It still doesn't; she doesn't speak unless she knows exactly what she's going to say.)

"I want to know more about you," I said softly. Fear, vulnerability, swirled in my stomach.

She pulled up to a red light and looked at me. "I could say the same about you."

We held each other's gazes until a honk told us the light had turned. She returned her attention to the road, and I studied her profile. Tall forehead, straight nose, thin lips, strong jaw, pointed chin. Ivory skin covered with freckles. Beautiful hazel eyes. Kind eyes. Intelligent eyes. But, wary eyes, too. Darcy was a watcher, and though she rarely shared her impressions of people, I knew she pegged a person within minutes of meeting them.

Frankly, I was shocked that she kept me around. I know me, and all my faults. Somehow I knew that the only way to know Darcy was for her to know me first. To trust me.

"My family made their fortune in railroads in the 1870s. We've managed to keep the family fortune intact by diversifying. My branch of the family is in newspapers. The *Chicago Express* specifically. My dad's the publisher. My mom is a philanthropist. My brother, Michael, rejected the family business and went into finance, cheating old people out of their pensions, probably. The Parsons name in Chicago will get you through any door you want to enter, will get you a last-minute reservation at the hottest restaurant, and will get you into the gossip section of the rival newspaper if you spit on the sidewalk. I'm here because no one gives a shit about the Parsons name in Texas, no one's after me for what I can do for them, what my family can do for them, and I've never felt freer in my entire life."

"That's why you're a photographer."

"What?"

"Being behind the camera gives you control over the narrative. It protects you, too. It keeps people from seeing your eyes and knowing how scared you are all the time."

If she would have punched me in the gut it would have hurt less. I looked out the grimy window and tried to fight back the tears.

"Hey." Darcy reached out and grasped my hand. I reluctantly met her gaze.

"You never have to be scared with me. I like you for you, and I'll never hurt you."

My breath caught. She squeezed my hand and returned her eyes to the road. But she kept holding my hand.

"You're the first friend I've ever had," Darcy said.

"What?"

"It's true."

"But you're amazing."

I felt the blush on my face and released Darcy's hand. A quick glance at her showed pink on her cheeks, too.

Darcy cleared her throat. "My mom was seventeen when she had me. Not married. She got kicked out of her mom's house. We lived with my Granny Evans until she died when I was five. Momma inherited the trailer house—" she glanced at me and I hoped my expression was neutral "—which is where she still lives. She's a maid."

"What about your dad? Do you—"

"Know him? Yeah. He's married. Deacon at the Baptist church. Recently elected mayor. He doesn't acknowledge me, though everyone in town knows I'm his." She pointed at her head. "The hair, you know."

Darcy gripped the steering wheel as if her life depended on it. I touched her shoulder. "You don't have to keep going if you don't want to. Where you came from, where you grew up, doesn't matter to me."

"I'm not ashamed of it."

I raised my eyebrows. "Then why didn't you tell me any of this eight weeks ago?"

"The same reason you didn't tell me. We both wanted to start over. We wanted—I wanted—to find out if Maddie Fucking Clarke had been right about me all these years, saying to anyone who would listen that I was a loser, a complete waste of space, a bastard, that no one would ever want to be friends with a pale skinned freckled freak who liked books more than people. I wanted to know if people would always see poor white trash when they met me. If the smell of cleaning chemicals had seeped into my skin so far that I would never be able to scrub Frio, Texas, and my miserable fucking life, off of me."

Darcy's voice had started low and slow and gradually risen as she spoke until her anger and hurt and fear resounded in the car, enveloped us, crushed us, connected us in a way I'd never been connected to another friend.

"Pull over," I said quietly.

She looked at me, fear in her eyes. "What?"

"Pull over."

We were on a shoulderless farm-to-market road east of Austin. Not many places to pull over, but Darcy found a cemetery and pulled off into the short drive. I got out of the car and walked around to Darcy's side. She was sitting in the car, still gripping the steering wheel, staring straight ahead, her cheeks wet with tears.

I opened the car door. She stared at my outstretched hand for a long time before looking up at me. "Trust me, Fitz."

Darcy pulled the emergency brake, unbuckled her seat belt, and stepped out of the car. I pulled her into a hug. Her arms hung loosely by her sides. "Don't make me beg you to hug me, Fitz."

Darcy put her arms around me and hugged me tightly. Neither of us moved to break the hug, and soon I felt Darcy shaking gently. I didn't shush her or offer words of encouragement. I was silent and let her cry. Finally, she sniffed heartily a few times and pulled away. She wouldn't look me in the eyes, but I saw enough to notice her eyes were even more stunning when glassy from crying.

"Darcy, you need to know something. You ready?"

She nodded and sniffed again.

"You're good enough, you're smart enough, and gosh darn it, people like you." I kept my face serious until Darcy laughed and grinned.

"Stuart Smalley? Really? That's the best you can do?"

"It's a truth universally acknowledged that kids are fucking cruel and who the fuck is this Maddie Clarke and where can I find her?"

Fitz scoffed. "She's at A&M, and she's my half sister."

"You. Are. Fucking. Kidding. Me."

"No. My chief tormentor for eighteen years was my sister."

"Did she know?"

"Everyone knew, Chloe, but no one admitted it."

I sighed. "Dammit."

"What?"

"I really hoped to get a bit more sympathy for my poor little rich girl story. To milk it a bit, you know. After all that it would just be pathetic."

"I'm familiar with pathetic, so I can relate."

"Hey." I grabbed Darcy's shoulders. "Shut up. You aren't pathetic, and I know for a fact that you never have been. That bitch Maddie is the one who's pathetic. It's called projection, and everything she said about you is how she felt about herself.

And look, if she turns up missing or dismembered, or dead in a ditch somewhere I had nothing to do with it. Okay?"

One corner of Darcy's mouth quirked up. "You'd do that for me?"

"Well, I'd definitely plan it out and fantasize about it. Whether I would go through with it is another story. I faint at the sight of blood."

"Some killer you'll be."

"It's the thought that counts. You have to admit that."

"Fine. Thank you for fantasizing about killing my arch-nemesis."

"You're welcome. Now, take me to Enchanted Rock or lose me forever!" I put my hand over my forehead and pretended to faint.

"You are such a dork."

"And that's why you love me."

"God help me, but it is." Fitz grinned and rolled her eyes.

We were back in the car and on the road when I turned to Darcy. "So, what's Maddie Clarke's nickname?"

Fitz cut her eyes at me. "Maddie Fucking Clarke."

I waited. And waited. "That's it?"

Fitz scrunched her nose up. "You don't understand how brave it was for me to say the f-word."

"Oh my God, I'm going to be City Girl for the rest of my life, aren't I?"

"Probably."

I lifted my face to the sky and groaned.

"Oh, stop being dramatic. Fine. I'll keep trying."

"Don't hurt yourself, Fitz. I'll still love you."

"You better. You're the only friend I've got."

And I have loved her. More than she's ever known.

Until two days ago when I confessed that I'd loved her from the start.

TWENTY

Chloe

I woke to the smell of coffee and the low murmur of voices. I looked around, discombobulated. That might terrify most people but waking up on assignment in foreign and far-flung places had been my life for nearly a decade. My forehead pressed against a cold car window covered in ice droplets, and a blanket I didn't remember covering myself with was mundane compared to an overcrowded bus jostling down a pockmarked dirt rode somewhere in Uzbekistan.

"How long have I been asleep?" I asked.

"Couple of hours," Jess said. She was leaned forward, her hands white knuckling the steering wheel.

Ella nudged my shoulder. I turned my head, and the heavenly smell of coffee met me. I took the travel mug and thanked her.

"Where are we?" I asked.

"Other side of St. Louis. Little over halfway there."

"Need me to drive?"

Jess shot me an incredulous look.

"I've already asked," Ella said.

"Neither one of you know how to drive in an ice storm. I'm fine," Jess said. "Your phone's been blowing up, Chlo."

I straightened in the chair and woke my phone. Missed calls from Mom, Michael, and Darcy, and a lot of texts from Darcy.

-You're driving?

-Jess and Ella are with you? I hope Jess is driving.

-I shouldn't have asked you to come. It was selfish of me and now all three of you are driving in this storm.

If anything happens to y'all...

-The dot is still moving on the map so I guess y'all are okay.

-Don't tell them about my mother. The fewer people that know the better.

-I mean, the gay thing is fine, I guess. Though I suppose it's her place to tell or come out or whatever. I mean don't mention the other stuff.

-The less Jess and Ella know the better. It's bad enough I told you.

-Actually, act like you don't know anything about the other stuff, okay? I would hate for you to have give up your life, too.

What the hell does that mean? Give up my life, too?

-Why aren't you answering your phone?

-Ella says you're asleep. You can sleep through anything and anywhere, can't you?

I chuckled. Yes, yes I can. I thought of the framed photo sitting on Darcy's dresser of me sleeping on a catamaran guy wire in Hawaii. Look, I'd been diving and taking underwater photographs for hours. It takes a lot out of me. Also, I like naps because I rarely sleep for more than two hours at a time on the best of days. I take a nap whenever I can.

"Well, Darcy is freaking out about us driving," I said.

"Yeah," Ella said. "I tried to calm her down. She wants you to call her."

Before I could, my brother's ugly face popped up on my phone. I showed it to Ella and Jess and answered the call.

"Hey, asshole."

"Nice. Why aren't you answering your phone?"

"I was asleep. Why are you calling?"

"I'm stuck in Vegas because of this fucking storm and I need you to meet with Mom and the caterer tomorrow."

"No."

"Jesus, are you still pouting?"

I inhaled, trying to center myself. It didn't work. None of that meditation bullshit ever worked for me. "No, Michael. I'm on my way to Carthage, Missouri. To Darcy."

Michael paused. "Why?"

"Because she called me freaking out and said she needed me."

"And you just had to run off and be her savior."

"Along with Jess and Ella. We're southwest of St. Louis right now."

"That's the epicenter of the storm. What are you thinking, Chloe?"

"I'm thinking my best friend is having a crisis and you're nowhere around."

"I'm stuck in Vegas. What crisis? I talked to her a couple of hours ago and she was fine."

I scoffed, pulled the phone away from my ear and muted it. "God, my brother is an asshole."

"What did he say?" Jess said.

"Nothing. Which is the point."

I unmuted the phone and put it back up to my ear. Michael was in the middle of saying something, but I interrupted him. "Can you repeat that?"

He sighed. "Is she pregnant?"

I could barely breathe but I somehow managed to say, "Why would you ask that?"

"Just something she said."

I waited. When he didn't continue, I said, "You didn't have the vasectomy, did you?"

Jess and Ella were both looking at me as I waited for my brother to reply.

"This is a conversation I need to have with Darcy."

I shook my head, and Ella and Jess both cursed quietly. "I don't know, bro, it's probably a conversation you should have had six months ago when you were supposed to have it."

"Do not talk to her about this."

I laughed. "Are you serious right now?"

"Yes, I'm serious. This is between me and Darcy. It has nothing to do with you."

"I would agree with you except for one glaring problem. She called me. She wanted *me*. She needs *me*."

"I told you I'm stuck in Vegas."

"You didn't even know she was in a crisis. She didn't ask you to come, did she?"

"I told you…"

"Did she tell you about the pregnancy test?"

That shut him up.

"I didn't think so."

"IUDs are 99 percent effective," Michael said. There wasn't an ounce of contrition in his voice, the bastard. I'd never understood how two amazing people like Eloise and Howard Parsons produced such a douchebag like Michael.

"I'm gonna stop you right there, because I'm not the one you lied to for months. Well, you lied to everyone, but what I think doesn't matter."

"That's a first."

"Fuck you, Michael." I hung up the phone and threw it onto the floor.

The sound of sleet clicking against the windshield and the low murmur of The Highwomen singing a Fleetwood Mac cover filled the silent car. Finally, Ella spoke.

"Do we tell her?" Ella asked.

"If she's pregnant, she knows," Jess said.

"We don't get in the middle of their relationship," I said. "We are here for Fitz. To support her. To give her a shoulder to cry on. To take her to an abortion clinic, if that's what she wants."

"In Missouri?" Jess said.

"Good point," Ella said. "I've been reading up on complications that might—"

"Let's not go there, okay?" I said.

"Sure. Yeah. You're right," Ella said. She sat back.

"I'm sorry, Ella. I shouldn't have snapped at you. I'm just worried."

"Sure," Ella said.

"Um, why are you so worried?" Jess asked.

"What do you mean?" I asked.

"Isn't her mom there?"

"Are you saying we shouldn't have come?" I said.

"No," Jess said slowly. She sighed. "Yeah, actually I am. Have you looked at this weather? I mean really looked? I'm going forty miles an hour, tops. My hands are cramping from gripping the steering wheel. We are the only idiots on the fucking road. If we were smart, we would pull over and find a hotel."

"Darcy wouldn't want us to put ourselves in danger," Ella said.

"I knew I shouldn't have let you two come with me," I said.

"Don't be a bitch, Chloe," Jess said. "She's our friend, too."

"Oh, that's the pot calling the kettle black."

"Guys," Ella said. "Fighting isn't helping."

Jess drove on, the silence in the car pressing in on me. My neck stiffened up, and I felt a tension headache starting at the base of my skull.

"I'm sorry, Jess. Ella. I'm sorry I dragged you into this. I should have been more logical than emotional. Darcy would have understood. I have a savior complex when it comes to Darcy. I've been working on it with my therapist. Obviously, I've got a long way to go. It's not just the pregnancy. She's got some stuff going on with Marja, too. She sounded desperate, and I had to come. I would have done the same for either of you. You know that, right?"

"Of course we do," Ella said.

Ella and I looked at Jess, who kept her eyes glued to the road. Finally, she said, "Yeah."

"Do you need some coffee, Jess?" I asked, offering an olive branch.

"That'd be nice."

"Here, Ella. Hand Stanley up here and why don't you get some shut-eye. I'll keep Jess company."

Ella handed me the thermos. "You two won't fight, will you?"

"No," we said in unison.

"Uh-huh," Ella said, clearly unconvinced. "Well, if you do fight, keep it down."

She settled down in the back seat, and I offered Jess the cap half full of coffee.

"That's a skimpy pour," Jess said.

"I can always add more, but if you spill it on yourself I'm afraid of what name you might call me."

Jess cut her eyes at me and returned them to the road. "I deserved that."

"Jess, have I done something to piss you off?"

"Besides this you mean?" She waved her hand at the sleet hitting the windshield.

"Again, you didn't have to come."

"Look out there, Chloe, and tell me how you think you'd be doing right now. Alone. Driving in this. In a fucking Prius."

I looked forward and, yeah, it looked pretty bad.

"You're wearing Birkenstocks, for God's sake."

"We left in a hurry."

"Admit you need me."

I crossed my arms over my chest. "Fine. I need you."

"See, was that so hard? What's your plan here?" Jess asked.

"I don't have a plan."

Jess didn't take her eyes from the road, but I saw her roll them. "Why does that not surprise me."

"That's not fair."

"It's completely fair, and you know it. For someone who is so detailed oriented with her job, you've always flown by the seat of your pants when it comes to your love life."

"I prefer go with the flow," I said. "Besides, as you well know, we hardly have a life for long term relationships."

"Plenty of travel writers have relationships. People like you and me just don't want one. Or, maybe I don't want one and you only want it with one particular person."

"Maybe." Jess did look at me now. "Okay, exactly," I said.

"Why the fuck did you wait so long to tell her?"

"I was too scared to in college and decided it would be worse to be rejected by her, to lose her friendship, than to love her unrequitedly. I told myself I loved her as a friend and slept with as many men and women as possible to keep that want at bay. It worked for a long time. Then, she started dating Michael and it didn't work anymore."

Jess hummed in understanding. She knew enough about my competitive relationship with my brother to understand why telling Darcy after she started dating Michael would be a huge disaster.

"I can't move on without her. Our lives are too intertwined. Friends, business. Maybe family."

"Please, she's not going to marry Michael and you know it. There's no coming back from a betrayal like that or a confession like yours. Not for Darcy."

"Michael can be pretty persuasive," I said.

"Are you seriously going to let her?"

"I cannot get in the middle of their relationship. I've told you that."

"You are in the middle of it whether you want to be or not."

"I'm trying really, really hard not to be, Jess."

"Now's not the time to stand back and pretend to be neutral." Jess pressed her lips together as if keeping herself from saying something.

"Go on," I said. "You're on a roll."

"Your relationship with Darcy is codependent, almost toxic. She leans on you too much, and you let her because it allows you to show her how much you love her without saying the words. It's allowed you both to ignore what's between you. She didn't really need you to come down here. She has her mother with her, for Christ sakes. Who doesn't want their mother when something like this happens?"

"She and Marja haven't been on the best of terms for a while."

"Before that they talked every day. You're telling me they didn't talk things out on the road?" Jess shook her head. "Did she ask you or did you just offer?"

"Okay, okay, I get it, Jess. You're pissed we're driving through this shitty weather to satisfy my ego or whatever."

"No, Chloe. Don't turn this back on me. Answer the question."

"What was it?"

She cut her eyes at me again.

"She asked," I said.

Jess nodded. Suddenly the car fishtailed. Jess's eyes widened, and I saw her intake of breath. I grabbed the dash and the edge of my seat and watched Jess turn the steering wheel into the slide, felt the car slow down, and finally the tires caught. Jess righted us on the road and exhaled slowly.

"We should pull over," I said.

"No, we're close. We can make it."

We rode in silence for a bit. I looked into the back seat and Ella was out for the count, mouth open, snoring slightly. The glow of the dashboard lights, the darkness outside, the low music, the warmth wrapped around me, made me drowsy.

"You can sleep, you know," Jess said. Her voice was quiet.

"No way am I leaving you to drive alone."

"Moral support, huh?" Jess said.

"I got you into this mess. I need to see you through it. Want some more coffee?"

"Sure." She gave the mug back to me. "You didn't get me

into this mess. You're not the only one with a savior complex," Jess said.

"That's a nice change, someone saving me," I chuckled.

"Oh, I'm here to save Darcy, not you, asshole," Jess teased. "Carthage, ten miles. We've made it."

TWENTY-ONE

Marja

"So that's what all the fuss is about?"

I lay on the bed next to Lena, naked and slicked with sweat, a pleasant stickiness between my legs. I licked my lips, tasted Lena, and throbbed with need. Again.

"Lesbian sex?"

"That, I suppose, but sex in general."

Lena turned on her side and propped her head on her hand and studied me. Her free hand gently caressed my stomach, my thigh, and back again. "Talk to me."

"And sound pathetic? No, thank you."

"Marja," she whispered, and gently turned my face to meet her gaze straight on. "Trust me."

I'm not good at the whole sharing thing. That's what happens when you alienate yourself from others. You get used to keeping everything inside, at comforting yourself, at working to exhaustion, at reading and learning and keeping your mind busy and full so that it's almost impossible to dwell on everything that went wrong in your life. It's almost impossible to remember the hopes and dreams of the naive sixteen-year-old that you once were.

But after what I'd just shared with this woman, how could I refuse her? I didn't want to analyze too closely what I saw in Lena's dark eyes as she waited, her fingers lazily tracing a random path across my body, touching me in a way that I'd never been touched. It was a simple caress, not overtly sexual, something that two people who cared for each other would do without thinking.

I traced my fingers gently across the back of Lena's hand, being careful to not make her stop.

"That feels nice. I bet you do this with all of your partners," I said.

Lena tensed.

"No, no. I'm not jealous. You don't think anything of touching me like this. It's probably instinctual, right? That's the kind of lover you are. Tender. Giving."

"I like to think so."

"You are. I've never had this kind of intimacy. With anyone. For me, pillow talk is a Doris Day movie."

Lena pulled me onto my side and intertwined her legs with mine. I pulled my head back a bit.

"Too close?" she said.

I tried to stifle a smile. "Only because I don't have my readers."

One of her glorious eyebrows crooked up. "I'm not even going to tell you where my mind just went."

"I'd much rather talk about that," I said.

"All in due time, *mi alma*."

I pushed away thoughts of the future, that Lena and I would say goodbye to each other forever in a matter of hours, and focused on the fact that this woman, beautiful inside and out, wanted me. All of me. Even the bad parts, it would seem.

I inhaled a shaky breath, cleared my throat. "I lost my virginity to Darcy's father when I was sixteen. It was the only time we had sex. I was the babysitter. I guess in today's parlance you would say he groomed me. There definitely wasn't any asking for permission."

"Did he—?"

"Rape me? No. I didn't particularly want to and I knew it was wrong, but I didn't say no."

"You were underage, he was in a position of power. That's rape."

"Not in the eighties it wasn't. Adult men fucking teenage girls was a goddamn epidemic in the eighties. Coaches were the worst. And adults just…shrugged. It was always talked about as if the girl was in charge, Sheila's sleeping with Coach Morgan as if it was consensual, as if the girl was the instigator. It was always just assumed." I scoffed. "God, it sounds so ridiculous, so awful now. We were kids, being preyed on by adult men, but no one saw it that way. We didn't even see it that way."

"It wasn't your fault."

I swallowed. "I know that now. Would have been nice for #MeToo to come along thirty years ago." I sighed. "Anyway, I was the unlucky one. I got pregnant. Who knows if the other girls did, too, but got abortions. I didn't, so I was labeled a whore when it all came out. Russell Clarke became a deacon of the Baptist church. Still is."

"Russell Clarke is Darcy's father?"

I nodded. "His hair has faded, and he's gotten gray, but it was easy to see the resemblance when he was young. He doubted the baby was his, which pissed me off. He knew very well I'd been a virgin. I told him let's wait for nine months to see if the baby had bright red hair. He punched me. That shiner was hell to cover up, let me tell you."

Lena's hand stopped its caresses and she tensed.

"He gave me money for an abortion. Five hundred dollars. Threatened me with all kinds of things if I didn't get it done." I scoffed. "If he hadn't hit me, I would have." I met Lena's steady gaze. "Darcy is in the next room because I back talked to Russell Clarke and he punched me in the face. Broke my nose. I wanted to get revenge. I thought having his bastard living in town would show everyone who he was, would ruin him." I focused on the hollow of Lena's throat, ashamed to meet her eyes. "It all backfired, of course. He's a pillar of the community. I was a white trash whore, high school dropout who made a living scrubbing shit stains from underneath the rims of other people's toilets."

"Hey." Lena tilted my head up, cradled my face. "You are not one of those things, Marja. You are the most wonderful woman I've ever met."

"No, I'm not."

"You are. I have a list of all the reasons I—" Lena swallowed, and my heart raced "—admire you."

I was disappointed, I'll admit. Did I want a declaration of love? I didn't think so until the moment I thought Lena would give it. I know, I know. I'm an idiot. I don't need you to remind me.

"Does Darcy know any of this?" Lena asked.

"She knows who her father is, and of course she knows my reputation, but you're the only person I've ever told why I kept the baby. I kept her out of spite." I tried to swallow the sob that wanted to escape. "Now you know why I'm a shit person. But once I held her in my arms in the hospital, I was so glad I kept her. I fell head over heels. I'll never forgive myself for all of the bullying and rumors she had to live with. I should have moved away from Frio, but I didn't have many options."

"She's turned into a wonderful woman," Lena said.

"I'm not sure how much credit I should get for that but thank you."

Lena traced a finger up my cleavage, back down to circle my belly button, and back up. "Is that bastard the only other person you've been with?"

"No, but I didn't have sex for eighteen years." Lena's finger stopped. "I told you I was pathetic."

"There's nothing wrong with being celibate."

"Celibate sounds so much better than frigid."

"You definitely aren't frigid, Marja Evans."

I leaned over and kissed her. "Not with you, I'm not." I stroked her cheek. "Tommy was the other, but you know that."

"I never liked him."

"Were you jealous?" I teased.

"One hundred percent."

"Oh, really?"

Lena chuckled. "Yes, really."

"Huh. Well, Tommy's not a bad guy."

"He started you laundering. He lied to you for years about whose money it was. He wasn't your friend."

"He isn't my enemy. That's Russell and Chelly Clarke. They put him up to it, and I'm still not sure why. Probably to set me up for a fall. I'll get the last laugh in the end."

"I have to get you safely to Chicago, first. I called an agent I know there, Stacie Anderson, gave her the DEA agents' badge numbers and phone info. She'll follow up to make sure Cooper's not on the take with the cartel. I'd be shocked, but they have a lot of money to throw around."

"Don't I know it."

"Anderson is going to extract us from here. Not sure how. There's an ice storm coming."

My throat thickened with emotion. "I won't get to go to Darcy's wedding?"

Lena's expression turned sheepish. "Cooper never had any intention of letting you go. It's too public."

"Of course not. And Darcy?"

"It isn't up to me. Though I do have an idea."

"What?"

"You give the codes to me and disappear. That was your plan, wasn't it? You have no intention of going into WITSEC."

"Yeah."

"I thought so. Darcy will be in protective custody for a while, but in a year, I'll meet you and we'll live on a beach somewhere far away from Frio and cartels and the FBI."

It took a moment for me to understand what she said. It was crazy. Insane, and the absolute last thing I expected her to come up with.

"You would do that for me? Leave your career and friends and parents? Your entire extended family. For me?" My voice went up an octave with every question.

"Yes. Since you missed all my signals last year, I'm going to spell it out for you. I love everything about you, your intelligence, your stubbornness, your loyalty to your friends, your big heart, I love your nose, your eyes, your chin, and your little elfin ears. I love the way you smell right here—" she touched the hollow behind my ear "—and I love the way you taste and how you sound when I'm doing something to you you particularly like. I love the look on your face when you come, I love how your come voice is a little squeak because you're fighting so hard to be quiet so your daughter next door won't hear you. I love that you're so incredibly sexy and don't even know it. I love everything about you, and I've been miserable for the last nine months without you."

Lena hovered over me, her eyes full of fire, her lips plump, her face flushed. Her eyes searched my face, waiting.

"Well? Aren't you going to say anything?"

"So, what you're saying is you love me?"

She stared at me, dumbfounded, then released my arms and sat up and threw her arms up. "Yes, that's what I'm saying. I love you."

I flipped her over onto her back and pinned her hands above her head, enjoying the expression of surprise on her face.

Fuck logic. Fuck my brain. I felt alive, whole, for the first time in my fucking life. I was going to enjoy it. Fuck the consequences.

"Good," I said. "Because I love you, too."

Between having sex and making plans, we were exhausted by the time a sliver of gray morning light peeked through the motel curtains.

"Shit," I said. "I hope Darcy is okay."

"I think I heard the door in the next room—" Lena leaned across me and looked at the clock "—eight hours ago?"

"I should probably check on her."

"Just another minute." Lena lay half on top of me and buried her face in my neck and inhaled deeply. She exhaled with a contented hum.

"You're so weird," I said.

"If loving the way you smell makes me weird, then I'll own it."

I put my lips next to her ear. "I love the way you taste."

"Hmm," Lena purred. "You were amazing." Lena stretched.

I tried to ignore the desire that was welling up inside me at the sight of Lena González stretching in bed next to me. Who have I turned into in the last ten hours? I needed to get a grip on myself.

"Get dressed, *mi alma*. We need to get on the road." She playfully tossed a shirt into my face. "Why the shocked expression? I told you how I felt last night."

"Yeah, but...are you sure about this?"

"The plan or disappearing with you?"

"Both."

Lena sat on the edge of the bed. "Marja, I left you once and it nearly killed me. There's no way I'm leaving you again. Especially after last night. Ever." She put her hands on my cheeks and wiped away my tears with her thumbs. "I love you, but more importantly, you deserve to be loved. Say it back to me."

"I love you."

Lena smiled. "That's great, but that's not what I meant. Say you deserve to be loved."

"You deserve to be loved, Lena González."

"You're not as funny as you think you are."

"I'm pretty fucking funny."

"Get your hot funny ass out of bed and dressed."

Lena knocked on the adjoining door. "Darcy? You up?"

I put on my shorts and T-shirt. Lena knocked again. "Darcy?"

"Do you have a key to the room?"

"No. It's in there," Lena said, pointing to the room. She knocked again, this time harder. It was my turn to call out.

"Darcy, honey. We have to get going. Helen?"

Helen barked and scratched at the door.

"Something's wrong," I said. Lena's expression said she agreed with me. It was a steel door and jamb, without a knob on this side. There was no way for Lena to force it open.

"I'll go to the office, get another key."

Lena was stepping outside when the adjoining door opened. I jerked back in surprise.

"Chloe?"

"Hey, Marja."

"What are you—"

Chloe opened the door the whole way. Darcy sat on the bed

with two other women. "Ella? Jess?" Fear coiled in my stomach when I realized what this meant.

Lena was next to me. "This complicates things," she said.

I looked closely at Darcy, whose eyes were red, and my eyes traveled to the bedside table where a pregnancy test lay, a white gash on the dark wood. My eyes went back to Darcy, and she nodded.

"I'm pregnant."

TWENTY-TWO

Chloe

When Darcy opened the door to the three of us, any questions we'd had about whether or not she needed us vanished. She was a mess. It was obvious she'd been crying most of the night. Her face was splotchy, dark half-moons like bruises under her bloodshot eyes. She grabbed my arm and pulled me inside and into her arms, and immediately started sobbing. I hugged her tightly and shushed her, saying it was all going to be okay, we were there now, and that there's nothing the four of us couldn't do.

"Damn straight," Jess said. I caught her eye over Darcy's shoulders. The stress of driving for ten hours in that weather was showing on her face.

"Have you eaten?" Ella asked. She was rubbing small comforting circles on Darcy's back.

Darcy pulled away from me, sniffed, and smiled, though it didn't reach her eyes. "A couple of candy bars last night."

"Ugh." Ella grimaced. Processed food was a personal affront to her. She would rather spend hours in the kitchen making a homemade "Snickers" bar than go to the bodega on the corner and buy one. Which means the four of us always ate very well. The fringe benefits of living with a chef.

"There's no microwave, and I didn't see a store anywhere close by." Ella was talking to herself, doing what she did best: nurturing the people she loved with food.

Jess was digging into her backpack. "Nothing will be open, even if we could drive, because I am not getting back out in that and none of you are, either. I've got this covered." She pulled out a mini camp stove and bags of dried meals that only needed hot water to be ready to go. Jess glanced at us. "You can talk while I do this, you know. Tell us what's going on, Fitz."

A knock on the adjoining door startled all of us. "That's my mom," Fitz said.

Jess straightened. "Yeah, don't take this the wrong way, but why the hell isn't your mom in here right now? From what little Chloe told us, you need your mother."

"She's, um. With someone. Lena."

Ella and Jess looked at Darcy with dawning comprehension. Jess's expression turned thunderous, and Ella looked embarrassed.

"She's been in there getting laid while we drove ten hours to help you? What the hell, Darcy?" Jess said.

"Who's Lena?" Ella asked.

"Darcy? Is everything okay?" Marja's voice came through the door.

"It's not like that," Darcy said. "She doesn't know. I didn't want to tell her because my mother deserves a little happiness."

"We can talk about this later," I said, shooting Jess a warning look, and opened the adjoining door.

"Chloe?" Marja said in astonishment. She glanced behind me, and I saw something like fear in her eyes. "Jess and Ella? What are y'all doing here?"

"Plan C then," said the woman standing behind Marja. She was tall, curvy, and beautiful and a little part of me that wasn't worried about Darcy thought, *Way to go, Marja.*

Marja stepped into the room. "What's going on Darcy? What's wrong?"

"I'm pregnant."

"That's great," Lena said. No one answered and Lena's smile faded. "That's not great?"

"I don't want kids. I never have. We agreed. I have an IUD and he got a vasectomy so we would be absolutely sure this wouldn't happen."

"Sometimes vasectomies don't work," Lena said.

"Sometimes people don't get them," Jess mumbled.

"What?" Marja said.

"Jess," I warned.

"Oh goodness," Ella whispered

Darcy leveled me with a steely glare. "Michael didn't get a vasectomy, and you knew?"

"No, I didn't know, and this is a conversation you need to have with Michael, not me." I motioned to the others. "Or any of us. We are here because you needed us. Tell us what you need."

Darcy looked at her three friends, speechless. "I didn't intend…" She trailed off, and everyone waited except Jess, who went into the bathroom and closed the door.

"I think I'll go get us all breakfast," Lena said.

"No, you won't," Ella said. "We're snowed in."

Lena opened the door to the room. A cold blast of air hit her. Ice coated the trees and power lines along the street.

"Y'all drove in this?" Marja asked.

"Yeah," I said. "Ten hours."

"Darcy, why didn't you come get me? I could have helped you," Marja said.

"I didn't want to bother you," Darcy said in a small voice.

"Instead you asked your friends to drive ten hours in terrible weather?" Marja looked appalled, and Darcy looked like she wanted to die.

I stepped forward. "Look, that doesn't matter now. We're here and we're safe."

"And snowed in," Lena said.

"With hardly any food," Ella said.

Jess came out of the bathroom with a small pan of water. She put it on the chest next to her little camp stove. "I can't believe I'm going to be the glass half full person here, but we have four beds for six people, two bathrooms, and enough dried camping food for two meals. Three if we stretch."

"She's right," I said. "We'll take over. Jess, you need to rest. You have to be exhausted after that drive," I said.

Jess nodded. "I am."

"You're all exhausted. Let me walk down the street to get breakfast," Lena said. "We can save the dried food if we get desperate."

"Thanks, Lena," Marja said.

"Oh, is that your name," Ella asked. She held out her hand. "I'm Ella Patel."

She took Ella's hand. "Special Agent Elena González." As soon as the words left her mouth, she grimaced.

"Special agent for what?" Ella said.

Lena looked at Marja, an apology written all over her face. "It's a habit."

"What the fuck have you gotten us into, Darcy?" Jess said.

The dog barked, scaring Jess, Ella, and me to death.

"Sorry," Marja said. "Helen barks whenever someone cusses."

Jess's eyes lit up. "Really?" She opened her mouth to test it out, I'm sure, but Ella put her hand over Jess's mouth.

"Not now, Jess," she said. Jess playfully bit Ella's fingers, and Ella blushed to the roots of her dark hair.

"It's not what I've gotten us into, it's what has Marja gotten us into," Darcy said.

Marja crossed her arms. "I'm not the one who asked her friends to risk their lives in this weather."

"Only because you don't have any friends."

"Okay," Lena said, stepping in front of Marja. "If you two are going to fight, go into the other room. These three don't need to know any more than they already do." She opened the adjoining door and motioned for them to leave. Darcy flounced off the bed and through the door. Marja followed. Before Lena closed the door she said, "Keep it down. We don't need the neighbors to know what's going on, either."

TWENTY-THREE

Darcy

Marja shut the door between the rooms and rounded on me. "Okay, let's have it."

"Let's have what?"

"Whatever it is that's been bottled up inside you all these years."

"I don't know what you're talking about."

"Bullshit. You've done a pretty good job of hiding it, I'll give you that. Get it off your chest once and for all."

My stomach dropped. I hated confrontation, arguments. I avoided having them with my mother for the first twenty years of my life so I'm not very good at them. Standing up for myself in business isn't a problem. I know my shit because I'm good at my job and I am always, always prepared. Standing up to Michael is getting easier, but I avoid it if I can. Chloe and I never fight. From the very beginning of our friendship, we've been able to talk through things.

Except after I kissed her.

I mentally shake my head. This is about me and Marja. The

very thought of standing up to my mother fills me with nausea. Or maybe that's the morning sickness.

Christ. How many problems can I have at once?

I crossed my arms, as if that would calm my stomach down. What I needed was a good puke.

Fuck it. I'm mad and I'm not going to take it anymore.

"I didn't know that standing up to you was ever an option. It's always been your way or the highway."

"Don't bounce it back on me, Darcy Elizabeth Evans. You're an adult, not a child. You want to lay into me about how shitty your childhood was? Do it. It's now or never."

"What's the point?" I asked. "You'll never admit you're wrong about anything. You're always right."

"That's not true."

I raised my eyebrows. "You don't say."

"Okay, fine. Touché." Marja rubbed her eyes and exhaled. When she looked at me again, I could tell the fight had left her, which was infuriating. I wanted to fight.

"I'm sorry you grew up dirt poor in a shitty town. I'm sorry I got you into all of this."

"Are you really? Or did part of you want this to happen—"

"Hell, Darcy, I didn't want to kill anyone!"

Helen's bark was faint through the wall. We lowered our voices.

"I don't mean that. I mean…you probably had something planned so that I would have to go into witness protection with you."

Marja twisted her mouth. "Okay, maybe part of me wanted you to come with me."

"I knew it."

"Do you blame me? When I leave that's it. It's a forever thing. I'll never see you again."

I couldn't hold it anymore. I barely made it to the toilet before puking up all the Snickers bars from last night. I flushed the toilet and sat back against the bathtub, my eyes closed. Marja turned the water on and off and handed me a cool washcloth. She sat on the edge of the tub next to me.

"I was sick as a dog with you for the first three months," she said. "Month four I craved Butterfingers and fried bologna."

"That's why you hate bologna, huh?"

"That and I learned what it's made of." Marja shudders. "Still like Butterfingers."

"They're impossible to find in Europe."

"Why are you buying American chocolate in Europe?"

I opened my eyes and looked at her. "Sometimes, you just want a taste of home, and Butterfingers make me think of you." She stroked my hair and smiled at me and I was right back in our trailer in Frio, my head in Marja's lap, reading a book. Marja rested her book on the arm of the couch and turned the pages with one hand; the other never stopped playing with my hair. It'd been years since I felt that connection with her.

Of course, I had to go and ruin it.

"What about the last three years, Momma?"

"We talked about that," Marja said.

"Yeah, we did, but I'm still hurt and pissed."

"I'm not apologizing again."

"Of course you aren't."

"What's the point, Darcy? It's over and done with. I've apologized. We don't have enough time for me to keep groveling about something I can't change, and if I could go back in time I wouldn't change it. Everyone in town needed to believe that we were estranged so that none of what I was doing would ever go back on you."

"Now I have to go into WITSEC with you. Do you realize how you've fucked up my life?" I said it quietly, though we could still hear Helen's faint bark. That dog must have Superman ears.

I pushed up from the floor and started pacing in the small room, biting my fingernails, a habit I'd stopped years ago.

"You aren't going into witness protection. Or your friends," Marja said firmly.

I stopped abruptly. "My friends? What the fuck are you talking about?"

"It doesn't matter. I'm going to fix it. I swear to you, I'll make this right."

"Oh really? How?"

Marja waved her hand in dismissal. "We don't have time. You have other fish to fry. Let me help you. Talk to me."

I paced again. I didn't even know where to start. I moved from biting my right thumb to my pinky.

"Darcy," Marja said in her best mom voice.

I stopped abruptly. "I think I'm in love with Chloe."

Marja stared at me and blinked a few times. "Well, I wasn't expecting *that*."

"I know, me either."

Marja nodded slowly. She opened her mouth to say something, closed it again.

"Not the reaction I expected of you, especially after last night," I said.

Marja scowled at me. "Don't be a bitch, Darcy." (Bark) "It says a lot that of all the things you have going on, Chloe was the first thing you mentioned."

I stopped pacing. She was right. My stomach was roiling again, but I couldn't tell if it was from my emotions for Chloe, the fetus, or the idea of never seeing Marja again.

"Why now? What happened?" Marja said.

"I kissed her Friday night."

I think Marja's eyebrows are permanently stuck halfway up her forehead. "Were you drunk?"

"No," I said indignantly. "Well, not drunk enough that I didn't know what I was doing. She told me she's been in love with me since college. I was shocked, obviously. But later, she said telling me was a mistake… I had to know. So I kissed her, and I can't stop thinking about it."

Marja's eyes were wide and her mouth gaped. "Um…wow. Okay. Um…"

"And then there's Michael. We haven't been getting along for a while. The wedding is huge and not what I wanted and did you know the Obamas are coming? The fucking Obamas are coming to my wedding. I don't fit into any universe where the Obamas know I exist in the world."

"Jesus."

"I know. But, whatever. Michael and I talked about kids early on in our relationship. I told him all the reasons I didn't want kids—my career, climate change, I don't want to bring kids into this fucked-up, cruel world—and he agreed. He said he didn't care. But here I am, with an IUD and a fiancé who was supposed to get snipped six months ago, and I'm pregnant. It's the biggest betrayal of my life, hands down. Between this wedding turning into what he wants with no regard to what I want, and this, how can I ever trust him again? Obviously, he thinks it's perfectly fine to ignore my wants and needs to satisfy his own."

I dropped onto the bed, drained of emotion and energy. I threw myself back on the mattress and covered my eyes with my arm. The urge to crawl under the bedcovers and sleep for days was unbearably tempting.

The bed dipped next to me and Marja placed her hand on my thigh and squeezed it. We sat in silence for a few minutes.

I hoped that Marja was gathering her thoughts so she could solve my problems for me.

Finally, she spoke, her voice low and with a hint of sadness. "I've realized I'm not the best person to give you advice about relationships or friendships. I've never had a romantic relationship, not really, and as you know friends weren't easy to come by when I was trying to eke out a living."

Great.

"The good news is I read a lot." I moved my arm from my eyes. Marja smiled. "But I'm not expert, and I can't make your decisions for you."

"You really could. I give you permission."

Marja laughed. "Not a chance in hell, baby girl."

I sighed. "It was worth a shot."

"Here's my opinion: Michael's never going to change. He's a rich white man, and he's used to getting his way in everything. He has no qualms about ignoring what you want. If that's the kind of marriage you want, then marry him. If not—" Marja shrugged a shoulder "—you need to break it off."

"Eloise has gone to so much trouble."

"Fuck Eloise. She'll be able to plan another one with the next future Mrs. Michael Parsons, and that will happen sooner than you think. They can afford it and besides, when they learn why, they'll understand. Or they should. That's a pretty big betrayal with lifelong consequences."

"Unless they knew," I said.

"It's possible, and all the more reason to break it off. You don't need to go through with something you clearly don't want to, for multiple reasons, just because you don't want to let anyone down. Be selfish, Darcy."

"Like you."

Marja's mouth tightened. I thought she was going to fight me on it, but she moved on. I could tell it was killing her.

"Do you want this baby?"

"It's a fetus, and I haven't allowed myself to think about that yet."

"Why?"

"I've never wanted children, and there is no way I want to be a single mother, and that's what I'd be."

Marja's gaze met mine for a long moment before she said, "You're making the right decision."

The truth I suspected—feared—my entire life pierced my heart as if it was paper-mache. Momma regretted keeping me. I knew I was a mistake—what sixteen-year-old intends to get pregnant?—but hearing Momma admit it…

I sniffed and looked at the ceiling to get my emotions together. I was going to have a lot to talk to my therapist about, that was for fucking sure. Hell, I might not even get to keep my therapist in witness protection, and who the hell would I be able to talk to about everything anyway?

I inhaled. "I never thought you'd admit it, Momma, but I'm glad you did."

"Admit what?"

"That you didn't want me. That I was a mistake. That your life would have been better off if you hadn't had to deal with raising a bastard in Frio, Texas."

Momma's face went white. "What are you talking about? I never said that. I've never thought that. Not even once!"

"Oh, please," I said. "Don't think I didn't know that you ate the cheap tuna out of a can when I went to sleep because you wanted me to have the leftover tacos or chicken or whatever you made. I know you made sacrifices because of me. I mean, my God, Momma, you didn't even date until I left. I would resent me, too."

"Whoa, whoa, whoa. I've never resented you, or regretted keeping you, and the sacrifices I made—" Momma swallowed hard "—were nothing compared to how much I loved you, or to the feeling inside me when you cuddled with me and looked at me as if I hung the moon. Once upon a time you were proud of me, and that was worth it all. And for the record, not dating wasn't that big of a sacrifice. I'd never been much interested in men, and now I know why."

"Why did you have me? I've never been able to figure it out. You are so smart. All my teachers that taught you talked about how smart you were, what a waste of intelligence it was for you not to go to UT, that you could have really been somebody."

Marja shot up from the bed. "Fuck them." It was loud and harsh, and I leaned back from the force of it. Helen was going crazy in the other room. "Where were all those teachers when I was alone and pregnant and trying to keep at school despite all the rumors and lies being told about me? The names I was called." She jabbed herself in the chest with her thumb. "Did any one of those teachers reach out to me to try to help me, to do what they could to help me make it as a single mom at UT? Did any of them shun Russell for knocking me up and throwing five hundred dollars at me to 'get it taken care of?' Hell no. They went to church with him. Heard him stand up and pray as a deacon. Voted for him for mayor. Made out like I was the one who was in the wrong, like I was some brazen hussy out to seduce all the married men in town and Russell was my first victim. Everyone forgave him right fast, but me?" Marja's face was red and she was breathing heavy. "No matter how successful I am, no matter how successful you are, they'll always look down on us.

"But none of that matters. We've risen above it. You've risen above it. I don't blame you for never going back to Frio. You wiped that shit stain of a town off your shoe years ago and haven't looked back. That's what I always wanted for you, and you did it. That's why I sacrificed. So you would have the opportunities I didn't, and when you were confronted with hard choices, I knew you would make the right decisions, that you would trust yourself and your intelligence and your independence.

"I'm so sorry for all the shit you went through living in Frio. That's the one thing I would do differently. I'd find a way to move us to Austin or San Antonio or Houston. But I was too stubborn and proud. I thought it would look like I was running, like I was as guilty as people said I was. And I wanted to rub Russell's nose in it." Momma scoffs. "That didn't work out like I planned, but I'm getting the last laugh."

My mind reeled. She'd answered every question, salved every worry, that I'd had for thirty-three years in a three-minute monologue. I didn't know where to start, so I started at the end.

"What do you mean, getting the last laugh."

"I didn't work for the cartel. Not directly. I don't have shit on them. I worked for Russell. He was the middleman."

"Russell Clarke works for the cartel? My dad?"

Marja shrugged one shoulder. "He's the one that came to threaten you three years ago. I'm pretty sure there's another layer."

"I'm sorry, my father threatened me and that's why you cut off contact with me?"

"Yes. I wanted out and he threatened to hurt you if I didn't keep working for them. He had to believe you were completely in the dark—"

"Which I was anyway."

"But he only knew our relationship when you were here, so he assumed I still shared everything with you."

"He really thought you'd tell me you were laundering money?"

"Russell is charming and good-looking, but he isn't the

sharpest knife in the drawer. Fuck Russell. He'll get what's coming to him."

We heard a knock on the door above Helen's nonstop barking. I opened the door and Helen shot through the door and jumped straight into my lap.

"You little traitor," Momma said to Helen, her voice full of affection. She scratched her behind the ears.

"Everything okay?" Chloe said.

"Yes," Marja said. "We're almost done."

"You can come in if you want," I said. Chloe's gaze met mine, and I knew what I needed to do. No, what I wanted to do. What would make me happy.

I smiled, relief and affection washing through me. I blotched, too, of course. Not from embarrassment, though.

Marja sat down and put her boots on.

"Where are you going?" I asked.

"To the store to get you some antinausea medicine."

"I feel better."

"Until tomorrow morning, you will."

"I'll go get it," Chloe said.

"No, you stay here. You two have a lot to talk about."

"She's right. We do," I said. Chloe smiled and reached out her hand. I took it and pulled her near me. Helen nestled into my lap as if to say, *I don't think so, chica*. Chloe raised her eyes and I laughed. "I guess you have competition," I said.

"I'll win her over." Chloe leaned down and kissed me gently on the lips, and lingered. Someone moaned, probably me. Maybe both of us.

Reader, I felt that kiss in all the right places.

"That is definitely my cue," Momma said.

She wore Lena's bomber jacket and slung a distressed leather messenger bag across her body.

"You look like you're going on an expedition. The drug-store is just around the corner."

"Need anything else from there?"

"Snickers bars. Multiple. Fred, the woman at the counter, will make sure you get a good deal."

Momma kissed me on the forehead. She stroked my cheek and looked down at me. "I love you."

"I love you, too."

She smiled, but it was a little tired and wistful. "Is Lena still next door?"

"She went to get breakfast," Chloe said.

"I'll eat it when I get back. Take care of my girl until I return," Marja said.

"With pleasure," Chloe said.

Helen jumped down from my lap and followed Momma to the door. "No, you need to stay with Darcy. She'll take care of you. Be good."

Momma straightened and opened the door a crack before pausing.

"And for the record, I didn't waste my intelligence. I started from absolutely nothing, not one nickel, and built up a successful small business with over thirty employees. I am somebody, the only person I've really ever wanted to be since the moment they put you in my arms, I'm Darcy Evans's mother, and fucking proud to be."

She smiled and walked out the door.

TWENTY-FOUR

Chloe

I wanted to take Darcy in my arms and kiss her senseless, but it wasn't the right moment.

All in due time.

Fitz had never looked at me like she did then, and all of the desire I'd pushed down and tried to ignore lit my body like a Roman candle.

Not now, Chloe. First, be her best friend.

I sat next to her on the bed. "How was your talk with Marja?"

Darcy inhaled. She took my hand and put it in her lap. "A lot to take in, to be honest. It's going to take a while to process."

"Okay."

"I'm not trying to brush you off, it's just my mind is a little fried with everything."

Darcy lifted my hand and kissed it, her lingering lips sending chills up my arm.

"She helped clarify some things for me."

"Yeah?" My voice was choked from the effort to keep myself

in check. Darcy's lips were impossibly soft and warm against my hand.

Her hazel eyes met mine. "I'm not going to marry Michael. He betrayed me and I will never trust him again. He's ignored everything I did and didn't want for the wedding, too. He's never going to change because the world is set up so that he doesn't have to."

"I'm sorry, Fitz." I put my arm around her and rubbed circles on her back. I was sorry for her and for my parents. I wasn't sorry for my douche canoe of a brother. I was mostly sorry for the scene that would happen when she broke it off, but it wasn't the time to bring that up.

"A part of me is sorry, too. But it's a very small part."

"Why?"

Fitz traced my jaw with her finger. "Because we have each other."

I exhaled all the uncertainty and tension I'd harbored since Friday night. "Does this mean that…"

"We're going to be a couple? No. Not yet."

"Oh."

She smiled. "It means we're going to take it slow and date and make sure that we work as a romantic couple before we jump in and do something we'll regret. Our friendship is too important to risk, even though right now I really want to take your clothes off."

"You do?" I laughed, giddy, warm, and incredibly turned on.

"I do."

"That's a coincidence, because I want to take your clothes off, too."

"I realized the last couple of days that you're the person I call automatically when anything happens, good or bad. If I was supposed to spend my life with Michael, it should have been him I wanted to call. I didn't, for a variety of reasons. Mainly though, I knew that you would support me unconditionally. He wouldn't. You're my person, and he's not."

Darcy's gaze dropped to my lips. "When I kissed you the other night—" her voice was low and intimate "—I never felt that way kissing Michael, or anyone else. That means something, and I want to find out what."

Darcy leaned forward and pressed her lips against mine. It was soft and sweet, and the tip of her tongue against my lips asked for more. I cupped her face and opened my mouth to her, letting Fitz take the lead.

For a few seconds, at least. Do you know how long I've been wanting to do this?

I let myself get lost in her, the way she felt, the way she smelled, the way she touched me, the way her skin was impossibly soft, the way her breast fit perfectly in the palm of my hand, the way she gasped when I lightly pinched her erect nipple through her shirt.

"My God, Chloe." Her voice dripped with want.

"Yes," I said, moving my mouth to her neck, my tongue tracing a line to her earlobe. Darcy groaned and arched into me.

She would have let me make love to her, and I wanted to, but I decided to let my better angels win. Plus, we had a room full of eagle eared best friends next door.

I pulled away. Her lips were swollen and wet, her eyes hooded and confused. "You okay, Fitz?"

"Um, yes. That was...um..."

"A lot to process," I teased.

Her eyes cleared and her mouth twisted into a smile. "Yes, a lot to process. But also something to look forward to."

"Oh my God, you have no idea," I said.

Fitz laughed. I love the sound of her laugh.

"You make me so happy," Fitz said.

"You make me happy, too." I cleared my throat. This was all great, but there was an FBI agent getting us breakfast. "What's this about witness protection?"

"Did you mention that to Ella and Jess?"

"No, but they're asking questions. You and Marja weren't exactly quiet when you were in here fighting."

Darcy inhaled and worry lines returned to her forehead. "Momma said she has a plan, that I won't have to go."

"What's her plan?"

"I have no idea. But I trust her."

I wasn't sure Fitz's trust was well-placed, to be honest, but she needed to believe in Marja. I kept my worries to myself.

"What about the baby?"

"I haven't decided."

My eyebrows raised. "You mean you might keep it?"

"I'm taking one thing at a time right now. Trying to."

A knock sounded on the door. Helen jumped from the bed and barked.

"Breakfast is here," Ella said.

"About time," Jess said.

"Oh my God, I'm so hungry," I said.

"Same."

With a gentle tug on my hand, Fitz pulled me to her for a quick kiss. "All I want to do is kiss you now. Let me know if it's too much."

I laughed. "Oh you sweet summer child, it will never be enough."

A few quick smiling kisses and laughter later, we opened the door. The smell of eggs and bacon made my stomach growl. "Get that food in my stomach, now," I said.

I'd opened a Styrofoam container and was about to dig in when Lena said, "Where's Marja?"

"She went to the drugstore for me," Darcy said. She took a

big bite of bacon. I guess her morning sickness was over. "She should be back soon."

Lena raised her phone to her ear. A phone rang in the other room.

Lena dashed off, the phone still ringing. It stopped midring. The four of us looked at each other in dawning realization.

"She forgot her phone," Darcy said.

"It has to be it," Ella said, though her expression said otherwise.

Lena stormed back into the room, her phone to her ear and Marja's phone in her hand. She handed it to Darcy.

The notes app was open with only two words in the top left-hand corner.

I'm sorry.

PART FIVE

TWENTY-FIVE

Darcy

The interrogation room in the Chicago FBI office looked exactly how I imagined it. Sterile, smelling of coffee and sweat, with a metal table bolted to the floor and uncomfortable metal chairs to match. Little red lights blinked from the cameras in all four corners of the ceiling. There wasn't a two-way mirror, at least.

Cold comfort, that. Agent Cooper had been asking me the same questions for at least two hours, and my answers never wavered.

"Marja didn't tell me anything."

"That's not what Agent González says."

"She's lying."

"Why would she do that?"

"To save her skin because she lost Marja? How should I know? I've barely known her a day."

"Marja didn't explain why she is going into witness protection? Why you are?"

"Nope."

"I was sitting at the table when we talked about it," Cooper said.

"You talked about it, sure. But Marja never said anything."

Agent Cooper glared at me, and I'm pretty sure that was when he decided to treat me as a hostile witness. Which I was.

Was I mad at Marja for leaving without a word? Yes, a little. But I trusted her. I knew whatever she was doing was to help me and Chloe and my friends. I also knew that she was five steps ahead of this asshole, and I intended to stall and lie and evade for as long as possible to give her a head start.

"I find it hard to believe she didn't say anything."

"Do you really? You've been investigating her for how long and you don't know what she's like? Stubborn and narcissistic? Arrogant and determined to do what she wants when she wants? Ghosting the FBI is exactly what Marja Evans would do."

"And ghosting you."

I shrugged. "She's done it before. I'm pretty used to it. She didn't give you what you wanted, did she?"

"She will," Cooper said.

I smiled. "It must sting to know that a little nobody maid from BFE Texas got exactly what she wanted and left you high and dry."

"It must sting you to know that whether you know anything or not, your life as you know it is over."

"I do hope these cameras work—" I twirled my finger in the air "—because that sounded a lot like a threat. Isn't it your job to help me if I'm in so much danger?"

"Considering the situation, you're awfully calm."

"I've watched a lot of *Law and Order*."

He didn't roll his eyes, though I could tell he wanted to.

"Where are my friends?"

Chloe

"Where the hell have you taken, Darcy?"

That was the last thing I said before I was marched off into this office by a blank-faced FBI agent. There's a desk with no computer or phone. A bookshelf with law books that look as if their spines have never been cracked. A photo of Joe Biden, grinning as if to say, *Hell yeah I'm finally President*, hangs above a very comfortable looking leather sofa, which is flanked by two matching chairs and centered with a coffee table.

A gorgeous FBI agent. Red hair, blue eyes, and very fit, lead Ella and Jess into the office. The modern-day Dana Scully smiled, and I knew that she was the "good cop." My defenses went up.

"Are you okay?" Ella asked.

"Besides being stared at by Uncle Joe—" I jerked my thumb in the direction of the photo "—and worrying about Fitz, I'm great."

"Yeah, where is Darcy?" Jess asked the agent, with only a bit of drool coming out of her mouth.

"She's fine. She's being questioned by Agent Cooper."

"And Agent González?"

"Being debriefed as we speak. I'm Agent Anderson."

I can't help but laugh. "Seriously?"

She rolls her eyes good-naturedly. "Yes, really. She was the reason I went into the FBI."

"She's the reason I'm a lesbian," Jess said.

Agent Anderson raises her eyebrows at Jess, but didn't respond. "Do you three want anything? Coffee? Water? Sodas?"

I was dying for a Dr. Pepper but I answered no. I didn't want to prolong this any more than necessary. Jess opened her mouth to reply, but I shook my head. We all declined, much to Agent Anderson's amusement.

She motioned to the couch and sat gracefully in one of the chairs, crossing one leg over the other.

"You've had quite a couple of days," she ventured.

We nodded and remained silent. We had that right, you know.

"Your friend must have been very distraught for you to drive to Carthage in that weather."

"She was," Jess said. "Chloe didn't want us to go, me and Ella, but there's no way Chloe could have driven in that ice. I have lots of experience, though."

I knew Jess well enough to know she wasn't talking about driving experience. Well, why not? It was as good of a deflection strategy as any, and watching Jess hit on Agent Anderson would be amusing to boot.

"Absolutely," I said. "Jess is the most experienced in our group in a lot of ways. Including driving. There's no one else in our group who can go all night like Jess."

"She sounds like a good woman to have around in tight circumstances," Agent Anderson said with a wry smile, clearly in on the joke.

Honest to God, it was tough to keep a straight face. I liked Agent Anderson immensely, and I think Jess was well on her way to falling in love.

"We all love Darcy like a sister," Ella interjected in her no-nonsense voice. She gave Jess a look, and Jess shrugged slightly.

Maybe it was the adrenaline running through my body, but I burst out laughing. Everyone turned their attention to me. "Sorry."

"We wanted to support her and make sure Chloe got there safely," Ella continued.

Sensing a weak link, Agent Anderson focused on Ella. "What was so urgent?" Agent Anderson asked.

"She's pregnant," Ella said.

I wished we were sitting at a table so I could kick her.

Agent Anderson tilted her head to the side. "That seems like good news. Not news that would make her three friends risk their lives driving in the earliest winter storm on record."

"Technically, it's autumn," I said.

Agent Anderson stayed focused on Ella. "I find it a little difficult to believe that's the reason."

"Darcy does—" Ella started.

"It's a long story," I interjected, "and something that is Darcy's to share if she wants."

"Look," Jess said, "we were surprised to find an FBI agent there at the hotel. But we don't have any idea why she was there, and we didn't ask questions. She, Agent González, didn't share anything either. We are as ignorant as little ducklings."

"And we don't want to know," Ella said.

"Darcy doesn't know anything either," I said.

"How do you know?" Agent Anderson asked.

"Because she told me."

"She told you what?"

"That she didn't know anything."

"When?"

"When she called."

"Was that the first time or the second time?"

"Both."

"So, Darcy called you twice to tell you that she didn't know anything about anything?"

Okay, yeah. It sounded stupid but I was in it, so I had to commit to it.

"Exactly."

"She didn't tell you that Marja killed a man in front of her?"

"What?" Jess and Ella said in unison.

Agent Anderson leaned forward and focused on me. "She did tell you, didn't she?"

"No."

"Then why weren't you shocked like your friends."

"I've known Marja longer than they have."

"You think she's capable of murder?"

"To protect Fitz? Absolutely."

"Is that what Darcy said, that Marja was protecting her?"

"No, she didn't tell me anything."

"Not that she is going into witness protection because of it."

"What?" Jess and Ella said again.

"Nope," I replied. "Not a word. We don't know anything. Fitz doesn't know anything either."

"I don't believe you."

I shrugged. "This is boring. Can we go?"

"Where's Helen?" Jess asked.

"Currently in the break room being fawned over."

"Lucky bitch," Jess said under her breath.

A distant bark sounded, and the three of us broke out into laughter.

It was obvious Agent Anderson didn't know what to think of us. A knock on the door was followed by Helen streaking into the room, when the door had barely opened a crack. She barked and ran around the office, looking in every nook and cranny before she stopped in front of Jess and sat. Jess leaned forward and rubbed the dog behind the ears.

"I know, Helen. You miss your human. Don't you worry, we'll take care of you." She patted the sofa between her and Ella, and Helen jumped up, lay down, and started licking her paw. Jess and Ella rubbed her back. "She's in distress," Jess said. "Marja is gone, and she can feel the bad vibes of this place."

The second agent leaned down and whispered something in Agent Anderson's ear. Her expression didn't change, but she nodded and stood.

"Looks like you three, and Helen, are free to go."

"What about Darcy?"

"That's up to Agent Cooper."

"I'm not leaving until Darcy does," I said.

Agent Anderson shrugged. "You can wait in the lobby if you want. Follow me."

As they waited at the elevator, Agent Anderson smiled down at Helen. "What kind of dog is she?"

"Mutt is my guess," Jess said.

Helen glared up at Jess and barked.

"I didn't cuss. Did I cuss?" Jess asked Ella.

"No."

Agent Anderson held the elevator door open for them. "Guess you aren't as charming as you think you are, is she Helen?" She looked down and winked, and Helen wagged her tail so hard I thought she was going to take flight.

Jess was stopped from replying by Ella's elbow in her ribs.

The door closed and Agent Anderson turned to Ella. "I love your cooking show. And restaurant. And cookbook."

"What a nice thing to say. Do you like to cook?"

"No, I'm terrible at it," Anderson laughed. "That's why I watch cooking shows."

"To learn?" Ella asked.

"Oh, no. I'll never be a good cook. I watch to marvel at your skill."

"Oh." Ella blushed and smiled. "Well, thanks for watching. And for buying my cookbook even though you won't use it."

Agent Anderson turned back to the front of the elevator just as it dinged, and the doors opened to let us out into the lobby.

"Hope to see you again soon," Jess said. Agent Anderson looked amused.

Ella gave her shy smile. "Mention my name when you call for a reservation. It should help."

"Hopefully the chef will visit my table," she said.

"I'm rarely there these days, but you never know." Ella waved. "Bye."

I turned to Agent Anderson, who was still holding the door open. "Christ, did you have to flirt with *both* of my friends?"

"That would be incredibly unprofessional of me."

"Trust me when I say, they know nothing."

"They?"

"We."

She nodded solemnly. "I'm sure I'll be seeing you again, Ms. Parsons."

"I really hope we don't see you again, Agent Scully. No offense."

"None taken. I love being compared to my idol."

"Not what I was talking about."

She leaned forward and stage-whispered. "I know."

I walked on, feeling she'd gotten the better of me somehow, and also suspected we would, in fact, be seeing her again.

As we walked down the hall, Ella hit Jess in the shoulder.

"Ow," Jess said, though Ella's hits were soft at worst. "What was that for?"

"You know very well. Flirting with the FBI agent at a time like this. Honestly."

"She looked like Gillian Anderson. I couldn't let that opportunity pass me by."

"You should have been focused on helping Darcy, not trying to get a date with her."

"I wasn't trying to get a date, Ella."

Ella sighed and rolled her eyes. We pushed through the exit and into the lobby.

"Chloe, girls, thank God."

My mother, father, and Michael stood up from uncomfortable looking chairs.

"Where's Darcy?" Michael asked.

"What are y'all doing here?" I asked.

"Where's Darcy," Michael asked again.

"Being questioned," Jess said.

"For what? Why?" Eloise said.

"Is Darcy in trouble with the FBI?" my father said.

"No."

"Where's Marja?" Eloise said.

"Where is Darcy?" Michael shouted.

"Christ, I don't know, okay?" I shouted back.

Bark.

Helen pulled away from Jess and ran to the other side of the room. Darcy stared at us, eyes wide, her neck and face splotchy from emotion. Helen went around and pushed through Darcy's legs, sitting between her feet.

"Shit," Darcy said.

This time, Helen didn't bark.

TWENTY-SIX

Darcy

Eloise and Robert tried to insist that we go back to their house, but I put my foot down.

"You're free to go wherever you want. I'm going home," I said.

"Exactly," Michael said. "I'll get us a cab."

"Not your place, Michael. Home. With Ella, Jess, and Chloe."

Helen barked, and danced on her toes.

"And Helen."

"We have a lot to talk about," Michael said in a low voice.

"We do. Come to the brownstone and we will."

"In private."

"Michael, I am not in the mood to be fucking bullied," I snapped. Helen growled at Michael.

He jerked his head back. "I'm not bullying you."

"Yes, you are, and I've had my fill with it for the day. I'm going home. Period."

"We're coming, too," Eloise said.

"Mother, I hardly think—"

"Chloe. We deserve answers, too."

"You deserve to know the truth, absolutely," Darcy said. "We will meet you three there."

A female agent stepped forward, scaring me to death. "I'll give you four a ride," she said.

"Where did you come from Agent Scully?" Jess said.

"The same door you did."

"Following us and eavesdropping, huh?" Chloe said.

I didn't care who this woman was, I didn't want to be in a car with Michael and his parents. "Yes, we will take you up on the ride," I said, Helen at my heels.

"This way," the agent said.

I didn't look at Michael or the Parsons as I left.

"Darcy?" Michael said, disbelief in his voice. "You're welcome for getting you out of here," he called out.

The agent stopped and turned. "She was never in custody, Mr. Parsons."

"What an asshole," Chloe said.

Helen growled, but I didn't get the impression she was growling at Chloe.

"I think I'm in love," Jess whispered to Ella, who rolled her eyes.

I slowed to let the agent get ahead of us, and my friends slowed with me. "Don't say anything in the car and say even less when we get home."

The main roads had been deiced and sanded, so the drive home wasn't as long or perilous as I thought. I stared out the window, wondering where my mother was, if she was safe, if she would contact me to let me know what was going on. Helen was asleep, with her head on my lap.

"I guess we have a new roommate," Jess said.

"Yes, we do," Chloe said.

"It's going to complicate things," Jess said.

"Nothing the four of us can't handle," Chloe said.

"There's nothing the four of us can't handle together," Ella said.

"Are you talking about the dog," Agent Anderson said from the driver's seat.

"Of course," Chloe said. "What else?"

What else, indeed.

Michael, Eloise, and Robert were waiting outside our door when Agent Anderson dropped us off. She gave me her card and said to call if I needed anything, or thought of anything that might be useful in their investigation. I didn't answer.

I hoped random sex toys and lingerie were scattered all over the house from the wedding shower, but I knew Jess better than that. It was spotless, of course. Helen immediately set to investigating every nook and cranny of the place. I filled a bowl full of water and set it down on the floor in front of her. She drank greedily, then returned to her snooping.

"Ella, I don't know where my bag is. The FBI is probably picking through your leopard skin tights as we speak."

"Agent Scully will be at your restaurant within the week, if so," Chloe teased.

"Anyone want some tea?" Ella said, ignoring the jab and no doubt hoping Eloise and Robert didn't hear.

"You'd think she grew up in England," Jess said.

"Tea would be lovely, thank you Ella," Eloise Parsons said. "Darcy, how are you doing? You must be exhausted."

I followed Ella into the kitchen and poured a healthy portion of Maker's Mark in a rocks glass. "I am." I lifted the glass in the air. "Cheers."

"Is it really a good idea to drink that?" Michael said.

"Why would it be a bad idea, Michael?" I downed the shot in one swallow and poured another.

"Darcy," Michael said.

"Michael."

"Let's just all have a seat and talk," Robert said, like the good CEO he was.

"I've been sitting for a while. I'll stand." I downed the second drink and put the glass down with a thud.

"Darcy," Ella said under her breath.

"You've made your point," Michael said. "You won't be bullied. You can do whatever you like."

"Am I trying to make a point? Or am I just really thirsty? And really fucking exhausted from the last three days, none of which would have happened if you and your mother hadn't gone behind my back and against my wishes to invite my mother to your wedding."

"Our wedding."

"Oh, no. It's been your wedding for a while now, Michael. Or maybe Eloise's. Y'all stopped listening to me from almost the moment I said I wanted to get married at the courthouse."

"That was absurd," Eloise said. "You must admit that."

"No, I don't. I should have known then. It should have been a red flag. But it wasn't. Or maybe I was just so happy to be part of a big loving family I ignored it. I can't anymore. This time, you've gone too far."

"What do you mean?" Robert said. "What is she talking about, Eloise? Is this about the Obamas, Darcy? I know it makes you uncomfortable, but it would have been rude not to send them an invitation. I didn't think they would come. I'm happy to talk to them. I'm sure they will understand."

"There won't be any need, but thank you, Robert."

"What do you mean, there won't be any need?" Michael said.

I looked at him fully for the first time. "Did you get a vasectomy, Michael?"

"You're pregnant, aren't you?"

"How could I be if you got a vasectomy like we agreed to. Like you promised."

"They don't always work," Eloise said.

"I have an IUD, Eloise. I'm not sure the exact statistics, but I'm sure the chances of getting pregnant with those two forms of birth control are miniscule."

"Are you pregnant?" Michael asked.

"Answer the question, Michael."

"What does it matter if you're pregnant?"

"Answer the question. Yes or no? Did you get a vasectomy?"

Michael stared at me for a long time. I knew him well enough to know he was thinking about lying. I expected it. "No, I didn't."

"Michael!" Robert said. "You gave your word to your fiancée to do something and you didn't do it? You willfully didn't do it?"

"I want children."

"Then you should have told me that!" I said.

"You would have broken up with me."

"Yes, probably. But we would have remained friends because we were open and honest with each other. Now, I'll never be able to trust you."

"You'll have to learn to when we are married."

I laughed. "I'm not going to marry you. I wouldn't marry you now for all the money in the world."

"I'll file for full custody," Michael said. "You've told enough people how you hate kids and don't want them that it will be easy to take it from you."

"Who said I'm keeping it?"

Michael's and Eloise's faces went white.

"You can't do that," Eloise said. "This is his child, too."

"Did you know about this, Eloise? That Michael didn't get a vasectomy?"

"Of course, she knew," Chloe said. "Michael doesn't do anything without Mommy's approval."

"Fuck off, Chloe," Michael said.

"Don't tell her to fuck off," I said. "Did you know, Eloise?"

Eloise Parsons is a shrewd woman, and I knew she was trying to figure out what to say so she would get what she wanted.

"I did, and I'm sorry we didn't tell you. Michael was distraught and I advised him to wait, not to ignore your wishes. None of that matters now that you have a precious life growing inside you."

"So, you're just pro-choice when it doesn't affect you?" Chloe said.

"Eloise, listen to yourself," Robert said.

"Everyone needs to listen to *me*," I said. I turned to Michael. "You impregnated me without my consent. You lied to me for months. Do you have any idea what the medical risks are for getting pregnant with an IUD? And ectopic pregnancy. The IUD being embedded in the uterine wall which, if I decide to carry the fetus to term, would be dangerous to both of us. At the end of it all, I might never be able to have children."

"You said you didn't want children!"

"I don't, but it's my choice not to have them. It shouldn't be a bad outcome from being impregnated without my consent!"

"We've been fighting for months, and even before all of this, I was having second thoughts. I'm not going to marry you. Not now. Not ever."

"Darcy—" Michael said.

"There's been a lot of money spent for you to back out now," Eloise said.

"Eloise, my God," Robert said. "Don't worry about the

money, Darcy." Robert had edged over to my side of the room, next to me and Chloe.

"I never asked for it and I never wanted it. Make Michael pay you back. Have a big party instead. I don't give a shit what you do, but I won't be there.

"As far as whether or not I'll get an abortion? I haven't decided. Honestly, between everything with Momma and finding out about your lies and betrayal, I haven't had a chance to think about it. But make no mistake. It will be between me and my doctor. No one else."

"Don't be so sure about that," Michael said.

"Do you really want it to get out that you lied to Darcy about getting a vasectomy?" Chloe asked. "I mean, everyone knows you're an asshole, but there's really no need to give everyone more ammunition."

"Oh, shut up, Chloe. Darcy is straight. She's never going to want to fuck you."

"Don't be so sure about that," I said.

There was a long moment of silence. "Chloe Parsons, what have you done?" Eloise said.

"You fucking bitch," Michael said to his sister. "You did this, didn't you?"

"Get Darcy pregnant without her consent? Nope. That's physically impossible. But I'm going to support her in whatever decision she makes."

"What happened between me and Chloe happened before I knew I was pregnant."

"How long have you been fucking my fiancée?" Michael stepped toward Chloe, but Jess stepped between them and Robert grabbed his arm from behind.

"Don't you dare, Michael," Robert said. "You need to leave. Now. You, too, Eloise."

"Don't talk to me like I'm a child," Michael said.

"Stop acting like one. Wait in the car. Both of you."

They left, and I sagged with relief. Chloe was there to catch me and lead me to the sofa. She sat next to me and held my hand. Helen, who had been uncharacteristically silent with all of the cuss words flying around, climbed into my lap and started licking my neck. "You okay, Fitz?" Chloe asked.

"I will be." I squeezed her hand.

"I'll run you a bath," Ella said.

"I'll help," Jess said.

When we were alone, Robert sat in the chair opposite the two of us on the couch.

"I'm so sorry, Darcy. I had no idea about any of this. Please believe me."

"I do."

"Don't worry about Michael's threats. I'll take care of it. If he does try to do something, I'll pay for your lawyers."

"You don't have to do that."

"Yes, I do."

Robert looked at our joined hands and smiled. "I wondered if you two were ever going to happen. I've seen it from the beginning. I'm glad you're seeing it, too, now.

"I was surprised when you started dating Michael, and even more so when you agreed to marry him. It wasn't my place to say anything. Besides. I was very happy to have you in my family as a daughter-in-law." He smiled. "It's nice to know that still might happen."

"It's a little soon to talk about that," Chloe said.

"I know, but I just wanted you to know that someone in this family is in your corner. Both of your corners." He stood. "Get some rest."

He turned when he got to the door. "I will support whatever decision you make about the baby. If you decide to keep it, you will have all the support you need from me to raise it on your own." He held his hand up. "I'm not talking about money but know that's always there if you need it. No, I meant that you will always have a babysitter a call away." He pointed his thumb at his chest.

"Thank you." I loved Robert and everything he was saying, but I really and truly wanted to get in the bath.

I stood, and Chloe stood with me.

"One more thing," Robert said.

I exhaled sharply and Chloe squeezed my hand in encouragement.

"When you're making your decision, remember that the baby has a piece of all of us in them. Including Chloe."

With that bombshell, he was gone.

Chloe

Darcy soaked in the bathtub for a very long time. I suspected she fell asleep. I knew that her fingers and toes would be pruny. Her skin would be soft and smell of lavender and rosemary.

I also knew she would crawl into her bed and sleep for days, which is why Helen was in my room, curled up on my bed, sound asleep. She snores, the little dove.

Darcy walked in, wearing her fluffy bathrobe and her wet hair tied up into a turban. I'd seen her like this thousands of times in the last fifteen years and yeah, I'd always felt a twinge at the sight. Tonight, though, an inferno erupted at my core.

"Don't you look comfy," she said to Helen, scratching her ears. "And very spoiled." Darcy picked up a lamb chew toy with raised eyebrows.

"Jess and Ella couldn't help themselves. You should see the basket of toys in the living room."

"That was fast."

"You were in there a while." I closed my computer, set it aside, and removed my glasses. "How do you feel?"

"Great…ish."

"Are you worried about Marja?"

"Yeah."

"Are you angry with her for leaving?"

"I probably should be, but I know she did it for me. She kept saying she was going to make sure none of us had to go into WITSEC."

"None of us?"

"She and Lena implied we all might have to go in."

"Good Lord. You have no idea where she is or what she's doing?"

"None. I don't want to talk about Marja."

"Okay. You'd best go to bed and get some rest. You've been through a lot."

"Good idea."

Darcy walked around my bed and got in, robe, turban and all. She lay on her side, facing me. "Do you mind?"

I swallowed hard. "Of course not."

I lay down, facing her. Our hands intertwined. "I knew your hands would be pruny."

"They are."

"And soft. And that you would smell good."

"Are you flirting with me."

"Maybe a little."

"I like it."

"Do you?"

Darcy nodded. "I've been thinking about what your dad said."

"I wouldn't hold out much hope on the babysitting. He doesn't know how to change a diaper."

"I'm sure he's a quick learner. He would be adorable with a baby."

"He would."

"That wasn't what I was thinking about. The other thing."

I'd been thinking about it a lot, too. The baby inside Darcy would have a part of me in it. It would be the closest we would ever come to having a biological child together. Now that I knew it, I couldn't get the idea out of my head, or the desire out of my heart.

"Me, too," I whispered. "You know I would never pressure you into doing what you didn't want. I mean it when I say I'll support you unconditionally."

"I know. You always have."

"If you want to talk about it, I'm here. But if you don't, that's fine, too."

"A lot depends on what the doctor says. I called in the bathroom and got an appointment."

"Want me to go with you?"

Darcy inhaled. "No, I don't think so."

"Sure. Whatever you want, let me know."

Darcy smiled and cupped my cheek. "I'm nervous. About us. Trying not to spiral."

I grinned. "Of course, you are. I'm an expert in helping you stop."

"I'm counting on it."

"Would a kiss help?"

"It definitely wouldn't hurt."

Our kiss was soft and lingering, more comfort than passion. I have always been protective of Darcy, but the emotion that surged through me was shocking. There was no whale too big to slay, no windmill too remote to tilt, no mountain too high… well, you get the idea. What Darcy needs, though, is support, not protectiveness. It goes a bit against my nature, especially with Fitz, but in that moment, when we kissed sweetly, I determined to be the partner Fitz needed, whatever that entailed.

We were staring at each other with goo-goo eyes and grinning at the sheer incomprehension of where we were in our relationship, and where it was going and not needing to verbalize any of it, when Ella called out and knocked on my door.

"Come in."

Neither Darcy nor I moved from our position, which didn't phase Ella in the least. Probably because she was holding out her phone to Darcy with wide eyes.

"It's Marja."

TWENTY-SEVEN

Marja

If everything had gone to plan, I would be on a boat in the middle of Lake Michigan on my way to Canada right now. New name, identity, Canadian passport, the works. But what they say about the best-laid plans is true.

Good news: I had a backup plan.

Bad news: I'm back in Frio.

Which has led me to sitting at my kitchen table, tied to a chair, being guarded by Tommy Fucking Baldwin.

"I guess this is the end of a beautiful friendship, huh, Tommy?"

"What the fuck are you doing back here, Marja? You said you were going to disappear."

"I've got to save Darcy."

"How, by getting killed?"

"Yes. Once I'm dead, they'll leave Darcy alone."

Tommy laughed, but there was no joy in it. "You are one crazy fucking bitch."

"No, Tommy, I'm a mother."

I shifted around in my chair.

Tommy shook his head and took a hit of his joint. He hadn't hardly looked at me since I'd arrived. He sat across the table, his leg jackhammering on the floor, shaking the trailer house.

"Care to share?" I asked, nodding to the joint. His nervousness was starting to seep into me, and I needed to take the edge off.

He held the joint for me, and I took a long hit, held the smoke in my lungs, slowly exhaled. I closed my eyes and sighed. "You always did have good stuff."

After a few minutes of silence, I asked, "Think she'll want to kill me herself, or have Russell do it?"

He scoffed. "She won't want to get her hands dirty. She needs Russell to give her cover as the doting wife."

"Which is why you're so nervous. You don't want to kill me."

His head jerked toward me. "No, I don't want to kill you. I don't want to kill anyone. I want to fight my dogs and drink and smoke weed by the river and be left in peace. They've decided, or Chelly's decided, I'm her security. Her muscle. As if I'm built to be a murderer like those cartel guys."

"Is that where you were all those months? In Mexico?"

"Yeah, and I don't want to talk about it."

He stood up and started pacing. He opened the blinds to look out the front window and released them with a clatter.

"What's taking so long?" I asked.

"City council meeting."

The clock said 6:30. I didn't have much time.

"Tommy, I can help you."

"How? Are you going to get me in on your deal with the Feds?"

"Any deal I had with the Feds ended when I ran. This is

better. All you have to do is untie me and leave. I'll handle Chelly on my own, and you disappear."

"How?"

"You have to untie me to find out."

Tommy side-eyed me. "You have the gun, Tommy. Not me. I wouldn't kill you anyway. But hurry up and decide because once Chelly gets here, it'll be too late." When he didn't answer, I said, "Make a decision, man. You can go live on a beach somewhere and smoke all the weed you want or stay here and kill me. You know that's what's going to happen."

He set the gun down on the table and opened his daddy's pocketknife. He cut the zip ties and I stood. "Go to my place in Tivvydale," I said, rubbing my wrists. "You remember it?"

"Yeah."

"On the worktable is a card for Philomena's Antique Shop. Call it from a burner phone. A woman will answer. Say you're looking for a set of six watermelon drink glasses from the thirties."

"What?"

"Six watermelon drink glasses from the thirties. She'll ask how soon you need them, and you tell her it's a last-minute gift for your sister. She'll tell you when and where to go. You get on my motorcycle and leave. Take back roads to where you're going, ditch your phone, and don't look back."

"This sounds like a TV show."

"Where do you think they get their ideas? Go. Now. Out the back." I gave him the keys to the car I bought from Fred at the CVS. Two thousand in cash for a beater and her silence. She thought it was a pretty good deal. I was relieved the Cutlass made it to Frio. "It's parked on Melvin Avenue. Give me your keys."

Tommy did and was gone.

"Not even a fucking thank you," I said.

Time was running short. But I would be ready.

TWENTY-EIGHT

Marja

Chelly came alone.

"Hi, Chells."

She stopped cold at the old nickname, and her face flushed. She hasn't heard that nickname from my lips for thirty-two years, the day she begged me to leave town. She'd lined up a job for me in Houston with a college friend of hers and had a wad of cash for me to live on for a few months. One of my biggest regrets is not taking the cash and the job. My pride and arrogance caused Darcy a lot of pain over the years, I know that. It's my greatest shame. I suppose that same pride, and my ability to hold a grudge, has landed me here, too.

Scorpios gonna scorpio.

I lifted my hands from the table. "I'm not armed."

Not yet anyway.

"Neither am I."

"Glad we've established that we aren't here to kill each other. Have a seat. Wanna beer?"

"Sure."

I opened the refrigerator and pulled two Shiners from the door and my gun from the milk shelf. When I turned around, Chelly was seated at the table, holding a gun on me.

"Well, well," I said. "We're both liars, then."

"Please, we've known that for years."

I shrugged slightly. I put the beers on the table and sat down. "Now that we've measured our dicks, let's enjoy one last beer."

She laid her gun on the table and opened her beer. I did the same.

"How did you get Tommy to leave?" Chelly asked.

"I promised him beautiful women and a lifetime supply of weed."

"That would do it."

"He's a man of simple tastes," I said.

"He knows too much."

"Maybe, but who in the world is going to believe that a stay-at-home mayor's wife runs the biggest meth business on the border?" I asked. I took a long drink of my beer. God, I'm going to miss Shiner Bock.

"It does seem far-fetched," she admitted with a sly grin.

"I've always wondered how in the world you got involved. You don't seem the type."

"Russell had gambling debts he couldn't repay. We were naive to think that once we laundered enough money through our real estate business that we could get out. But, as you well know, there's only one way you leave the cartel."

"Dead. Once I'm gone, all your problems are solved, and you would finally, finally, be free of your nemesis."

Chelly drank again and when she put the bottle down, she said, "One of them, anyway."

"I can't believe I admired you, once. You were beautiful, intelligent, fun. I thought we were friends."

"We were. You were the first person in this town I connected with, that I enjoyed spending time with. Russell thought it was weird that I was friends with a sixteen-year-old, though that ten-year difference doesn't seem like much now, does it?"

"No."

"You always were an old soul." She tilted her head and studied me. "He did it on purpose, you know. Seduced you. Because he hated that I had a friend, and he wasn't the center of my attention."

"That's fucked up."

"I know. You actually did him a favor when you didn't get an abortion...he said you were demanding he pay you, and that was where the money was going." Chelly scoffed. "I was a fool to believe him. It took me years to realize it was a gambling problem."

"He'd charm the fangs off a rattlesnake, that's for sure."

"Russell was too big of an idiot to launder money, so I stepped in and was good at it. I let it go to my head, the power I had over Russell. He'd had so much over me for all those years, it was nice to see him squirm when I even alluded to the fact I could make one phone call and his debts wouldn't be paid."

"Jesus Christ, Chells."

"Don't act like you don't know what it's like to be independent, to feel you finally have power for the first time in your life. The money was what it was all about. I'm better at laundering than you are, Marja."

"I doubt that. Why did you have Tommy use me? Was it to tie it all around my neck in case you got caught?"

"I'm not going to say that thought didn't cross my mind. No one wants to go to jail, after all. Nope, it was guilt."

"Guilt. You?"

"I believed Russell for years when he said that our money was going to you."

"How could you believe that? You saw how poor we were."

"It was easier to believe you were drinking and smoking your money away than to believe my husband was lying to me. When we needed more businesses to run money through, I asked Tommy to use you."

"To pay me back for all the shit Darcy had to put up with from your daughter."

Chelly looked down and nodded. "Yes." She scoffed. "I was a pretty big idiot for a long time." She looked me in the eye. "I'm really sorry."

"You know I can't forgive you."

"I didn't think you would. Why did you come back?"

"To keep Darcy from having to go into WITSEC."

"How are you going to do that?"

"I'm going to give you the access codes to all of the evidence I have against you, and you're going to kill me."

Chelly's eyes widened, then narrowed. She took a long pull from her beer, her eyes never leaving mine.

"Am I?"

"Yes. You take that info back to the cartel, and my dead body, and your problems are solved. Then, you're going to convince them to leave Darcy alone."

"You're serious," she said.

"One hundred percent."

Chelly opened her mouth to speak, then shut it. Finally, she said, "Why would you do that?"

"Darcy's pregnant."

It was obviously the last thing Chelly expected me to say. "Congratulations."

"If I keep my deal with the Feds, they'll make her go into

WITSEC. She's survived too much, worked too hard to build her life to have to give it up because of my stupid mistakes."

"Don't you think you're taking the whole *do anything for your children* a little too far?"

"Old habits die hard," I said. "The only decision I've ever made for myself was laundering money for extra cash. That's led me here, sitting in my own damn kitchen asking my mortal enemy to kill me. It's not the storybook ending I would have picked, but there you are." I drank the rest of my beer and set the empty bottle down on the table. "Let's get this over with."

"If I kill you, you'll never see your grandchild," Chelly said.

"They'll be better off without me."

"Don't be ridiculous. They'd be lucky to have a grand-mother like you."

I shook my head. "I'll probably fuck them up like I did Darcy."

"Marja," Chelly said quietly. "We all made mistakes, wish we could go back and do things differently. But Darcy is pretty amazing, even I see that. She has more of you in her than Russell, thank God. Jesus, you're sacrificing yourself to protect your daughter and unborn grandchild. How can you even think you're a terrible mom? You're the best mom I've ever known."

My throat thickened, and tears burned my eyes. Grief at never seeing Darcy again, at never getting a chance to hold my grandchild, welled inside me. It was unfair, but my life has always been unfair. The best thing I could do for Darcy and my grandchild was to protect them, to ensure their safety, to make sure they had long, happy lives. This was how to do it. Regrets and sadness were luxuries I didn't have time for.

I stood and wiped my eyes. "I've got plastic on the bed in the back so it's easy to clean up."

Chelly stared at me for a long moment then burst out laughing.

"Stop laughing," I said.

Chelly leaned forward and dipped her head, slapping the table to emphasize her laughter.

My face turned red. "Stop laughing," I said.

Chelly didn't, couldn't, stop. All the years of people talking about me behind my back, the rumors and lies, the stopped conversations, the side-eyed expressions from people at the grocery store rushed over me on a wave of white-hot anger.

I picked the gun up from the table and pushed it roughly against Chelly's head. "STOP LAUGHING!"

Chelly stopped and her body went completely still. Her eyes widened, and she held her hands out in front of her. "Okay, okay, Marja. I'm sorry."

"You're not going to get out of this, Chelly," I growled. "There's no one here to do the dirty work for you. If you want me dead, you're going to have to look me in the eye and pull the trigger yourself."

"I don't want you dead, Marja. I've never wanted you dead."

"Then why did you send a cartel hit men after me and Darcy?"

"I didn't send the last two. That *was* the cartel. I swear I had nothing to do with it. They decided we couldn't get it done and took matters in their own hands. The last two was Cooper. He's on the take and has been for years. Look, Marja, just put the gun down and listen to me, okay?"

"Why should I listen to you?"

"Because I've been trying to get you out, to save you, for the last three years. I sent the first man, yes, but he wasn't with the cartel, and he wasn't a hit man. We were going to help you disappear. But it needed to look like you were taken, to sell it to Cooper. I told her we should have let you in on the plan, but she said it was too risky, you would have never trusted either one of us."

"What the hell are you talking about? Who?"

The screen door opened.

"Me." Lena stood at the door, holding a gun on me.

"Lena? What the hell?"

"Plan C," Lena said, and pulled the trigger.

TWENTY-NINE

Darcy

It's been two weeks since Marja's late night phone call. She told me I might not hear from her again, and I haven't. I don't know if she's alive or dead, or if the FBI has her stashed somewhere torturing her into telling them all she knows about money laundering for Russell and Chelly Clarke.

I've memorized our conversation and replay it in my head every day.

"Momma, where are you?"

"Where everyone would least expect. Listen, I don't have much time. I figured the chances of them monitoring Ella's phone was the least likely."

"Smart."

"I just wanted to tell you how much I love you. You've been the brightest part of my life and I'm very proud of you."

"Stop talking like this." My throat thickened with emotion, and Chloe put her arm around my shoulder. I leaned into her, felt her strength coursing through me.

"I have to. We might not ever see each other again."

"Momma, stop it."

"Listen to me, Darcy, if anything happens to me, you might not know about it for a while, if ever. Just imagine me sailing around the world, the wind blowing through my hair, a kicking tan, and a beautiful woman by my side."

"Momma, you don't know how to sail."

"I read about it in a book."

My laugh was half a sob. "Of course you did."

"I love you. You and Chloe are going to make fantastic parents to my grandchild."

"But, I haven't de—"

"If you ever meet a guy named King, trust him."

"What?"

"Love you baby girl. Gotta go."

And she was gone.

I haven't heard from her or anyone for two weeks. The FBI is ignoring my calls. Every time the door to a bar or café opens, I turn my head and expect to see Marja walk through the door.

Today is Friday. The holidays have come and gone with no word from Marja. I do as she says and imagine her sailing around the world. Maybe it's because I've thought of her that way for so long, she really seems to fit that life. I hope she's happy, wherever she is.

This is our last day working in the co-op space. We move into our offices near Grant Park next week. Chloe is there putting the finishing touches on everything, which means hanging her award-winning photos with exacting standards. I feel sorry for the workmen.

I didn't see King for a couple of months after our ill-fated road trip, had completely forgotten about him to be honest. It crossed my mind briefly that he was who Marja was telling me about, but what were the chances? It turns out his real name is Richard Ryan, and he goes by King because he's a fan of the LA hockey team. Besides, how in the hell could Marja have ever met him?

I am packing up for the day; I have an hour to get to my doctor's appointment. At the exit, I run into Special Agent Anderson. Quite literally collide with her.

"Oh, hello. Agent—" I almost said Agent Scully. It has nothing to do with the fact that the four of us have been marathoning *The X-Files* for months.

"Anderson, but you can call me Stacie."

"Oh. Okay. What brings you here? Or has the FBI figured out this is a hot bed of digital nomad tax evaders and decided to lull them all into a sense of awe by sending Agent Scully to work among them?"

Stacie Anderson laughs. "No, but that's a pretty good idea. I'll pass it on to the IRS."

"Well, good to see you. I have an—"

"I came to see you. This will only take a minute." She motions for me to go back through the door, and when I do, she asks me to follow her.

She leads me through the common area, where she turns more than a few heads, though maybe the sight of two smoking hot redheads walking through the office is rare enough that people notice. (Chloe has called me smoking hot enough that I'm almost starting to believe it.)

Yes, things are going great.

No, I'm not going to tell you about our sex life.

Agent Scully leads me to the back stairwell, and we go up a floor, down another long hall.

My imagination is going crazy. Momma's here. Agent Scully's taking me to see her and has to be clandestine about it because Momma's in WITSEC. Oh my God, is she about to kidnap me into WITSEC because I know too much? It's been nearly four months, why would they come for me now?

My heart is hammering, palms sweating, when Agent Anderson opens the door to an office. I walk in behind her and my heart plummets. It's empty. Completely bare except for tangled cords coming out of the wall and the stale smell of coffee and cigarettes.

"Sorry for the subterfuge. There really is no privacy in those co-ops, and I didn't want you to have to gather yourself to walk through the common area."

Stacie's gaze latches on to mine.

"She's dead then."

"Yes."

I took a deep breath. "When?"

"Two days after she left you."

"What? Why am I only being told now?"

"I just found out. The agents on the case were reassigned, and the new agents assumed you had been told."

"How did you find out?"

"Lena called and asked me to check in on you."

"Where is she?"

"Alaska. I'm sorry for your loss, Darcy."

"Thank you."

"Is there anything I can do for you? Get you?" Stacie said.

"How did she die?"

Stacie's mouth twitched slightly, before her professional mask returned. "She was shot."

"You saw her?"

"The photos, yes."

"And they're authentic?"

"Seem to be."

I nodded, staring at the jumble of cords.

"Are you sure I can't give you a ride somewhere? Maybe call your girlfriend?"

"No. I just want to be alone for a minute."

Stacie nodded and went to the door. Her hand on the knob, she said, "It was weird, though. After she died, the new agents shut the case down within a week."

"Shut it down?"

"I guess her cartel secrets died with her."

"She didn't have any cartel secrets. She only worked for a local couple in Frio. They were the real connection."

Stacie raised her eyebrows. "Interesting. That wasn't in the final report."

"What happened to her body?"

"Cremated."

"Without my permission?"

"She'd signed a statement with the Bureau for what was to happen with her body in the event something like this happened. It must not have mentioned calling you."

Pain pierced my heart. "I've heard enough, thank you."

"You haven't been contacted by anyone at all? Anyone new come into your life recently?"

"Besides investors, no."

"Let me know if you do. Something doesn't add up."

"That's Marja for you, irritating you from beyond the grave."

Stacie smiled and was gone. I leaned against the wall and slid down to sit on the floor. Marja is dead. Gone. I knew I was sad more than I felt sad. I'd been preparing myself for this news for months. I suppose that had blunted its impact. My life has been insane, and I've barely had time to breathe, let alone mourn. I'm sure it will come at the worst possible time.

The door opened and I jumped. King closed the door behind him.

"Hey, Darce." His voice sounded weird. It sounded…normal. Not like the beach bum, douchebro voice he'd been using for months.

"Did Marja send you to watch out for me?"

He smiled. "Marja told me you'd sniff me out. I felt sure the surfer dude 'taxes are tyranny' would throw you off the scent."

"She said if I met a man named King I should trust him. You should have used a generic name like Jay or Gary or Kevin."

He chuckled. "What did Gillian Anderson want?"

"She told me Marja's dead."

King nodded solemnly. "How are you doing?"

"I've been better, but I've been worse, too. It's complicated."

He nodded. "I hear ya." He cleared his throat, reached into his messenger bag, and pulled out a slim 4″ x 6″ envelope. "Marja wanted me to give you this." He crouched next to me and whispered, "It's account numbers and passwords for you. Website addresses, too. You know how to use the dark web?"

"Why would I know how to use the dark web?"

"I can teach you."

"This is my last day here."

"Yeah, I know. Very cool, getting new offices. Here's the thing, I'm a bit of a jack-of-all-trades when it comes to computers and finances."

"You're a money launderer."

"The PC term is cleaner, Fitz, and that's not what this is. This money is clean, and in accounts that are private. Marja wanted to make sure you were taken care of if something happened to her."

"So, she's giving me money I can't use unless I want the IRS to be on my ass."

"Again, I can help you with that at work."

"At work?"

"Did I mention that I've been hired by your VC company to create your new and improved Wander Women website?"

"No, you have not."

"We'll be working together a lot."

"So, it seems."

"I'm one of the good ones. I promise."

"The proof is in the pudding, dude."

He stood. "I love pudding! Will there be pudding in the break room?"

I laughed. "I'll see what I can do."

"Excellent. You're late for your doctor's appointment."

"We're going to have to talk about privacy and boundaries, King. First, help me up."

He held out his hand and heaved me up off the floor.

"I haven't hacked your computer. I'm just an excellent eavesdropper."

"Boundaries."

"Got it. Oh, one more thing." He reached into his backpack and pulled out a postcard. "This came to my address, but I think it's for you." He handed me the card and with a wink, walked out the door.

The front of the card was a photo of a catamaran in full sail on a crystal clear blue sea, a sandy beach in the background. The opposite side was blank, save a postmark from Tahiti dated January 1.

I was the last one to the OB's office, which was a problem since I was the patient. Chloe stood as soon as I walked into the waiting room.

"She's here. That's her," Chloe said to the receptionist.

The woman smiled. "Thank God you're here. We were about to have to take your partner back and put her on oxygen."

"I wasn't that bad."

"Yeah, you were," Robert said.

"We told Chloe she was being ridiculous," Michael said. Robert and Eloise stood behind him, nodding.

"You're a grown woman and can take care of yourself, Darcy," Eloise said.

"Are you okay?" Michael said. "Feeling sick or anything?"

"No, not as bad as I was."

"Good to hear."

"Okay, Eloise. I think we should go," Robert said.

"No, I want to wait in the lobby until they're done."

Robert sighed and sat down, mumbling, "We're taking up 20 percent of their chairs but okay. Fine."

The months after I broke it off with Michael were tense, to say the least. My decision to keep the baby wasn't easy or quick. After the initial sonogram confirmed it wasn't an ectopic pregnancy and that the IUD hadn't had time to grow into the uterus, the device had been removed and I had a decision to make. I talked to Chloe, Jess, and Ella, and decided that my situation was completely different from my mother's. I would have help from all sides. Michael had been chastened by his father, the threat of taking away his trust fund was a pretty big stick, and Michael and Eloise agreed to every condition I set. Between the Parsons, me, Chloe, Jess, and Ella, this baby would be well taken care of.

That was all well and good and a huge relief off my shoulders. But the deciding factor was Chloe. We would never have the chance to share a child in the same way as this one. Since I planned to spend the rest of my life with her and trusted her with my life, and our child's, it was an easy call. It was difficult to understand how little I cared about giving up my long-held intention of never getting pregnant. I suppose being in love and being loved makes all the difference.

Chloe pulled me a little aside. "Are you okay? You weren't answering your texts."

"I am now. I saw Agent Scully."

Chloe's face dropped. "Oh no."

"Yes."

"Fitz, I'm so sorry." She pulled me into her arms and her energy and strength surged through me. I would feel weak, needing this from her, if she hadn't told me that hugging me made her feel the same way.

"Thanks, Coco." She pulled back and smiled. The nickname was new, and she really liked it. I did, too.

"I'll tell you all about it tonight, but I also got this today."

Coco took the postcard in confusion, which only grew when she looked at the back addressed to King.

"Is this that libertarian douche at the co-op?"

"Yes. Look at the postmark."

She did and flipped the card back over. A huge smile broke across her face.

"Holy fuck she did it."

"Apparently she did. I have no idea how."

"Oh my God, what, who, when? I'm so confused."

"Just as Marja would like it."

"She really is a piece of work."

"She is."

A door opened and a nurse called for Darcy. Michael and Chloe followed me to the door.

I smiled at them both. "Let's go meet our baby."

EPILOGUE

Bali in December is the perfect spot for a wedding. At least according to Wander Women's star founders, Fitz and Coco. For the last three years, they have been traveling the world with their toddler daughter, Julia Fitz-Coco (not her real name, or is it?), writing about how to travel with a child and an evangelical dog named Helen. And making it look easy.

Helen, of course, has her own Instagram and more followers than Fitz's or Coco's accounts, combined. It has gone to her head, as well. Bless her.

Wander Women is a phenomenon. A few men try to troll them for focusing only on women, but more men come to their defense, especially solo travelers, happy to get the female perspective on travel. They've started a travel line of luggage for each vertical—family, adventure, and wine suitcases (their best seller by far)—and are partnering with a designer to create a travel capsule wardrobe for all seasons and adventures, to take the stress out of packing.

Darcy, Chloe, Jess, and Ella have been going a mile a minute for three years, but for the next two weeks, they're taking a break. The website might be updated, there might be a podcast, but no one is promising anything. The entire Wander Woman team is invited and coming to the wedding. They are there to have fun, not work. But let's be honest, everyone's Instagram will be blowing up with images of the hotel (which is hosting and excited for the free publicity) and all of the fun they'll be having. King is in charge of all of that. He is excellent at organizing parties, it turns out. Darcy and Chloe are focused on each other, getting married, and spending time with their precocious daughter, who resembles her maternal grandmother in personality more and more each day.

I've followed it all.

I've anchored my catamaran in the ocean within sight of the resort where Darcy and Chloe are getting married. Every morning I get up, take care of my boat, eat breakfast, and settle in a chair, with a pair of high-powered binoculars trained on the beach. King has been feeding me information about the wedding and all of the events, and I've read it so many times, I know it by heart.

My heart clenches every time I see Julia. My God, she is so beautiful and radiant. She laughs constantly and charms the pants off of everyone, even the cabana boy who doesn't speak a lick of English. Julia speaks Indonesian only a little, King says, not as well as Spanish and French.

She's three, and she's the most brilliant child in the world.

My arms ache to hold her, but I know I can't. Not yet. Maybe one day, but it doesn't seem that the FBI and DEA want to pull the trigger on charging the cartel. Instead, they are risking Chelly's and Russell's lives by making them continue to feed information to the government.

I don't really give a shit about Russell, but I'm sorry that Chelly can't escape.

Today is the wedding day, and I've watched the hotel employees set up for a sunset wedding. I have champagne chilling and a charcuterie board ready to celebrate during the reception.

It's cold comfort, but it will have to do.

The sun is starting to set. It's almost time.

A cold beer is pressed to my neck. I look up. Lena smiles down at me, a huge straw sunhat blocking out the sun behind her.

"Hello, beautiful."

She leans down and kisses me. I can't help it, I sigh with pleasure. It never gets old, being kissed by Elena González.

Between us, she puts a standing wine bucket with champagne and two flutes buried in the ice. She sits in the chair next to me and raises her own binoculars.

"This is great and all, but I liked our ceremony better," Lena says.

"In the middle of the ocean with no witnesses?"

"The whale was a witness."

"True. You're lucky I agreed to even that considering you shot me."

"With a tranq dart. You didn't even feel it."

"Oh, I felt the betrayal of the woman I loved shooting me in those milliseconds, believe me."

"It worked, didn't it?"

"I suppose so."

I'd woken up, twelve hours later, on a private jet on my way to I didn't know where, with Lena hovering over me with a smile.

"Plan C worked."

It took me a moment for my head to clear and realize what was going on. Actually, I still didn't know what was going on.

"It would have been nice to fucking know what plan C was."

"If I would have told you, it wouldn't have worked."

"Explain it to me. Use small words. My head hurts like a motherfucker."

"I realized early on that you were far down on the pecking order, that you didn't have a direct connection to the cartel. It took me nine months to figure out it was the Clarkes, one more to figure out it was Chelly, and two weeks to figure out how to turn her. That's when I left.

"When Tommy told Chelly you wanted out, she was going to make it happen. She thought there were enough layers between you and the cartel. But Russell let it slip to someone, and the cartel was going to kill you. She sent Russell to scare you to stay. I think she was relieved when I caught her. Getting you out was part of the deal, and making sure Darcy was safe."

"You planned to fake my death all along."

"Yes. We sent the first guy to kidnap you, not hurt you. I didn't know you had a gun."

"You were doing this all behind Cooper's back?"

"Yes, which complicated things."

"Is he in jail?"

"No. We don't want to alert the cartel that Chelly's working for us. They don't have a chance."

It took months to sink in, to reset all my interactions with Chelly over the years into a new paradigm, a new perspective. My perceptions were so solidified against her, it took quite a bit of soul-searching to accept that she was more complicated than I gave her credit for, that maybe she was a victim of Russell Clarke, too.

I turn to gaze at Lena, my beautiful partner. She'd given up her career for me, but not before making sure Marja Evans was dead and buried. She met me in Zihuatanejo a year later, and we've been sailing around the Pacific since. One day we will make it to Europe. Maybe. I've become rather fond of East Asia. I might never leave.

The wedding is about to begin. Julia and Helen are ready to walk down the aisle. Chloe and Darcy are holding hands, waiting for their cue to walk down the aisle together. King goes up to them and whispers in their ears. Their faces show shock, then happiness. They look out to the ocean. Toward my boat, *Clean Livin'*. They grin and wave. I wave back, though I know they can't see me.

Darcy kisses Chloe and they start walking down the aisle. I've never seen Darcy happier.

Peace settles over me, and I am whole.

★ ★ ★ ★ ★

ACKNOWLEDGEMENTS

This is my COVID book. And my divorce book. And my coming-out book. And my empty-nester book. And my digital-nomad book. And my buying-a-home book. And my first-girlfriend book.

It shouldn't come as a surprise, then, that it took me four years to finish and included three partial drafts, an 85K completed and trunked MS, and a from-scratch rewrite. That rewrite is the book you hold in your hands. In pure word count, I could have started and finished three books. I love these characters and I hate these characters. I love this book and I hate it.

I am, in a word, ambivalent.

On a good day, writing is hard. This book was brutal for all the reasons above and the tiny little details and life events that fan out from the big events like limbs on a tree. But I finished it and lo and behold, when I reread it during edits, it was much better than it had any right to be.

I started this book so long ago I should probably do a blanket thank-you to everyone I've talked to since 2018. So, thanks.

But there are those who need specific shout-outs.

To my sons, Ryan & Jack Lenhardt, for your love and understanding and being such amazing men. Raising you two is, and always will be, my greatest achievement.

To my family for the unwavering support and love you gave me during a very difficult time in my life: Linda Whitley, Stephen Whitley, Tommy & Tricia Teague, Brandon & Lia Brewer, Whitley & Jordan Teague.

To Jenny Martin, for everything and more. I seriously don't know what I would have done without your friendship these last four years. And to Chris & Conor, for welcoming a virtual stranger and making me feel at home.

To everyone at DFW Writers' Workshop, but especially Leslie Lutz, John Bartell, Brian Tracy, Brooke Fossey, & Katie Bernet.

To Blake Leyers & Christine Carbo, for long-distance professional and personal support. Wish I could see you both more!

To my divorce lawyer & my therapist. Obviously.

To my Winnsboro peeps for being there for me: Kelli Geraci, Jo Porterfield, Jane St. Romain, Diane Connor, Brenda Morey, Rachel Conner, CJ Thatcher, Cyndie Ewert, Mary White, & so many others.

To Diane & Walker Fenci & Kim & Terry Conaty, for encouragement, support, and lending an ear to listen or a shoulder to cry on.

To old friends who supported me, and new friends who've reminded me that I am a friend worth having: Jill Grawe, Sara Pearson, Jennifer Jackson, Donna Ledbetter, Melanie Walz, Autumn Van Volkenburg, & S.

To Carrie Frisbie, for being the person I can talk to for hours at Katy Trail Ice House and it seems like thirty minutes. To James Frisbie, for not freaking out too much when our happy hour turned into happy six hours.

To Michele Bidelspach & everyone at Graydon House, for

being patient through so many ups and downs and versions of a very simple "what about a mother/daughter road trip?" pitch.

To Rebecca Slorach and the entire Mills & Boon team, for your love and enthusiasm for *The Secret of You and Me* and *Run Baby Run*. You guys are the best!

To Alice Speilburg, my agent extraordinaire. It's been a roller coaster these last few years, I know. Thanks for being there for me professionally and personally. *Thanks* doesn't seem like a big enough word, to be honest.

To Janie Milman & Mickey Wilson, for welcoming me to Chez Castillon and creating the environment and space for me to finish this book. I love you two to bits!

To Hazel, you big, beautiful galoot.

Last but certainly not least, to Julie Cohen. You've brought such happiness and joy to my life. I love so many things about you, but I especially love the way you look at me when you think about dogs.

Thank you all so very much.

I have loved Marja from the first moment she walked into my head, and I knew that hers was a story I wanted to tell. In the end, this is a story about being a parent, choosing to and not choosing to, and about unconditional love and sacrifice. I hope it makes you laugh and cry, and maybe surprise you here and there.

Happy reading!
xoxoxo
Mel

Loved **Run Baby Run?**

Try another uplifting romance from Melissa Lenhardt
The Secret of You and Me

Turn the page for a sneak peak at chapter one.

MILLS & BOON

nora

I'm not a war hero, nor have I ever claimed to be. I'm a war hero like anyone who wears the uniform is deemed a hero, by merely doing the job we signed up for, volunteered for, or were, sometimes, persuaded into doing.

I stared down a never-ending line of people who knew me, but whom I couldn't remember to save my life. I smiled and shook hands and listened to them shower me with platitudes, and thank me for my service, though I'd been out of the army for eight years. Seemed like yesterday. Seemed like forever ago.

"Your father was proud of you."

"Proudest day of his life when you deployed over to kick some Saddam Hussein ass. Thank you for your service."

"To hear old Noakes talk you'da thought you toppled that statue yourself. You didn't, did you?"

"Talked about you all the time."

"Loved you so much."

"So proud. Thank you for your service."

"He missed you but understood how important your job is."

"Kept everyone up-to-date on your career."

I caught Emmadean's eye with a clear *What the hell are these people talking about?* expression.

She shrugged a shoulder and took the man in front of me off my hands. "Earl, thanks for coming."

Mary, on my opposite side, leaned near me and whispered, "Rest assured, Pop hated you. Emmadean's who talks you up." She leaned away and smiled at the woman in front of her. "Hello, Mrs. Wyatt. Thanks for the enchiladas."

"They weren't too spicy, were they?"

"No, they were perfect."

My stomach twisted. *This* woman I knew. Joyce Wyatt's hair had gone from a dark brown *Steel Magnolias* football helmet to a blond *Steel Magnolias* football helmet. Her solution to going gray, I supposed. It wasn't a bad look on her, but hair dye couldn't mask the fine wrinkles mapping her still-lovely face. She held her purse tightly in front of her and looked at me with a hesitant expression as if she wasn't sure how she would be received. I held out my hands. "I should have known those enchiladas were from you. They were delicious."

Mrs. Wyatt sagged with relief. Holding hands wasn't enough for her. She pulled me into her arms. "Nora. I've missed you so," she whispered in my ear.

"I've missed you, too," I said.

She pulled back. "When you left so suddenly, then didn't call...?"

She waited for the explanation that never came, and one I would never give. "Mrs. Wyatt, that was all a long time ago."

She nodded and sniffed as if struggling to hold back her emotions. "I suppose so." She turned her head and stared into the distance behind me, at my father's coffin. "I can't believe it's been nearly twenty years." She shook her head, returned her attention to me and said, "You didn't break only Charlie's heart, leaving like that."

"I would have been a terrible daughter-in-law and an even worse wife."

"Couldn't have been any worse th—" Good manners took over, and Joyce Wyatt didn't finish.

I forced a smile and remained silent. Mrs. Wyatt sighed, understanding that was as close to an apology as I was going to give.

"I'm sorry about your father."

"Thank you."

"Are you staying in town long?"

In my peripheral vision, I saw Mary turn her head slightly in my direction, though she continued to talk to Mr. Wyatt. "I'm not sure. It depends on what needs to be done."

Mr. Wyatt stepped towards me. "Nora. We hope to see you again before you go. Stop by so we can catch up."

The Wyatts nodded and moved on to console Emmadean and Dormer. As sweet as the Wyatts were, and as much as I had loved them when Charlie and I dated, I had no intention of going over for a visit. I didn't want to have to lie to them and try to avoid their questions.

In the brief break between the Wyatts and the next mourner, I looked down the never-ending line. "Christ, is that Jamie Luke?"

Mary leaned over. "It is. And Tiffany Williams and Kim Stopper." Kim saw us, grinned and waved vigorously from her hip as if trying to hide her excitement at seeing me. The other two waved more demurely, in keeping with a Texas funeral visitation where the deceased lay in repose in the open casket not ten feet away. It had taken longer to wrangle the kids than I thought—those DQ dip cones had probably been a mistake—but there had been a silver lining: I hadn't had to pay my respects to my father's body before mourners started lining up to tell us how sad they were to see old Ray Noakes go before his time.

A stout man wearing a polyester Western sports coat and buff-colored cowboy hat, and smelling strongly of Stetson cologne, stepped forward and greeted Mary and me together. When he held out his hand to shake Mary's, I saw the gun holstered on his right hip, next to his Ranger star.

"Rick Michaels," he said, shaking our hands in turn, and wheezing as if he'd just climbed ten flights of stairs. "Worked with Ray for fifteen years or so. Started just after you enlisted. Thank you for your service."

I gritted my teeth and nodded my thanks.

"Pop spoke of you often, Mr. Michaels," Mary said.

"He was a good man. Solid. Trust him with my life. And my wife."

Though he and Pop were sworn peace officers—Texas Rangers—they worked the cases involving farm and ranch crimes through the Texas and Southwestern Cattleman's Association, a surprisingly busy beat since meth heads had taken to stealing and selling cows and farm equipment for drug money.

"Is your life in danger often, chasing cattle rustlers and tractor thieves?" I said.

Michaels lifted his chin, offended, but willing to let it pass because I was grieving. Condescension oozed from him. "We caught the tweakers who killed your dad."

"Thank the Lord," Emmadean said.

"Just took them into custody this morning after they tried to sell the tractor they stole the night Ray died. They were so high that night they didn't even remember Ray was there. Doubt we'll ever know what happened exactly."

"At least you caught them," Dormer said.

"Oh, they'll be put away for a long time, rest assured. Sorry for your loss. Ray's gonna be sorely missed."

The Ranger had barely moved away when Jamie, Tiffany, and Kim were on me, hugging me like I was their long-lost friend. The truth was, there had been a long-running competition between all of us. I'd assumed it had fizzled with time, but if the way Jamie and Tiffany were sizing me up was any indication, the game was still on for them. Nor had the dynamic between the three seem to have changed; Jamie and Tiffany controlled the conversation, while Kim hung on, desperately trying to get a word in edgewise, and be noticed.

"My God, Nora Noakes, you look *exactly* like you did in high school," Tiffany said.

Jamie looked me up and down. "It's good to see being in the military didn't turn you butch."

"Depends on your definition of butch. One definition, my personal favorite, is being able to kill a man with your bare hands. In that regard yes, the military turned me butch."

Mary barked out a laugh. Jamie was stunned into silence (mission accomplished) so Tiffany jumped in.

"You're just as pretty as the day you were crowned homecoming queen. Same haircut, I see," Tiffany said.

"I was football sweetheart," I clarified.

"That's right," Tiffany said. "Sophie was homecoming queen. You two won everything, didn't you?"

"We tried," I said.

"Have you seen Sophie?" Jamie asked, her eyebrows arching.

Of the three, Jamie had always been the cattiest, the one with the instinctive ability to know someone's soft spot and poke at it until it was inflamed. I smiled at her, feeling nothing but pity. She was trying to psychologically torture the wrong person.

"Not yet."

"I'm sorry about your dad," Kim said, grasping my forearm. "I lost my father a few years ago, so I understand how difficult…" She swallowed. "If you want to talk—"

"It's hardly the same thing," Tiffany said. "You adored your father. You lived next door to him, for Christsakes. Nora hasn't been back to Lynchfield in, what? Twenty years?"

"Eighteen. The anniversary is next Saturday. I celebrate it every year. Maybe we can celebrate it together this year?"

Jamie, Tiffany and Kim stared at me, their smiles fixed somewhere between amusement and anger. Kim finally said, "That's Charlie's fund raiser. He's running for State Senate, you know."

"I did not."

"I'm sure Sophie and Charlie would love to have you there."

My smile froze, and there was a spark of triumph in Jamie's eyes. I forced my smile to relax, leaned forward and whispered, "Every fund raiser I've been to in DC has free-flowing alcohol. Think Charlie will too, or are the Baptists around here still pretending not to drink?"

"Oh, I don't think—" Kim started.

"Are you implying we're hypocrites?" a cold female voice said from behind the trio. Jamie, Tiffany and Kim parted, eyes wide, to make way for Brenda Russell: tall, elegant, dripping with gold jewelry and stinking of Chanel No. 5. I struggled to swallow the bile that rose in my throat, an automatic reaction the scent had triggered in me since I was eighteen years old.

"Brenda."

Brenda Russell's nostrils flared at my use of her Christian name. Check that, her first name. Though professing to be devout, there was nothing Christ-like in the woman. I looked for her husband. "Where's Doug?"

"He died of cancer three years ago."

"Did he?" Everyone waited for me to offer my condolences,

but I merely stared at the woman. I'd rather be waterboarded than offer her an ounce of sympathy.

"How are you doing, Mrs. Russell?" my sister said.

"As well as can be expected. I'm sorry for your loss," Brenda said to Mary. "Your father was a fine, Christian man. Moral and always willing to do what was right, regardless of the consequences."

I clasped my hands in front of me and kept my expression placid. I might have envisioned her face a time or two during my sparring sessions, but the woman who stood before me bore only a passing resemblance to the woman from twenty years earlier. Her hair was the same style, but entirely gray. Her face, once perpetually tanned and smooth, was lined with wrinkles and freckled with sunspots her foundation couldn't mask. The deepest wrinkles were around her pursed mouth and looked strikingly like spokes on a wheel.

"How's Sophie?" I didn't care or want to know the answer. But, I wanted to see the expression on Brenda's face when I said her daughter's name. Brenda Russell didn't disappoint. I smirked, and she knew I was baiting her. From the corner of my eye, I saw Jamie look on with an admiring expression. Approval from that corner made me feel petty and small, but not enough to apologize to Brenda Russell.

The line was backing up, so Brenda moved on to Emmadean, as did the other three, though reluctantly. I placed a hand on Kim's arm. "Thank you for the offer. I appreciate it, and I'm sorry to hear about your father."

Kim grasped my hand and smiled. She swallowed thickly. "Thank you, Nora. It's so good to see you, I wish it wasn't under these circumstances…"

"It's good to see you, too, Kim."

"I've always liked your hair," she said. "It's classic. Don't let Jamie give you shit. You should see some of the hairstyles she's gone through in the last twenty years." She winked at me and went to pay her respects to my father. I smiled at the sight of Jamie and Tiffany scurrying after Kim for a change to find out what we talked about.

I ran my hand down my hair. It wasn't the same haircut, though it was a variation on the same theme. A *lob*. Long enough for a ponytail but not so long that it took forever to dry. Simple and professional. I'd gotten bangs after getting out of the army. Big mistake. Now I settled for tucking my hair behind my ears and, if I was trying to be fancy, letting it drape across one eye. I was rarely fancy.

"Your hair is fine," Mary said.

Fucking Jamie Luke.

"Why do you hate Brenda Russell?" Mary asked. "She didn't cheat on you; Charlie and Sophie did."

"It's complicated."

"To not offer condolences is incredibly rude, especially for you. Brenda Russell loved you."

It was true. There was a time when Brenda Russell treated me like a daughter. I practically lived at their house each summer from the time I was ten years old. Brenda and Sophie got along better when I was around, and I'd acted many, many times as a buffer when we were young, and a go-between when Sophie and I were teens. I'd admired Brenda, with her beauty and poise and her generous heart. Doug had been a quiet man who worked all the time. He gave me distracted smiles and pats on the head, and always cheered the loudest at my tennis matches, seemingly as happy for my successes as he was for Sophie's. I think he was making up for the fact that my father rarely came. It had been a shock when the Russells turned on me so thoroughly, and cut me out of their lives.

My stomach clenched at the memory, at the lingering—or

was it imagined?—scent of Chanel No. 5. "Not at the end, she didn't."

"Hey, look down the line. Charlie's here. No Sophie, though."

I followed Mary's gaze and still only saw a bunch of vaguely familiar strangers. "Where?"

"Last in line."

"The bald guy?"

"Yep. Charlie's still got those eyes, though."

I felt those eyes on me as we went through the remainder of the mourners, willing it to be over, but dreading the final greeting. Charlie Wyatt shook Mary's hand. "I saw Jeremy outside with the kids. They were pretty wired for a visitation."

I tried to look as innocent as possible.

"I better go check on him," Mary said. She looked as exhausted as I felt. My cheeks were sore from holding an appropriately sad smile, one that said it's nice to see you but the *circumstances*. Putting people at ease was a strength of mine, but today's performance had been taxing in unexpected ways.

"Emmadean, Dormer. Sorry for your loss," Charlie said. He leaned in and hugged Emmadean.

"Charlie, thanks for coming," Emmadean said.

Everyone moved away to give us privacy, and I was left alone with my first boyfriend, my first lover, the person I'd thought I'd spend the rest of my life with. He was familiar and foreign all at once. When he looked at me with those eyes and that smile, he still managed to make my stomach flutter, after all this time.

He inhaled, his gaze roaming over my face. "NoNo."

I gritted my teeth at the nickname, but smiled and said, "Hi, Charlie." My gaze landed on his shiny bald head. "What the hell happened to your hair?"

He laughed, the corners of his pale blue eyes crinkled and

that damn dimple appeared on his left cheek. The Deadly Dimple, Sophie and I had called it. It still was. "How many times have you heard 'You haven't changed a bit' tonight?" Charlie asked.

"With you, over a thousand."

"Well, you haven't."

"I live a pure life."

"Ha. I doubt that." He put his hands in his suit pants pockets. The top button of his shirt was unbuttoned and his blue tie, which set off his eyes in a mesmerizing way, was loosened. I wondered if Sophie had picked it out. "How have you been?" he asked.

"Good. Fantastic. How about you?"

He shrugged and looked around. "I'm still in Lynchfield."

"Wasn't that the plan?"

A sheepish smile. "Yes."

"I hear you're right on track. Law practice, now running for State Senate?"

"Yep." He nodded. "It wasn't always easy." He caught my eye and looked away.

"Anything worth having is never easy, is it?"

"I suppose not."

The funeral director walked into the room on soft feet and with a polite, grieving smile. He met Emmadean and Dormer at my father's casket and spoke in a low voice about whatever was next on the list of tasks for a grieving family.

I steeled myself to ask about Sophie when a young woman walked down the aisle, her head buried in her phone. Her dark hair hung down past her shoulders, save a small braided portion near her hairline. She was tall and thin, with coltish legs jutting from beneath her thigh-length black sundress. The sleeves of a pale pink summer sweater were pushed halfway up her forearms. When she finally looked up from her phone, I inhaled sharply, and loudly enough for Charlie to notice.

"I know, right?" he said.

Sophie's daughter stopped by her father and appraised me with aquamarine eyes that she'd obviously inherited from Charlie. But, the Bette Davis eyes, the thick lashes that curved almost to her dark eyebrows, the full lips, those were pure Sophie.

"Nora, this is my daughter, Logan."

"I've heard a lot about you."

I shuddered to think of what she'd heard. "Nice to meet you."

"Logan's a junior," Charlie said.

"Rising senior," Logan corrected him. "School just ended. I'm sorry about your dad. That's gotta suck."

"Logan," Charlie chided.

"What? It does. I don't know what I'd do if you died."

Charlie pulled his daughter into a one-armed hug. "You won't have to worry about that for years."

"You don't know that. I'm sure Mr. Noakes didn't expect to be run over by a bunch of cows, either." She snapped her fingers. "It can happen just like that."

"Well, my pop *was* sixty-five years old," I said.

"True," Logan said. Her mouth twisted into a crooked smile, and I almost burst into tears at the sight of the familiar mannerism. "Still, what a way to go." She appraised me again. "So. Why haven't you been back to Lynchfield?"

"Logan," Charlie said, pulling his daughter into a playful headlock.

"No, it's okay." She was direct and bold, and utterly guileless, just like her mother had been. I liked Logan immensely. "My father kicked me out of the house. Told me never to return. So I didn't."

"Harsh," Logan said, at the same time Charlie said, "What?"

I ignored Charlie. "Is Sophie hiding in the car?"

"No." Logan became interested in her phone again and said, dismissively, "She doesn't feel well. A migraine." She was lying. Unsurprising, under the circumstances, but Logan's embarrassment at her mother's absence was interesting.

"She'll be at the funeral tomorrow," Charlie promised.

"Excuse me. Nora?" The funeral director had impeccable timing. "We're getting ready to close the casket, would you like a few moments before we do?"

"Yes," I lied. "Thank you."

"We should go," Charlie said. "See you tomorrow."

I smiled and offered a half-hearted wave.

Emmadean and Dormer came up beside me. Emmadean rubbed my back. "You okay, honey?"

"Yes. Where'd Mary go?"

"The kids."

I rolled my eyes. The kids were Mary's built-in excuse for everything.

"Come on, Emmadean," Dormer said in his soft drawl. "Let's give Nora some time alone with Ray."

He nodded, his gentle eyes full of understanding. Dormer was a soft-spoken, solitary man of few words. He rarely offered his opinion, so when he spoke, everyone took his word as law and obeyed almost without question. When Dormer closed the door behind them, I sank down into the nearest chair, exhausted. My head hurt, and my face ached from smiling. I rubbed my stomach, trying to massage away the squirming bundle of emotions that woke at the sight of Charlie and Logan Wyatt.

I inhaled and forced myself to look at my father's polished cherrywood casket. Rather showy for a salt-of-the-earth man like Raymond Noakes. Mary's doing, no doubt. It would have been more appropriate for the bastard to be propped up against the wall in a pine box like the bandits of the Old West. I chuckled. "You would have loved that, wouldn't you?"

From my vantage point, I could only see Ray in profile, his broad forehead beneath a thick mane of hair, his nose arching up and dipping down to point to his handlebar mustache, which had gone completely gray in the last two decades. Emmadean told me Ray had been found facedown, his arms covering his head, which explained why his face was unmarred by hoof prints. The back of his head, set deep into a soft pillow, hadn't been so fortunate, but Dormer said you couldn't tell at all. Ray looked like he was taking a power nap, something he'd done in his recliner at lunchtime for forty years. The Mardell Funeral Home always had done nice work.

The crown of Ray's straw Stetson poked up from his stomach, covering his hands, most likely, or possibly his hands were clutching the brim. I had no intention of finding out. I was here to bury my father, not to grieve for him, to make up with him or, God forbid, cry over his cold body.

I sighed and rose. I buttoned my blazer and pulled down the cuffs of my crisp white shirt. I tucked my hair behind my ears, turned around and walked away, praying with every step that Sophie would feign another headache tomorrow, so I could escape Lynchfield without seeing her.

Don't miss The Secret of You and Me *by Melissa Lenhardt*

OUT NOW

Copyright © 2020 by Melissa Lenhardt

LET'S TALK
Romance

Follow us:

 Millsandboon

 @MillsandBoon

 @MillsandBoonUK

 @MillsandBoonUK

For all the latest titles and special offers, sign up to our newsletter:

Millsandboon.co.uk